S0-AKY-495

Cauldron of Evil

Other Five Star Titles by Marilyn Ross:

Cellars of the Dead
Curse of Black Charlie
Death's Dark Music
Waiting in the Shadows
Don't Look Behind You

Cauldron of Evil

The Stewarts of Stormhaven-5

Marilyn Ross

Five Star • Waterville, Maine

Published in 2004 in conjunction with Maureen Moran Agency.

The text of this edition is unabridged.

Set in 11 pt. Plantin by Carleen Stearns.

Printed in the United States on permanent paper.

Library of Congress Cataloging-in-Publication Data

Ross, Marilyn, 1912–
Cauldron of evil / Marilyn Ross.
p. cm. — (The Stewarts of Stormhaven ; 5)
ISBN 1-59414-240-8 (hc : alk. paper)
1. Young women—Fiction. 2. Scotland—Fiction.
3. Manors—Fiction. I. Title.
PR9199.3.R5996C38 2004
813′.54—dc22 2004053224

To our good friends Joe Hickman
and his charming wife, Tuckie!

Prologue

The year is 1854. Prime Minister Lord Aberdeen has yielded to the warmongers in his cabinet, allowing England to become involved in the Crimean War—an engagement which turned out to be a sordidly wretched affair and the war of the most magnitude since the epic struggle with Napoleon. Men of commonsense were forced to ask themselves why Britain, France and Sardinia were sending armies to the Black Sea to help Turks fight Russians? Why were Christian Englishmen joining with their former French foes to support Mohammedan Turks against Christian Russians?

It was an utterly ridiculous struggle, waged in the name of religion, and most of the good people of Britain believed it a disaster. Queen Victoria, with her tendency to understate, called it, "a quite unsatisfactory war." As indeed it was. It ended without victory with a treaty in 1856 and resulted in the unseating of Lord Aberdeen's government. Out of all this unhappy business there emerged the heroic deeds of Florence Nightingale and the beginning of nursing as we know it today. A more minor but still memorable achievement was Lord Alfred Tennyson's epic poem, *The Charge of The Light Brigade!* Someone had blundered!

These events provided a background to this episode in the history of the Stewarts of Stormhaven, but they play only a small part in the story itself. Most disturbed by the war was Ernest Stewart, grandson of Ian Stewart, the elder, and son of Roger, who had turned the management of his father's business over to someone else so that he might head the family bank.

This is the story of Dr. William Davis and his young wife, Ardith. William Davis was the son of Ishbel and Henry Davis. Ishbel Davis was the daughter of the late Dr. Ian Stewart. William's early years were spent in London where his father was a prominent tea merchant. It also happened that his parents came under the shadow of the opium traffic in which many of the English merchants were dabbling. In deference to the wishes of his wife, Henry Davis abandoned the tea business and moved to a village near Edinburgh to operate a cattle farm.

So William Davis was educated mostly in Edinburgh, the city of his mother's people. He attended Edinburgh Medical School and married the lovely, though frail, Ardith Ross. This is an account of their marriage and the many weird adventures which they experienced in a small coastal town in the Highlands where a belief in witches was still prevalent.

William's sister, June, was married to Emery Sanders, and they lived in London where the Sanders were as prominent in banking as the Stewarts were in Edinburgh.

Stormhaven Castle still stood in majesty towering above the great city. And it was there that the assembled family saw the New Year in! That fateful year of 1854!

William and June had journeyed up from London with their spouses. William and Ardith also brought along their three-year-old son, Ian. June and Emery were childless although several years married. Ishbel and her husband, Henry Davis, were there, Henry in a state of noticeably failing health. James Stewart and his wife, Inez, had sent letters of greetings from America, but were unable to be present. Ishbel's brother, Ernest, and his wife, Jean Stewart, with their only child, Flora, hosted the occasion which greeted the momentous year!

Chapter One

The London winter of 1854 was notable for a succession of cold, rainy days. Ardith Stewart found herself influenced by the weather and felt it increased the apprehensions which she already felt. For the past six months she had been troubled by a nagging cough and a feeling of utter weariness. In the beginning, she had tried to hide her condition from her devoted husband, William, but since he was a young doctor serving on the staff of the noted Bishop's Hospital, this had not been easy to do.

She had gradually turned the care of her beloved three-year-old son over to Mrs. Murray, their housekeeper, and spent much of the time, when her doctor-husband was away from the small house in Court Street on his duties, resting. Yet, with all the rest, her condition had not improved.

This frightened her, since as a girl of twelve she had suffered from a mild attack of consumption and had been confined to her bed for all of twelve months. She had been quite frank in telling William about this when he'd asked her to be his wife.

"I do not have a strong constitution," she'd warned him with a quaint earnestness. "I fear I might not make a good wife for a doctor!"

The brown-haired, good-looking William had taken her in his arms and with an adoring look in his keen, brown eyes had laughed and said, "You'll be the ideal doctor's wife! When you are ill I shall be able to attend you and not charge you any fee! What a saving! You dare not marry anyone else!"

She'd smiled up at him ruefully. "I knew you would not listen."

"Of course I won't listen to such nonsense!" he'd said. "Your Aunt Madge is willing to have you marry me, and if you agree we need only set the date for the ceremony."

Both her parents had died in a fire which had swept through the country house of a friend whom they'd been visiting. Fortunately, she'd been left with her Aunt Madge in London. So her doting aunt became her foster parent and raised her to a charming young womanhood.

She was twenty-one when William asked her to marry him. By then she had lost her look of frailness and was a lively, raven-haired beauty. Her sparkling green eyes and the faint patch of color on her cheeks gave every evidence of health. But it was an illusive picture of her true condition. The slim, charming girl worked at seeming vivacious when she was often actually weary.

After Ian was born she had a brief sick spell, but she was soon on her feet again, managing the affairs of their small household with a vigor and shrewdness which one did not look for in a girl so young and lovely.

Now, after four years of marriage, she knew she was on the brink of a health-breakdown. She was terrified, not so much for herself as for her husband and her little boy. The really bad period had begun when she and William and the boy had gone to the Stewart family seat in Edinburgh. Ernest Stewart and his wife, Jean, had sent them an urgent invitation to attend a family reunion to see the New Year 1854 in with them. Since William's father and mother were to be there and William's father was not too well, they decided to make the long winter journey by railway and stage.

Ardith had never seen Edinburgh before and she was duly impressed by the great Scottish city cloaked in snow and the towering gray edifice of the family castle known as Stormhaven. William had come to have a great fondness for the city and had taken her on a tour by sleigh of his favorite Edinburgh places. She saw the great Cathedral of St. Giles, the High Street, which she was surprised to hear called the Royal Mile. She thought there was little of royalty about its hodge-podge of old and new, of seventeenth century corbels and pepper-pot turrets, of tiny, ancient shops. She saw a vast parliament hall where there had not been a parliament for more than a century. But there was also great character and beauty in many of the old buildings.

The house party at Stormhaven had been a happy occasion. June, William's older sister, and her banker husband, Emery Sanders, had made the journey from London to be there with them. June had a distinctive beauty about her, though she was not truly perfect of feature. She was a tall, attractive person whose brown hair was a shade lighter than William's. She had thus far been unable to bear children, and this had given her a good deal of concern.

Emery Sanders, her jolly husband, seemed not perturbed about their childless state at all. He liked children, as he showed by his constant attentions to young Ian, during the trying journey the two couples had made from London to Edinburgh. But the stout, good-natured young man was not one to fret much about anything. He enjoyed his career in his family's London bank and adored June.

Ernest and Jean had been perfect hosts. And their teenage daughter, Flora, had also labored to make everyone feel at home. It had been a jolly time with blazing log fires in immense fireplaces, great feasting and drinking with many

Edinburgh friends joining their family circle. There were toasts to the New Year, the stirring sound of the bagpipes to fete 1854, and an orchestra to provide music for dancing until the small hours in the grand ballroom of Stormhaven.

There had also been a mournful touch to the occasion. William's father, former London tea merchant Henry Davis, had suffered a heart seizure a few months earlier and was still in weakened health. His wife, Ishbel, privately confided to Ardith that her husband was truly unwell.

"You must not be surprised if word of Henry's death comes at any time," she'd warned her daughter-in-law. "Our doctor says that Henry cannot survive another such attack."

"We must pray it doesn't happen," Ardith had said.

Ishbel, gray of hair but still softly lovely of face, had nodded. "I have not given up hope."

Still Ardith knew that her father-in-law's condition was grave. Henry Davis had left the dinner table on one of the many evenings of feasting, and he had not been able to join in the dancing or other later festivities.

In the privacy of their bedroom at Stormhaven, a worried William had sat by the fireplace with tow-headed Ian sleeping in his arms and told her worriedly, "I can't bear to see my father so failed. I find it hard to believe."

"He did have a bad heart seizure," Ardith reminded him.

"I've talked with his doctor," William said gravely, "and I do not like the history of his illness. There could be more trouble ahead."

At the time she'd been secretly troubled by her own feelings of weakness and so had rather quickly put concern for the ailing Henry Davis out of her mind. She felt it was best to be cheery about it all for William's sake. Her husband was devoted to his father, and his death would cause him much unhappiness. And if she should be stricken at the same time it would make matters worse.

So all through the cold and wet January and February she fought to hide how badly she felt. Then her masquerade came to an end without her being able to help it. One evening, as she got up from the dinner table to stroll to the living room with William, she collapsed.

When she came to, she was in her bedroom and an older colleague of her husband's, Dr. Layton Thomas, was in attendance by her bed. The white-haired doctor had his pince-nez balanced on his prominent nose, which dominated his rather long dour face, and he was studying her.

The old doctor addressed her in his stern fashion, "Well, madam, you have been playing a pretty game on us, haven't you?"

"What do you mean?" she'd asked, gazing up at him. At the same time, a concerned William came to stand within the glow of the lamplight from her bedside table.

Dr. Thomas said, "You have been troubled by your old illness. No need to lie to me. I have listened to your lungs. You have had a relapse of the lung fever once again!"

"No!" she said, raising herself frantically on an elbow.

William came close to her and touched a hand on her shoulder. He said, "The doctor only wishes to be helpful."

Ardith gazed up at her husband with fear-stricken eyes. "By telling me I have consumption again?"

"No need to make so much of it!" William protested.

She looked up at the old doctor who was still staring at her. "Do you take it so lightly, Dr. Thomas?"

"No," the veteran said in his stern fashion. "It is my opinion that if you remain here in London your lungs will grow worse, and you will live no more than a year or two."

"You see!" she told William.

William's handsome face had gone pale. Her husband had been used to giving death sentences to others, but when he heard her being discussed in the same fashion he showed shock.

He took her hand tightly in his and, holding it, turned to the older doctor to ask, "What do you suggest?"

"Your wife must leave London and have a rest," Dr. Thomas said. "Otherwise, I would not care to be responsible."

She protested, "But William's work is at the hospital."

"Then he must change his place of work," was the old man's grim advice.

"I can't ask him to do that," she protested.

"No need to," William reassured her, still holding her hand. "I've been thinking for some time I'd like to set myself up in a small country practice in the Highlands beyond Edinburgh."

She worried. "You're doing so well here! And learning so much at the same time!"

"I know enough," William said. "Your health comes first. I will send a letter to an Edinburgh realtor today and ask that he try and find me a likely location for a practice."

Dr. Thomas regarded her sternly, "The Highland air, madam, might do a good deal for your condition. I can offer you medicine, which you must take faithfully, but nothing so healing as the air which you would breathe up there."

"It really would make that much difference?" she asked.

The old doctor nodded his white head. "It would," he said. "I shall write some prescriptions for you. You must take more bed rest for a period at least. And I don't know what to say about the boy."

She stared up at him open-mouthed. "The boy?"

"Yes," the old doctor said. "His welfare must also be taken into consideration. It may not be good for him to be so near you!"

"I am his mother!"

William pressed her hand a bit more firmly in his. "I'm sure Dr. Thomas does not mean to part you from Ian. But we must also realize your disease can be communicated, and you would not want to have Ian ill."

"Surely if I keep him at a distance," she said unhappily.

Dr. Thomas shook his head. "I don't know, madam. I do not think that as easily managed as you suggest. It might be wise to place him in another's care until you are in better health."

"Send him away?" she asked with a hint of a sob.

"There is no doubt someone," Dr. Thomas said.

"No one!" she protested. "Aunt Madge died two years ago. She was my only relative."

William eyed her with surprise. "You can't have forgotten June?" And he turned to the old doctor to explain, "My sister. She is young and childless and, I may say, devoted to Ian. She would be glad to look after him for a little."

Ardith's eyes brimmed with tears. She had forgotten June in her grief. Yet the knowledge there was someone who would care for the child did not make her feel any happier. She said, "I would prefer to keep him here."

Dr. Thomas removed the pince-nez and thrust them in his upper jacket pocket, the broad black ribbon dangling from them. He said, "If the idea makes you so unhappy it will probably be better to allow the youngster to remain here. At least until your plans are settled. But do take precautions. Restrain your kissing him, and let your husband and housekeeper have the major care of him!"

"Anything, doctor!" she promised, elated at his giving way in this matter. He was noted for being grim in his decisions.

The old doctor and William strolled out of the room after a little, talking seriously. She waited alone in the silence and the soft glow of the room's single lamp. She heard the downstairs door open and shut and next the sound of the doctor's carriage going on its way. Then William's footsteps as he came back up the stairs and finally joined her in the bedroom again.

He came and sat with her on the bed. He touched his lips to her fevered brow. "You ought to have told me earlier," he said.

"I hoped I would be better!"

"You will be!"

She gave her handsome husband a troubled look. "I do pray so. I've always been worried!"

"Dr. Thomas is very hopeful that a change of air can work miracles in your case. It is too damp here and the air is foul with chimney smoke and all the rest. Once you are in the country you will be better."

"You won't take Ian from me?"

"Of course not," her husband said. "If you feel so strongly about it I'm sure we can manage. We will, I promise!" And he kissed her again.

In the weeks which followed, William was most considerate of her. Occasionally they would have company, and often his sister, June, came and sat with her. Ian became used to not seeing his mother as frequently as before. Mrs. Murray kept him busy with toys and childhood games, and William gave him every minute he could spare. It was not easy, but they somehow carried on.

Ardith felt her strength grow very gradually and her

coughs became less racking and less frequent. Dr. Thomas came regularly to see her and indicated in his stern way he was satisfied with her progress but impatient to get her away from London. William had been in correspondence with an Edinburgh realtor and was considering several towns in which he might locate. Ardith studied the descriptions of the property offerings as they came by post from Scotland and found it exciting to visualize what they might be like.

William said, "Of course, I will have to personally visit the areas before we make a final decision."

Then one afternoon in April when spring seemed to have arrived with its promise of warm and sunny days ahead, June appeared suddenly in a stricken state. Ardith had only to greet her to see that something had badly upset her sister-in-law.

June confirmed this, saying, "I have just received a special telegraph message from Mother! Father had another seizure! He's dead!" And the blonde girl sank into a nearby chair and, with head bowed, began to weep.

Ardith placed a comforting hand on the older woman's shoulder. "I'm so sorry! Does William know?"

"I have had Emery go to the hospital. I imagine he's had the word by now!" June said, touching her eyes with a hankie.

"You will be going to the funeral, of course," Ardith said.

"Yes," June agreed. "Mother said she would delay burial until we arrived. Uncle Ernest long ago offered that Father might be buried in the Stewart family lot, and my father was delighted with the idea. So he and Mother will both be buried in Edinburgh."

"They were devoted in life," she said. "I'm sure your

mother is relieved by the knowledge they will one day rest side-by-side again."

June gazed up at her apologetically. "I'm sorry to bring this bad news. Especially when you're not well."

"I had to know. I doubt that Dr. Thomas will allow me to make the long journey to Edinburgh and back again. The last one tired me so greatly."

"It would be most unwise for you," June agreed. "No one in the family could sensibly expect it of you."

"But William will go," she said. "And perhaps he will have an opportunity to visit some of the properties we've been offered in the Highlands."

"I hate to think of you going there! So far away!"

"Dr. Thomas thinks it my best hope."

"Then there is no question," June sighed. "And I'm sure William will enjoy small-town practice. He has been in London long enough to have a good background of medicine."

"I'm certain of that."

"But Emery and I will miss you," June said. "We will be the only ones of the family left in London. You will surely visit some of the Edinburgh Stewarts occasionally."

"That is true," Ardith agreed. "But you and Emery must come and visit us at least once a year, even though the distance may be great."

June gave her a meaningful look. "It will be good for Ian."

"Yes," she said quietly. And then she went on, "If it doesn't work out . . . I mean, if I don't get better . . . I'd like to think that you might help William in raising Ian."

The blonde young woman at once got to her feet. "You mustn't think of such things."

"It could happen," Ardith said, trying to appear braver

than she truly felt. She was anxious to get this settled at a moment when their mutual grief allowed them to speak frankly to one another.

"I shall pray that it won't," her sister-in-law said. "But you have my solemn promise that Ian will never know neglect as long as Emery and I are alive."

"Thank you," Ardith said sincerely. Her eyes blurred with tears. "And now I must call Mrs. Murray to get us some tea."

William along with June and her husband made the journey to Edinburgh to attend his father's funeral. He also planned to look into the matter of purchasing a Highland property before he returned. Meanwhile, Ardith remained in London with Ian. She took her medications regularly and was feeling so much better that she often went with her son for long walks in a nearby square on sunny afternoons.

She missed her husband and, knowing the grief his father's death had brought him, regretted that she had not been able to go to Edinburgh with him. Perhaps it was her upset state of mind which brought on a series of weird nightmares which she started to have during William's absence. She would wake from them perspiring and terrified, they were so vivid! Never had she known such strange dreams!

The dream seemed to always begin with her strolling in a garden behind a grim-looking stone mansion. The mansion appeared to be on the edge of a cliff near the ocean, because the wash of waves on the beach below could be plainly heard. Then, all at once, there were other sounds, the murmurings of many angry voices. And these hostile, approaching voices filled her with a sudden fear, as if she knew what they meant. At once she ran from the gardens into the house.

As she entered the dark hallway of the house, she came face to face with an elderly woman, whose age-weary features wore an expression of utter terror. The woman, apparently a housekeeper by her apron and cap, touched the fingers of a hand to her trembling lips and stepped back in the shadows.

Ardith had no time for her beyond giving her a despairing glance. She ran up a narrow back stairway and then another to a bedroom on an upper floor. It was a large room with a huge canopied bed. She bolted the door of the room and leaned against it, listening nervously. At first, there were no sounds, but then the voices came again from within the house.

Her fears increased as she realized the angry band were mounting the stairs! They were coming directly to the room where she was seeking refuge. All at once, a loud pounding on the door made her stumble back in terror. She gazed at the door with fear-stricken eyes as the voices outside grew louder and more threatening. She was too paralyzed by her fear to move further or cry out.

There were more angry shouts, and then great pressure was exerted on the door. She watched as it wavered under the blows, until the bolt burst away and the door swung open to reveal a group of men with angry faces. Their leader uttered a shout of triumph and came into the room and roughly seized her.

It was then she began to scream for help. But it did no good! Other hands seized her and it all became a blurred terror. She was walking through a misted wood to the accompaniment of a chanting chorus of taunting voices. She knew that she was doomed. There could be no help. No escape.

She closed her eyes and the angry voices surged high in a

chorus of hate. When she opened her eyes again, she was bound to a tree, it was growing dark, and the group of vindictive males were throwing brush and other pieces of small combustible wood at her feet and beside her. Then someone came forward bearing a flaming torch and, with a derisive cry, touched the torch to the dry brush. It ignited at once and she was caught in a circle of leaping, searing flames! Beyond the flames came shouts of mad glee.

It was at this point in the nightmare she always awakened. The first time she experienced the eerie dream was about a week after William left for Edinburgh. It was so unusual and she remembered the details of it so well that it haunted her waking hours. And when she began to experience the same odd nightmare over and over again, she began to think it had some significance.

Could it be an ominous warning of her own approaching death? This thought worried her a good deal. Or did it mean that her young son or her husband were in danger? She felt it was too unusual not to have some mystical significance. But she could not interpret it. Nor did she dare to mention it to stern old Dr. Thomas. So she kept the nightmares to herself until her husband arrived.

William arrived back from Scotland looking more tired than she had ever seen him before. Over their first meal together, which was dinner on the evening of his return, he began to talk of his experiences.

In his brown velvet jacket and vest and his fawn checkered trousers, he gazed at her across the table. "I want you to know I have made excellent use of my time."

"I'm sure you have," she agreed.

"I have found a town most suitable for us and for my practice; it's a small coastal fishing town named Harwick."

"Did you go there?"

Her young husband hesitated. "No. I had it on the word of the Edinburgh representative for the property that the price is excellent. It is actually a large estate with much farm land which has gone unused. The local squire has wanted to buy the place, but it appears he is a mean fellow and has only offered a fraction of what it is worth."

"Yet you say it is cheaply priced?"

"It is," William went on. "I talked to Uncle Ernest about it, and he was most enthusiastic."

"And the town needs a doctor?" she asked. She was wearing a dress especially chosen for the occasion with a full skirt of golden cloth and a white top. She had wanted to make this first night of William's homecoming a special one. Mrs. Murray had excelled herself with a special steak and kidney pie and her marvellous trifle for dessert. Now they had finished the ample meal and lingered over their tea.

William frowned slightly. "That is rather awkward. But I'm sure I can handle the situation. There is a doctor there now by the name of Carr. But he is elderly and given to drink. He neglects his patients for days at a time, and they have been trying to prevail upon another doctor to establish there to right this unhappy business."

She listened wtih a small uneasiness. "But won't that mean strife?"

"I hope not," William said with assurance. "And if there should be any I'll take no part in it. I'll build myself my own list of patients by giving them good care. If this fellow does as well, he may be able to stay on. If he refuses to reform I shall soon take over the entire town."

Ardith said, "There are bound to be those who will take sides."

"The real estate man assured me because of this other

doctor's drinking I will be made welcome."

"But he is bound to present the best side of it, since he is interested in selling the property."

William smiled good-naturedly. "What a Doubting Thomas you are becoming. Surely you will trust my judgment in this?"

"Naturally!"

He leaned forward and touched his hands on hers. "Then have no fears. I will be able to manage things. I have already made payment for the property, and it now remains for me only to wind my affairs up here and at the hospital. Then we shall be on our way north where good health awaits you!"

She smiled. "I hope that will be true."

"Bound to be," William said. "Mother, though desolated by my father's death, was pleased to hear of our going to Harwick. It means we shall be nearer to her and will be able to visit back and forth more often."

"What are her plans?" Ardith asked.

"She is going to turn the operation of the cattle farm over to the present manager who is most competent. And she is coming in to Edinburgh to live at Stormhaven with Uncle Ernest and Aunt Jean. It is a vast place, and she can have her own apartment while at the same time being able to enjoy their company when she wishes. I consider it an ideal arrangement."

Ardith nodded. "I agree it is better that she not be alone at this time. And I'm certain Uncle Ernest will welcome her."

"He and Aunt Jean made the suggestion. They have only one child, and I think they must get lonely in that big place. By the way, I understand that Wyndmoor is fairly large, at least a third the size of Stormhaven."

"Wyndmoor!" she exclaimed, repeating the name.

"Yes. That is what it is called. Don't you like it?"

"It's not that," she said. "It's just that it somehow sounds familiar to me. Wyndmoor." She repeated the name again in a puzzled tone.

Her young husband laughed. "How could you have heard it before? You've never been to Harwick!"

"Perhaps I've read about it somewhere."

"I doubt it is that famous."

"Or perhaps there is a house somewhere else by that name, and I have heard it mentioned," she said.

William showed amusement. "What an odd little person you can be, when you wish. I think it is being shut up here in London. You'll bloom when you get to the fresh air of the Northland."

"I've been going out a good deal," she told him. "Ian and I have gone for walks in the square. We meet the nannies with their baby carriages, and Ian likes to stare in at the babies. He calls them funny little animals!"

William said, "You haven't been overdoing yourself, I hope."

"Not at all," she told him. "Dr. Thomas approves of my walks. And I take my medicine regularly, three times a day. I do feel ever so much better!"

William got to his feet. "Then that is all right. I must get a quantity of that medicine from Thomas before we leave. We don't want to be caught short of it, and it takes a while for packages to get up where we are going."

Suddenly, she felt a small panic. "I know I shall miss London!"

He came to her and, taking her by the hands, waited for her to get up from her chair. Then he took her in his arms and kissed her gently. "You must get away from this foul city air. We know your weakness and happily there is a solution for it. Ian will also thrive in the country! It will be good for all of us!"

Ardith wished fervently that all his predictions would be proven true. She dearly wanted to return to full health, and she wanted her young son to have a happy, normal life. But it did mean going far away to what must be a rather isolated spot. And, from what William had told her, it appeared he would have to compete with another doctor in the town, who even if a drunkard might prove a barrier to their cherished plans.

They were in the upstairs bedroom and preparing for bed when she paused in a routine nightly brushing of her raven hair before the dresser mirror to turn to him. He had donned his dressing gown and was smoking a final pipe before bed in an easy chair near her.

He gestured, saying, "Go on with your hair brushing! I enjoy watching you!"

She smiled. "Do you?"

"Honestly."

"I was afraid I was boring you," she said.

"Not at all."

"And I suddenly thought of something I've been meaning to tell you."

"Oh?"

She hesitated for a moment, embarrassed now that she had brought the subject up. Yet she knew she must mention it or she would be troubled in mind. This would not be good for her. She had worried enough as it was.

The brush still in her hand, she said, "I've had a series of odd nightmares since you left."

"Nightmares?"

"Yes."

He removed his pipe from his mouth and gave her a questioning stare. "What sort of nightmares?"

"Unlike anything I've known before," she said, not sure what his reaction was going to be. Often he was sympathetic in such matters, but he could be bluntly male without any true understanding of her sensitive nature.

William's handsome face shadowed. "For goodness sakes, continue! You have caught my interest without troubling to satisfy it."

"I'll tell you the nightmare," she said. And she went into a long account of it, ending with her being burned by the angry marauders.

William frowned as she finished. "You must have read all that in a book! Some trashy novel!"

"No! I haven't!" she protested.

"It doesn't make sense," he said in the impatient tone which she had feared he might use. "Where could all that have come from if you haven't read it somewhere?"

She shook her head. "I don't know. I only know I awake terrified, drenched with perspiration!"

Staring at her, her husband asked, "How many times have you had this dream?"

She shrugged. "I can't say exactly. Perhaps six or seven times."

"Always in the same detail?"

"Yes. It always begins and ends the same. I'm walking in the garden and then I hear the angry voices. And I wind up being burned at the stake or whatever."

"In your condition, you're bound to have a night fever," he said. "It's part of the illness. Did you mention these odd nightmares to Dr. Thomas?"

"No."

"Why not?"

"I was afraid to."

"That was childish of you!" William reproached her. "I think this has some bearing on your condition, and he should know anything that has such importance."

"I decided to wait and tell you," she said unhappily, staring down at the brush. "I hoped you'd understand and help me."

William heard her rueful words with a new look of compassion on his face. He got up and came over to her. "Forgive me! I didn't mean to be cold about this. I guess I reverted to my clinical attitude. You became a patient and I the doctor. Sorry. I do understand and I shall tell Thomas about it. It's merely a symptom of night fever."

"You think I will get over those horrid dreams?"

"I'm certain you will," he promised her, standing by her so she could see his smiling reflection in the mirror. "It is without a doubt something you've read long ago and which you've retained in your subconscious. I've known other such cases."

"Then you don't think it's anything to worry about?"

"No. When these unnatural fevers leave you I'm certain the nightmares will vanish as well. Now go on with your hair brushing so we may get to bed. It's been a long day for me!"

So the discussion ended there. But many hours later, just before the gray of dawn, she had a repeat of the nightmare! When she wakened in her usual state of near hysteria, she saw that her husband was sleeping placidly at her side and she could not bring herself to rouse him. He would only pass her fears off as being childish things in any case.

But what especially terrified her now was that she was almost positive that in this latest version of the grisly nightmare one of the voices filled with hatred had called out the name of Wyndmoor!

Chapter Two

It was seven weeks later. William was helping Ardith descend from the train compartment in the bustling Edinburgh railway station. Ian was clutching her by the hand, and she had the panicky feeling that she might faint at any second. The noise and confusion of the railway platform along with the sooty smoke which filled the air there made her head reel. She knew the journey had taken much more of a toll than she'd expected, and she wanted to hide this from William.

Her top-hatted young husband took her by the arm and eyed her worriedly. "You are dreadfully pale! Are you ill?"

She shook her head and attempted a wan smile. "Just the noise!"

"Blasted awful place!" William agreed. "The air is filled with the stench of soot and oil. Give me a moment and I'll have you away from it all."

"I'll be all right," she assured him, though she was far from certain of this.

"Mother and Aunt Jean are supposed to be here to meet us," he said.

Ian raised his small, happy face and in a childish tone said, "Grandmother!"

William laughed. "You've mastered that word very well, old chap! You're quite right! It's your grandmother we're looking for."

People brushed by them, intent on their own problems; a porter shouted and came rattling by with a cart loaded with bags. Somewhere close by an engine issued several loud, warning blasts. The three made their way along the wooden platform, jostled on all sides by passengers coming and going, and Ardith decided this was as close to the Inferno of Dante as she had ever managed to get.

They reached the comparative quiet and fresh air of the railway building itself, and two pleasant ladies in flowing skirts and wide-brimmed hats detached themselves from the crowd and came towards them. Ardith saw that it was Ishbel Davis, William's mother, and Jean Stewart, his aunt. She thrust an eager Ian towards them to be lifted up and kissed by the two older women. And then, all her resources drained, she turned to William with a plaintive look and collapsed in his arms.

She did not revive until she was in the grand carriage, indicative of the wealth of the Stewarts, and on her way over the cobblestone streets to Stormhaven. William was seated by her with his arm around her and holding smelling salts beneath her nose.

As she opened her eyes, he said, "You gave us all a scare!"

Weakly, she said, "I'm so sorry! I think it was the noise and the foul air!"

From the seat opposite, Ishbel Stewart said, "The journey was a long one for you! No wonder you fainted!" The older woman had Ian seated like a little old man between her and Jean.

William said, "The train was stuffy the last few hours, and we have travelled a long way."

Friendly Jean Stewart showed a smile on her round, pink and white face. "Had I to travel so far, I'd have fainted long before Ardith did!"

Ian gazed at her with a troubled look on his tiny face. "I'll get Dr. Thomas," he decided.

His words made Ardith smile again and sit up. She reached out her hands to her manly little son and told him, "Thank you, Ian, but I shall be all right now. And I'm afraid Dr. Thomas is much too far away to call on."

"That's certain," William said, glancing out the window. "I find it hard to believe I'm back in Edinburgh again, so soon."

Ishbel Davis showed a pleased look on her still lovely face. "I wish you could remain here and not go to the Highlands."

"It is all arranged," he said.

"But you could change the arrangements," his mother persisted. "Your grandfather was a well-known doctor here and you'd soon have a fine practice."

Aunt Jean nodded. "I promise to send all my friends to you. And most of them are ailing!"

William smiled. "That's kind of you, Aunt Jean. But we must go on to Harwick. Ardith needs the fresh, Highland air."

His mother said, "Well, I promise you are not moving from Stormhaven for a week at least! Ardith must have a good rest before she goes off to the Highlands and the care of a big house."

"I'm really quite well," Ardith assured her, knowing that William would not take a week's waiting patiently. He was on edge to get to Harwick and see his new property.

William said, "In any case, Ardith will have little to do. The lawyer looking after the property transfer at the other end is assembling some servants for us and having them prepare the house for our arrival."

"Nevertheless . . ." his mother said firmly, and Ardith

had a feeling Ishbel would have her way. They would remain at Stormhaven for a week.

Their visit to the impressive stone castle was a pleasant one. William's mother had recovered from the most poignant period of mourning for his recently deceased father, though there were moments when she would hesitate in the midst of some other talk to make a sad reference to him. It was obvious that, while she concealed it, her lost mate was still much on her mind.

Flora enjoyed romping in the gardens of the castle with Ian. And the lad seemed to look on Stormhaven as his second home. Ardith rested a good deal of the time, sunning herself in the glass enclosed conservatory, and having afternoon naps in her bedroom. Aunt Jean had wisely declared against any visitors, and so the family had quiet dinners by themselves.

Not that any dinner attended by the robust Ernest Stewart was ever that quiet. He was a bluff, hearty man with a loud manner of speaking and a friendly air. He enjoyed presiding at the table. And when he laughed he could be heard many rooms away. Yet it was said in Edinburgh that he was as shrewd a banker as his uncle Walter had been.

The seventy-six-year-old Walter now never left the upstairs room in which he'd been a captive since a stroke had laid him low in 1852. Heather Rae, his wife, had predeceased him in 1851, and his only son, James, had crossed the broad Atlantic to live the life of a wealthy plantation owner in North Carolina. James and his father had never gotten on well, and some felt it was the old man's unhappiness about this which had brought on his crippling stroke.

Ardith had not known the banker in his prime. She had tiptoed into his room at Christmas time with Ishbel to visit briefly with him. The once shrewd, energetic man was reduced to a wasted shell with vacant, staring eyes. He did not appear to recognize anyone nor was he able to communicate in any way. Yet his attending doctor claimed his heart was still strong, and it could be that the unhappy Walter might live on a long while.

Ernest had assigned three servants to care for the old man around the clock. James wrote from far-off North Carolina at least once every month to inquire about his father's health, yet he gave no indication of planning to pay a visit to him. Ardith found it pathetic that a man of so much authority and power should be so humbled. To all intents, Walter Stewart was dead to the world of banking and his family, yet he lived on as an unhappy shadow of his former self.

On the night before she and William were to begin their journey to Harwick, Ernest lingered longer than usual at the dinner table. He seemed in a less happy mood than usual, and they soon discovered the reason.

"I fear our nation is now involved in what could well be a disastrous war," he solemnly informed them. "I have it on the word of one of Her Majesty's most trusted advisors."

William frowned. "I don't understand it at all. Yet I know the fleet has been sent to the Asian area. How did we get into this mess? Find ourselves fighting the Russians with the Turks as allies?"

Uncle Ernest raised a hand in a frustrated gesture. "I wish I could tell you why. No one seems quite sure. We have stumbled into it through one treaty and another. Lord Aberdeen has been a good prime minister, but I'm certain this war may ruin his political career."

"You think his government will come down?" Ishbel asked.

"If we lose the war or there is no conclusive victory it will have to," Ernest Stewart said. "And the project looks doomed from the start."

Jean spoke up, saying, "I understand one of the first military regiments being sent to the Crimea is a Scottish one."

"That's true," her husband agreed. "But they are having trouble with their present recruiting in Scotland. Few wish to take the Queen's shilling. And I don't blame them."

"A bad business," William said. "I'll be glad to lose myself in the Highlands. London is bound to be seething with war excitement from now on."

His uncle gave him a knowing glance. "Don't be so certain you will escape all links with the war in Harwick. I hear there was a riot there when a recruiting officer visited it recently. Sir Douglas Gordon, the local representative of the Queen, took the platform with the recruiting officer and they were not only booed but stoned!"

Ardith looked at her husband with a wry smile. "Is this the quiet village you have promised me?"

"I don't think things like that happen there often," William said. "I think the trouble rests with Sir Douglas. He is not popular in the district. At least that's what I've been told."

"I met him once," Ernest Stewart said. "My advice is to watch out for him. He could make a vicious enemy."

"I will keep that in mind," William said.

Ardith turned to Ernest Stewart at the head of the table and informed him, "I fear we may already have incurred his anger. As I understand it, William outbid him on a large estate which he was attempting to buy cheaply."

Ernest Stewart offered her a grave smile. "I must claim some guilt for advising William to make the purchase. I would hope Sir Douglas Gordon is not so unreasonable as to start a feud because he was bested in a fair business deal."

Ishbel said, "From what I've heard, he might well do just that."

William frowned at his mother. "Please don't encourage Ardith in her fancies; she has far too many as it is. I have every hope that Sir Douglas will behave like a gentleman. There is no point in expecting anything else."

His uncle said, "I agree. But it might be wise to avoid any further problems in that direction."

After they rose from the table, William took Ardith aside and told her, "You're to come along to the library. Mother and I want to have a chat with you there."

"What about?" she asked.

"You will know soon enough," her husband told her, leading her out of the dining room and down a long hallway to the library.

When they reached the book-lined room, they found Ishbel standing there by a table which held a lamp with a fancy, pink shade. The older woman nodded to them and said, "Why don't we all sit down and be comfortable?"

The two women sat down, but William remained standing with his hands clasped behind his back. In spite of his thirty years, there was still a trace of boyishness about him. He stood there rather awkwardly in his black frock coat and his striped trousers.

His mother spoke first, addressing herself to Ardith, "I have a proposal to make which I hope you won't resent."

Ardith stared at her. "What sort of proposal?"

"I would like to keep Ian here with me for a little," her mother-in-law said. "You know I am lonely and his company would be of value to me. Also, he will get the best of care here."

She protested, "But I don't want to be parted from my child!"

Ishbel sighed. "Of course, I understand your feelings and I won't blame you if you refuse to agree. But wouldn't it be better for you and everyone else if the boy remained here until you adjusted to living at Harwick?"

Now William joined in the argument, "I must confess, I agree with Mother. You are not too well yet, as evidenced by your collapse when we arrived here the other day. Suppose you should have a similar collapse after we get to Harwick?"

"I won't!" she said.

"Who can be sure of that?" her husband asked. "I think it wise for the boy and for us to leave him here where he is happy and safe, and let us get settled at Harwick."

"Then I can visit you and bring him to you," Ishbel suggested. "I promise that, as soon as you let me know you're ready for him, I'll come with him."

"What Mother says make sense," William urged.

Ardith sat there silently for a moment. Hurt stabbed at her throat. And yet, as much as she wanted to keep Ian with her, she knew that William and his mother were probably right. The best plan would be to leave him at Stormhaven until they were settled in this new home. It would be that much less strain on her, and she knew Ishbel could be trusted to give the lad every care.

At last she replied in a small voice, "Very well. I agree. But only with the understanding that you bring him to me as soon as I ask."

Ishbel said, "You know I will do that!"

William's handsome, boyish face mirrored his relief. He told Ardith, "I thank you, darling, for being so sensible in this matter. I've been worried from the start."

Ishbel said, "It takes about a week to get a letter from Harwick. So be sure to write me regularly and give time for the letter to reach me. I will write to you as well."

Ardith stood up. "I'm not at all sure about Harwick," she said. "Now that we're ready to go there, I worry about it."

William reminded her, "Dr. Thomas told you that mountain air is necessary for the restoration of your health."

She sighed. "I hope it isn't a vain effort."

Her mother-in-law rose and placed a comforting arm about her. "Of course it won't be a vain effort. I have every belief that you will fully recover."

"And so have I," William said. "If only she'll be easy on herself. She insists on making everything difficult when there's no need."

Ardith accepted this reproach from him without a reply. She was worried and she couldn't help it. And when her recurrent and terrifying nightmare returned that night, she put it down to the strain which she'd undergone. She said nothing about it to William as she lay awake thinking about the next day and her parting with Ian.

Actually, it turned out to be much less painful than she had anticipated. Ian enjoyed playing with Flora in the gardens of Stormhaven and he liked his grandmother. He was perfectly willing to remain there without his parents. This brave display on the part of the lad forced Ardith to take on a braver mood. She kissed Ian good-bye and told him that soon his grandmother would bring him to a wonderful new house by the sea.

"Will there be fishing boats there?" Ian wanted to know.

"Dozens of them," William told his young son.

"I will like that," Ian said.

He stood in the driveway holding his grandmother's hand and waving them good-bye with his free hand as they drove off. Ardith smiled and waved back as she fought her tears, then she settled close beside William for the start of their journey to the Highlands.

The first part of the trip was made by rail, a short side spur which headed up into the mountains. It ended at a small village, and there they took a stage. They rode all day in the uncomfortable stage, and when evening came broke the journey by an overnight stay at a tiny, country inn. Ardith was so weary she slept in spite of being in an upset state. William assured her they would reach Harwick before noon the next day.

Ardith sat by the window of the stage the next morning and watched the scenery. It was hauntingly beautiful, with pale blue mountains looming in the distance and the bright green of the trees and grass contrasted very often by swift, dark-blue streams frothed with white. And soon they would be close to the sea, for Harwick was perched on the cliffs high above the restless water.

She and William said little to each other. And the only other passenger in the coach was a rather seedy-looking man in his forties who had joined the stage at the inn. He wore gray tweeds and a gray top hat. His oval, slightly jowled face showed a tiny stubble of gray beard, although he seemed to have brownish hair.

His face was notable for his speculative blue eyes, which seemed to look out on the world with a kind of gay cynicism. At last, he addressed himself to them, "May I inquire if you are going to Harwick?"

William nodded with some dignity. "That is the destination of the stage, I believe."

Their fellow traveller laughed. "That it is! But I don't

find many strangers going there. Do you and your good lady plan to stay long in Harwick?"

"We plan to make our home there," William said.

The shrewd, cynical eyes of the man opposite brightened. "I know who you must be," he exclaimed. "You're the new doctor and his wife."

"I am Dr. William Davis," her husband said somewhat stiffly, "and this is my wife, Ardith. May I inquire as to who you might be?"

The seedy man in the gray tweeds chuckled at this. It seemed to touch his sense of humor. He said, "Indeed, you might, doctor. And may I congratulate you on the beauty of your wife." He removed his hat and bowed to her.

Ardith returned the compliment with a small smile and tried to decide what to make of the somewhat impudent man. He had not taken long to begin his questioning of them.

William said, "And your name is . . . ?"

"Henry Gordon, Esquire," the paunchy man said with a kind of amused importance. "I reside in Harwick. I have come to the town only recently after an absence of some twenty years. Years which I have spent on the Continent, pursuing my studies and career as an artist."

"An artist!" William said.

"I do mostly landscapes," the tweed-clad Gordon said. His tricky eyes focussed on her again and he added, "Though a pretty face such as your wife's could well inspire me to attempt a portrait study."

William said, "You are Henry Gordon. Could you be any relative of Sir Douglas Gordon?"

The paunchy man looked at them with a sly smile. "I wondered how long it would take you to get to that. I am Sir Douglas's younger brother, though not all that young, you understand."

Ardith said, "We've heard about your brother."

"Nothing good, I'd venture," Henry Gordon said at once. "He and I don't get along. He considers me the black sheep of the family, and what I consider him should not be said before a lady like yourself."

"Then you don't live at the estate?" William said.

"Not likely," Henry Gordon said. "I have a cottage at the other end of the village, which I share with a lady companion whom I met in Edinburgh. A young woman of great talent as a singer called Jeannie Truffin."

William seemed amused by the man's roguish charm. With a smile, he said, "Then I expect we'll see something of you in Harwick."

"It's a village, doctor," Henry Gordon said. "The kind of place where people can't help meeting. Makes it awkward for Sir Gordon and his Lady Mona. I'm afraid Lady Mona doesn't approve of me or my Jeannie; you see, Lady Mona is one of those pale blonde sorts who spends a great deal of time in prayer. We Gordons are Catholics and the village priest, Father Craig, knowing on which side his bread is buttered, pays a good deal of attention to my titled brother and his wife."

William said, "Does your brother have any children?"

"One little girl of thirteen, name of Margaret," the man opposite said. "She's not a bad sort. We get on well enough, though her father and mother drag her off whenever they find her talking to me."

"You're being very frank with us," Ardith said, wondering if this were truly so, or whether he was merely pretending frankness.

The man smiled at her. "I place great stock in frankness, madam. This way you know exactly where you stand. And I'm happy to greet the new owners of Wyndmoor. You know my brother wanted to buy the estate?"

"Yes, I know that," William said.

The man opposite winked at him. "Didn't exactly put Sir Douglas in a joyous frame of mind when he learned that you had bought the place."

Ardith said, "He had his chance."

"Oh, I know that, madam," the paunchy man said. "But Sir Douglas isn't the sort who takes defeat easily. Nor is he beloved by the people of Harwick. I dare say you've heard about the scandal of the recruiting episode. They stoned both him and the recruiting officer from the platform!"

William said, "I was told that."

"No secret," the artist said. "It was reported in all the papers. Scotland is not taking to this new war any better than the people of England. What's your opinion of it, doctor?"

"I think it an unfortunate venture," her husband said. "But unhappily the protests of the public are generally ignored."

"And that's a fact," the man opposite them said, bracing himself as the stage hit a bumpy spot in the road. "We could do with some road improvements up here, but that's not likely to happen."

William asked him, "Do you know Dr. Carr?"

The man nodded. "I've known him for years. He was my doctor when I was a lad. Poor old chap isn't worth much now, what with age and his drinking. There are days at a time when he isn't able to see patients. Your coming to the town will be a blessing."

"I hope that will be the general opinion," William said.

"Bound to be a bit of friction," Henry Gordon said. "But that will soon end, and you'll have plenty of patients."

Ardith continued to observe the talkative Henry Gordon

and speculate about him. He had been very quick to tag himself as the black sheep of the Gordon family, no doubt because he felt they would hear this soon in any case. In a small village, this sort of gossip went on continually. The fact he disliked his titled brother was also apparent. And he seemed to have nothing but good will for them. Perhaps he was a friend on whom they might count.

William looked at his pocket watch and said, "We should be nearing the town by this time."

Henry Gordon leaned over and looked out the other side window. He said, "As a matter of fact, we are close to Harwick. I recognize this part of the road. I'll soon be leaving you, as my little cottage is on the outskirts of the town."

William told him, "I've enjoyed meeting you. I'm sure we shall see each other soon again."

"Not a doubt about it," the man said. "I hope you find the estate and the town to your liking. And one evening you must come and have dinner with my Jeannie and me. I'd like to show you some of my Italian paintings. I spent four years in Italy and did a lot of painting there."

"That would be most interesting," Ardith said.

The man nodded and then, half-rising in his seat, knocked on the window which opened by the driver's back. When the driver opened the small aperture, Henry Gordon told him, "Let me out at my gate, Jock. I don't want to go on into the village."

It was only a few minutes later that the stage came to a halt by a lane surrounded by evergreens. The paunchy man doffed his hat again and took her hand in parting, then shook hands with William. He next left the stage and waited to be given a satchel from the rear where baggage was kept. Once he had the satchel he waved to them and started up the lane with it as the stage drove on.

"What did you make of him?" William asked her.

She hesitated. "I don't know."

"I found him amusing. We have rogues come to the hospital in London every day, but none I enjoyed more than that fellow. He may be a black sheep, but he's an interesting one. And as for his brother, Sir Douglas, not liking him, I'd say that was all in his favor."

Ardith gave her handsome husband a questioning glance. "I wonder if he didn't try a little too hard to win us over? He seemed to me to be playing a game the whole time he was in the stage."

"I'm amazed," William said. "And I'll make you a bet."

"What sort of bet?"

"That he becomes one of our closest friends and strongest supporters in Harwick!"

"You could be right," she said.

"I'm positive that I am," her young husband assured her. "I think fate was kind in having us meet him as we did. And I have an idea he'll be on our side if only to annoy his titled brother!"

Ardith glanced out the window and saw a group of cottages along the road replacing the evergreens. She said, "I think we've arrived!" And so they had.

As it turned out, Harwick had only a single street which led directly from the hills to the ocean. The street was a continuation of the road they had been following and had no more paving than the road itself. But as they came to the central area of the village, the buildings were often of two stories and closer together. The street itself leaned towards the ocean directly ahead and ended in a wharf at which there were a cluster of small fishing vessels.

The stage came to a stop outside a tavern and ale house

which bore the sign, *The Fife and Drum.* A weathered brown sign depicting a fife above a drum swung overhead from the door of the stone building. And as the stage halted, a stout bald man wearing a white apron came out of the door of the tavern to greet them.

The driver had descended from his seat and opened the door for them. William stepped out first and then helped her to the cobblestoned sidewalk. The odor of fish assailed her nostrils, and this was mixed with the smell of the salt ocean. There could be no doubt of the source from which most of the Harwick folk derived their livelihood.

The innkeeper bowed to them. He showed a smile on his fleshy, crimson-cheeked face as he asked, "Do I ken right? Are you no the new doctor and his lady?"

William was playing at being his most professional self. With boyish dignity, he said, "That is quite correct."

"Aye, I knew it!" the innkeeper declared. "John Macree asked me to meet you. He is at the county seat defending a case, and he will not be back until later in the day."

"But Lawyer Macree was to meet us," William said in mild protest.

"So he claimed," the innkeeper said. "But the court was called unexpectedly, and so he had to go to it. He asked that I see you had a clean room to refresh yourselves in and a meal of my good food before he came by to pick you up."

William looked a little less displeased. "Well, that was very good of him. But we did wish to see our new home. We are weary at the end of a long journey."

"Aye! I hae no doubt of that," the innkeeper said solemnly. "But Sir Douglas Gordon called the court for this day, and there was little Lawyer Macree could do about it."

William gave Ardith a significant look and then with a grim smile said to the innkeeper, "I perceive the point of our difficulty now. Very likely Sir Douglas knew of our arriving and that John Macree had a client to defend, and so held the court deliberately to make it more difficult for us."

The innkeeper rubbed his chin thoughtfully. "Now that could be, though I admit the thought had not occurred to me. Sir Douglas is a powerful man in these parts."

"I'm sure he is," William said. "What about our luggage?"

"The stage may leave it here," the innkeeper said. "I'll see a wagon takes it on ahead to Wyndmoor."

Ardith ventured to ask nervously, "Do you know if the house has been opened as Lawyer Macree promised?"

"Yes, madam," the innkeeper said. "It was opened days ago, and the servants Lawyer Macree engaged have been working to make all ready for you."

William turned to her and said, "It would seem Lawyer Macree devised this plan in lieu of meeting us. I think we had best follow it. We can go inside and freshen ourselves and then enjoy some food."

She nodded. "Yes. It sounds most practical."

The innkeeper looked pleased. "Lawyer Macree will keep you waiting no longer than he has to. If you will come with me I'll show you to your room."

They followed the bald man in the apron into the inn and up a dark flight of stone steps, him leading the way and breathing laboriously as he ascended the steps. They reached a narrow hall and he opened a door, stating, "My best room! Wash and rest and come down for food when you like." With that, he bowed and started down the stairs once again.

She led the way into the room, which also had a small anteroom for dressing and washing off the main bedroom. It was rather pretentious for the tiny inn, but she noticed that the room and the clothes on the wooden frame bed were spotlessly clean.

She said, "Lawyer Macree apparently meant that we should be comfortable."

"This place isn't bad at all," William agreed as he looked about, inspecting it. "And you realize that the delay has been deliberately caused by Sir Douglas Gordon."

"You're assuming that!"

"I'm certain of it," he said. "But never mind. We will succeed here in spite of him!" He went to her and regarded her with fond eyes. "You have borne up well these last few days. I hope you aren't too weary and discouraged."

She returned his smile. "I feel surprisingly well. And I only wait for the day when I can write your mother and have her bring Ian to us."

He nodded. "If all goes well, it shouldn't be long. And now make haste to wash up so we may go down for some of the landlord's good food. I'm ravishingly hungry!"

Ardith laughed. "I'm sure we'll be served fish. Did you smell the air as we got out of the stage?"

"I did," William agreed. "It's a true fishing village. But the air will be sweeter when we're away from the town itself."

She refreshed herself from the journey, and then William took advantage of the room's facilities. After which they went down to the large square room with ceiling beams which was the main public room. Here they sat at a worn table of broad planks and had a delicious meal of broiled haddock. The fish was fresh and sweet. William had a tankard of ale to help the food along, and she had a glass of sherry.

The innkeeper hovered by their table, making suggestions about all their food choices. He brought out some fine old cheese to top the meal and then stood by for their compliments.

"You have fed us well, sir," William told him. "And I'm sure my wife agrees."

Ardith smiled. "Perhaps it was because I was truly hungry, but I have seldom enjoyed a meal more."

"The house is known for its food and good companionship," the innkeeper said, clearly pleased. "We have many of the men of the village here at night and a few of the lasses as well. Of course, it's not for the gentry like yourself at such times!"

"Who knows?" William asked. "We might enjoy ourselves!"

"It is good to have Wyndmoor open once again," the old innkeeper said. "Will you work the farm?"

"I'll follow John Macree's advice about that," William said. "It will depend on whether I can get help or not."

"You'll have no trouble finding lads to work there," the innkeeper said. "Grim McLeod has taken over the post of caretaker, and he's there now."

"What a strange name," Ardith commented.

The innkeeper chuckled. "Well, it's not his true name at all. His right name is Glen, but he is a kind of solitary, quiet man, unlike his brothers, and he has six of them, so they took to calling him Grim and it caught on!"

"So everyone calls him Grim now," William suggested.

"That's it, sir," the innkeeper said. "You're lucky to get him. He's a good man, though I can't imagine why he decided to give up his fishing to work on land. He's always been a man of the sea!"

"Perhaps he is getting older," Ardith said.

"It might be that," the innkeeper agreed. "At any rate, he's a fine worker and he'll have things in order for you, I'm sure. The Bray place has been deserted for far too long."

"How long?" William asked.

The innkeeper frowned slightly. "It must be close to twenty years, sir."

William looked surprised. "I didn't know that. Why would it remain empty such a long while?"

The innkeeper looked uneasy. He said, "It's a large property, sir. And when John Bray left to go to Canada, no one seemed to want it."

"A wonder the house hasn't gone into decay," Ardith said.

"No, madam," the old innkeeper said. "Wyndmoor is too well built for that. And it should have some fine furniture in it. I was there once in John Bray's day, and he had furnished it like a castle for his young wife."

William asked, "What made him leave here?"

"After she died he had no more interest in the house or in Harwick," the innkeeper said.

Before William could go on questioning the old man, the door opened and a tall, spare man with gray side-whiskers decorating a flat face entered. The newcomer wore a shabby black suit and a black top hat. He came directly to them to doff his top hat and show a balding head.

"I'm John Macree, your lawyer," he said. "I'm sorry to have kept you waiting."

William was on his feet. "We understand you had no choice. And we have been most royally entertained."

"Excellent," Lawyer Macree said, a thin smile on his flat face. "My carriage is outside, and if you are ready we can proceed to Wyndmoor without further delay."

"We've been looking forward to this moment," Ardith said, rising.

The tall lawyer showed a shadow of a smile. "I'm sure

you will not be disappointed."

They left the inn and joined the lawyer in his carriage. It was an open rig, and he swung the horse around and drove along a lane leading from the main street. Within a short distance the lane widened to a small road. They continued along this dusty road; there were thick growths of evergreens flanking either side of the road and no sign of houses.

William asked the lawyer, "How did you make out in court?"

"Not well," Lawyer Macree said dourly. "The lad I was representing was up for poaching. And Sir Douglas is cruel when it comes to such cases."

"He found the boy guilty?" William said.

"Yes and gave him the alternative of a jail sentence or joining the army. Of course, the boy volunteered at once. Another lad to be sacrificed in the Crimea," the lawyer said with anger.

They turned a corner in the road and ahead she saw a tall stone building of some distinction rising above the evergreens. She did not ask, nor did anyone need to tell her; she knew at once this tall, graystone building was Wyndmoor. She knew it because it was the exact image of the house she had known in all her terrifying nightmares. Involuntarily, she began to tremble!

Chapter Three

Lawyer Macree drove his carriage up to the wide oaken door which gave entrance to Wyndmoor, and almost at once the door swung open and an enormous man came out, followed by a small lad. The lad ran to take hold of the horse's head in preparation to leading it to the stables, and the big man stood ready to help them step to the ground.

Ardith was fighting to control the attack of nerves which she'd had on seeing the old house in its woods setting. She did not want her husband or any of the others to notice her shock. She gazed down at the big man in the rough clothes of a fisherman waiting for them to leave the carriage. He must have easily towered more than six feet, and he was broad of shoulder as well. His graying hair was thick and long and parted on the side. His face had the melancholy look of a bloodhound, so it was not hard to understand why he had been nicknamed Grim.

William alighted first, and it was he who helped her down, with John Macree following. The lawyer paused to introduce them to the big man, who was indeed Grim McLeod. No sign of a welcoming smile showed on the giant's lined countenance, but he did nod to each of them.

"I trust you will find all in order," Grim McLeod said in a kind of rusty voice.

Lawyer Macree asked, "Did you get Mrs. Nellie MacDonald to come as housekeeper?"

The dour McLeod nodded. "Aye! She is here! But she would not come without her girl, and I refused to offer the daughter any paying work since she's daft."

Lawyer Macree at once turned to them with an embarrassed expression on his flat face. He said, "It's not as bad as it sounds. Mrs. MacDonald is a most competent woman, and she worked here years ago as a maid. So she knows the house. Her daughter is a mute and seemingly retarded, but she is a harmless child of twelve. I doubt that her presence in the servant's quarters will give you any trouble."

William took this all in and turned to her, "I'm sure it will be all right. Don't you agree, dear?"

She had been lost in a welter of troubling thoughts, and so she'd barely heard what had been said. So she ventured a nervous, "Yes, I think so."

Her young husband eyed her with concern. "You are all right, aren't you? You're not overtired?"

"No," she replied quickly. "I was merely taking note of the house and its surroundings. I wasn't listening carefully."

"Oh!" her husband said. And then by way of explanation to Lawyer Macree, he added, "My wife is of frail health. That is our main reason for coming here. Her London doctor thinks the good air here will help her."

"The air is pure!" Lawyer Macree assured them. "No one can deny that. And I hope it does you good, Mrs. Davis."

"Thank you," she said, determined to get more of a hold on herself. To pay attention to what was being said and not let memories of those terrifying nightmares plunge her into a condition of fear in which she'd not be able to tolerate the house.

Lawyer Macree turned to question the big man once

again, asking, "And did you get the other servants I suggested?"

"Most of them," Grim McLeod said. "I was able to hire Meg Johnson as personal maid to Mrs. Davis."

"Excellent," the old lawyer sounded pleased. And he turned to Ardith to explain, "Meg has been in service in Edinburgh to some of the fine families. She returned here because she was homesick. She is one of the few available trained as a proper ladies' maid."

William smiled at Grim McLeod and said, "I'm sure we are chiefly fortunate in having a competent man like yourself to head our staff."

In his dour way the big man said, "I will serve as best I can, sir."

"What made you decide to give up fishing?" William asked him.

For the first time the giant showed an uneasy look. He said, "It was not an easy decision for me to make, sir. But the fishing has been poor the last two years, and there have been barely enough cleared from the catches to provide food for the families of my brothers. As the eldest, I felt it my duty to look for some kind of employment elsewhere."

William listened and seemed to be impressed. He said, "We will try and make you glad you came to the decision, McLeod."

"Thank you, sir," the big man said. "Mrs. MacDonald is inside. And the baggage came from *The Fife and Drum* a little while ago."

Lawyer Macree turned to them with a thin smile on his weathered face. "Then I should say the moment has come to cross the threshold of your new home!"

"So it has!" William said with enthusiasm. Smiling, he swung Ardith up in his arms and headed for the wide entrance of the old mansion. "This, I understand, is the proper approach."

She laughed, protesting, "I'm not a bride and this is not my first home!"

"It is the most impressive one we've had, so we may as well follow the ritual," William said, and he carried her in and put her down again at the sight of the waiting Nellie MacDonald and a petite, yellow-haired girl in a maid's uniform who stood at her side.

William extended his hand to the pleasant looking matron and said, "You must be our new housekeeper, Mrs. MacDonald?"

The woman nervously returned his handshake. "That I am," she said. "And this is Meg, who will be personal maid to your wife."

William smiled at the attractive girl who blushed wildly and looked down at the floor. He said, "I'm sure Mrs. Davis and I will be pleased with everything."

Mrs. MacDonald at once exclaimed, "The house has been shut up for so long and the furniture and other things let go, that I have had a hard time getting it properly cleaned. But I have done my best."

Ardith summoned a smile for the woman. "I'd say you'd done a praiseworthy job, Mrs. MacDonald."

"Thank you, madam," the older woman said. "There is fine furniture here, and it deserves better care than it had. But at least the house is liveable now."

Lawyer Macree said, "Since I'm familiar with Wyndmoor, I can show them through it. You and Meg may return to your duties."

Mrs. MacDonald looked relieved at not being called on for the task of tour guide. She said, "You will be remaining for dinner, sir?"

The lawyer turned to William, "If you and your wife care to have me join you?"

"I consider it an excellent idea," William agreed. "We have many things to settle and it is already late in the afternoon."

Mrs. MacDonald said, "Very well, then. I'll have dinner ready for seven." And she and the girl went off down a long hall which led to the rear of the old mansion.

Lawyer Macree became the dry professional as he turned to them and said, "This house is, as you will see, extremely well built. Constructed by the family of John Bray some seventy-five years ago. I may say only the Bray family have occupied it up until now. John Bray was the last to live here."

Ardith said, "The innkeeper said he left the house after his wife died."

"Yes," the lawyer said and cleared his throat. "As you can see, the reception hall is ample. There is a large drawing room to the left and a good-sized dining room on the right. The library and study are to the rear as are the sewing rooms. And the bedrooms, excluding those of the servants in the rear and cellar areas, are all on the second and third floor. But then you can best decide about your property by seeing it. All the furnishings were included in the price which makes it an exceptional investment from any point of view."

The lawyer's voice droned on as he took them from room to room of the imposing old mansion. Ardith could not help but be impressed by the thorough way in which the house had been cleaned in a short time. She continued to fight her terror about the place and the fact the house in her nightmares had been so remarkably like it. She tried to tell herself that all old mansions of this sort bore many similarities. But she could not completely conquer her fear of the house as she clung to William's arm on their tour of the many rooms.

They were on the second floor now, and Lawyer Macree opened a door to a richly appointed bedchamber decorated in a shade of dark blue. He said, "This is the master's bedchamber and there is an adjoining bedroom much like it." He moved to a door which connected the two and showed them the bedroom beyond, which was almost the same size but decorated in gray.

William said to her, "We shall each occupy our own bedroom here. It will be better for you! Should I be called out to see a patient in the night, which is all too likely, you need not be bothered."

Ardith at once felt a new uneasiness about sleeping alone in the large blue room with its massive canopied bed. She said, "The rooms are so huge for only one person."

Her young husband said, "All the better for your health. And since there is but a door between the rooms, we will always be close to one another. Doubtless we will spend much of the time in your bedroom. But with all this space, it would be silly not to take advantage of having separate sleeping quarters."

She saw that William had made up his mind and it would do no good to argue the point. Lawyer Macree stood by, discreetly silent during this domestic debate, a bland look on the flat face with the gray side-whiskers.

They went on upstairs to an area of guest rooms and rooms meant only for storage. Most of these had remained locked for years. They stepped onto a small balcony which looked out onto the sea. And after they had studied the unruly dark waves and the cliffs they returned downstairs. Lawyer Macree led them into the living room which had a massive cut-glass chandelier and paneled walls of dark walnut. The room was furnished with exquisite taste and clearly much thought and money must have been spent to make it so nearly perfect.

Ardith took in the fine pieces of furniture, the rich carpets and finally the impressive oil paintings which lined the walls of the room. She said, "The former owner must have had a great interest in art."

Lawyer Macree nodded. "John Bray was a man of cultivated tastes."

"And he left all this to emigrate to Canada?" she asked the lawyer.

"Yes," the lawyer said. "He left here twenty years ago with his sister, Mary. Neither of them have ever returned."

William said, "And the property has been for sale all that long while."

"It has," the flat-faced Macree said. "It seemed we would never find a buyer. In fact, Sir Douglas Gordon was so sure of this he didn't make any proper bid for the property, although he made it known he wanted it."

Ardith said, "Why didn't he make a true offer for the place if he really wished to buy it?"

Again the lawyer took on an evasive air, saying, "I don't think Sir Douglas thought it was necessary. He was so sure he would eventually get the property for a pittance."

William said, "And I ruined any hope of that."

"You most certainly did, doctor," Lawyer Macree agreed.

Ardith was still mystified by it all. "Why should it take twenty years to find a buyer at a proper price?"

The lawyer's eyes turned to a large, magnificent painting on the wall close by where he stood. Ignoring her question, he said, "That is a portrait of Fanny Bray, the wife of John

Bray, whose death was the cause of his leaving Wyndmoor. He had completely refurnished and redecorated the house for her when she came here as a bride."

Ardith went over to study the painting of a regal, black-haired girl with intelligent eyes in an even-featured face. The girl in the portrait was wearing a low cut white gown with flowing skirts. She had a band of white satin around her hair with roses of red set in the satin. The beauty sat on an ebony chair with low arms.

Lawyer Macree turned from the painting to study her. And he told her, "I think it remarkable. You know you bear something of a resemblance to the late Fanny Bray!"

"By George, she does!" William said with some awe, his eyes fixed on Ardith, "Just now I became aware of it myself. Their eyes are a lot alike and the jawline!"

She stared up at the large painting with mixed feelings. She could not see the marked resemblance which they were suggesting, but she could see the woman's features were of her same general type.

"I don't truly resemble her," she protested. "Or at least only in a casual way."

"You may not see it," William said, "but there is surely a resemblance."

Lawyer Macree told her. "You ought to be flattered, Mrs. Davis. Fanny Bray was one of the loveliest looking women I have ever met."

"I'm grateful for the compliment," she said, "though I must question it."

Lawyer Macree stared at the portrait again with almost a worshipful air. "You know, there were men who fell so completely under her spell their whole lives were changed. John Bray was one of them. And we have another still here in the village. She was a famous concert singer, of course.

Appeared in theaters and halls over the British Isles and on the Continent as well."

Ardith asked him, "Did you ever hear her sing?"

"Many times," the lawyer said with a hint of nostalgia in his tone and manner. "But in the year before she died, she changed a good deal. And one of the ways in which she changed was turning her back on her singing. But there is still a fine pianoforte in the conservatory."

It seemed to Ardith that the lawyer had a special feeling for the woman in the portrait — the lovely woman whose death had sent her husband away from this old mansion. She was certain there was some legend connected with Fanny Bray and her death.

She said, "She must have died young."

"Relatively," the old lawyer said. "I'd say she was about your age when that portrait was painted. And she was dead two years later."

Like a flash those nightmares she'd had came rushing to fill her mind. She eyed the thin lawyer with the gray side-whiskers and asked him tautly, "What caused her death?"

"Yes," William said, also turning to the lawyer. "You never did tell me that."

Lawyer Macree wet his lips with the end of his tongue. Then he said, "I suppose I skipped the matter because it is not all that pleasant. Mrs. Bray died as the result of an unfortunate misunderstanding."

A chill coursed down Ardith's spine. "What kind of a misunderstanding?"

The lawyer took a white handkerchief from his coat pocket and patted his brow with it. "You will excuse me," he murmured. "I'm subject to heat flashes. The truth of it is, the poor lady was murdered by a group of madmen!"

"No!" she said, feeling faint and clutching her husband's

arm. Now she was going over her nightmare, sure it fitted whatever had happened here. The nightmare had been a forerunner to her coming to this place. A kind of warning! A warning which they had ignored by buying Wyndmoor!

William turned to pat her hand and show concern. He said, "You mustn't let it bother you. All of this happened many years ago. It has nothing to do with us!"

She paid no attention to him but gazed at the old lawyer accusingly as she said, "This is why the house remained empty so long. Why no one offered to buy it. That's what made Sir Douglas think he would eventually get it at his own price!"

The old lawyer raised a hand in a pleading gesture. "There is some truth in what you say."

She said, "Why didn't you tell all this to my husband?"

"It didn't seem needful," Lawyer Macree replied. "I do not think what happened here two decades ago should in any way harm the property."

"Some people must have thought so. The place has been empty and deserted for twenty years," Ardith reminded him unhappily. And turning to William, she added, "I'm afraid we've made a terrible mistake in coming here!"

"Don't get that in your head!" William told her. And he turned to the old lawyer to say, "My wife has not been enjoying good health. It does not take too much to upset her. I'm sure you understand."

"Certainly, Dr. Davis," Lawyer Macree said. "But let me assure you that never could you have found a place anywhere else of this quality for the price which you paid for this."

William said, "I'm sure of that. Though I do wish you had confided the history of the house to me."

"You should have done that," Ardith said unhappily.

"I'm sorry if you feel I have in any way taken advantage of you," the lawyer said. "And I think that now Sir Douglas Gordon has learned his lesson and would be glad to take the property off your hands for what you paid for it."

"No," William said. "I have made my choice in coming here, and I will not let silly fears change my mind."

"Are you certain that is wise?" Ardith asked him. "We know so little about this place and what really happened here!"

"Whatever happened, it is no concern of ours," her young husband said almost in anger. "Let me decide this!"

"I will not be happy here. I know it!" she warned him.

"Nonsense," William said. And he confided to the lawyer, "My wife is weary from her journey. I think what we all need is some food in our stomachs and then an early bed."

"I'm sure Mrs. MacDonald is ready to serve dinner at any time," the lawyer said.

"Then let us have it now," William said. "And during the meal you shall give us an account of this dark business you've mentioned."

"I shall be happy to offer the details," the lawyer said.

The meal Mrs. MacDonald served was a notable one. And Ardith felt that if it were a sample of what was to come she could not complain about the food being offered or the way it was prepared. For this first dinner the housekeeper had found some wild partridge and each of them had a luscious, tiny bird roasted with wild rice and a stuffing made tasty by a special mixture of wild herbs.

Every course of the dinner was excellent, and three wines graced the table. Candlelight provided the warm glow which gave them the right atmosphere for such a dinner. The dessert was a rich pudding and tea was served along with it. Fine as the meal turned out to be, Ardith enjoyed it only a little. Her thoughts wandered from the dinner table, and she worried that the old house might have some horrible spell on it which would now twist their lives in some tragic fashion. The old lawyer had yet to explain the way in which the former mistress of the mansion had met her death.

Both William and Lawyer Macree produced long-stemmed clay pipes which they filled with tobacco and lighted. Ardith felt she could wait no longer and so directed herself to the lawyer, saying, "You have not yet explained about Fanny Bray."

The flat face showed a grim look. He held his pipe in one hand and with the other he uneasily rubbed one of his gray side-whiskers. Then he said, "She was thought to be a witch, ma'am. One of those in league with the Devil!"

She was astounded. "That lovely creature a witch! I don't believe it! I can't think that even in this remote place such accusations would be made in this day and age."

"It happened twenty years ago," the lawyer reminded her. "And up here in the Highlands there is still a good deal of superstition. You have surely heard of the mother witch? She is said to be the Gyre Carline or Nicniven, a Hecate of the countryside! And then there is the Devil's Mark, somewhere on the body of the evil one, usually a scar in the shape of a hoof print!"

William looked astounded. "You're saying such beliefs continue to exist?"

The lawyer looked embarrassed. "Not among the educated few. But among the lower classes there is still a deal of witchcraft. There are many who believe in 'dark looks,' unmentionable powers and spells."

"Incredible," William said, sitting back in his chair.

Ardith asked in a strained voice, "What made people think Fanny Bray was a witch?"

"It is a grim tale," the old lawyer said. "No man was more happy than John Bray when the lovely Fanny agreed to marry him and he brought her here to this house."

"And then?" Ardith said.

The lawyer gazed off into space as he recollected the events. In a sad voice, he said, "The happiness was not to last long. John Bray had an older sister, Mary. She was a spinster and had seen to the running of the house until her brother's marriage. At his urging, she remained on and continued to look after the household which should have been his new wife's responsibility. Fanny was too pleasant a person to make anything of this. But she must have felt lost, no longer having her career and having nothing to occupy her."

Ardith asked, "Didn't John Bray realize that?"

"He didn't seem to," the lawyer said. "Not even when the man she had spurned to marry him appeared on the scene. His name was James Burnett, a handsome man and a sculptor of note. He followed Fanny all the way to this remote village and begged her to leave John Bray and go off with him. He insisted his love for her was as great as ever, and he warned her that this was no proper life for her."

"But she wouldn't listen to him?" she suggested.

"No," Lawyer Macree said. "She was in love with John Bray and so she was prepared to live the lonely life which he offered her. James Burnett couldn't believe it! He bought a house here and continued to plead for her love at every opportunity. She finally refused to see him, but he stayed on. And the story is that his love turned to hate. He became a recluse having little to do with the village, going away by times to visit London or Edinburgh, but always returning.

He still lives here and the yard behind his house is filled with his sculptures."

Ardith said, "You haven't explained how Fanny Bray came to be regarded as a witch."

The lawyer took his pipe from his mouth. "That didn't happen for a year or more after she came here to live. John Bray didn't make any attempt to introduce her to the local people, which I thought a mistake. He kept her here, shielded from the town. And after a while, there began to be whispers about her. Some said she was mad in spite of her beauty. Others claimed she was a witch who remained shut up here weaving spells. All nonsense, of course. I met Fanny Bray, as lawyer to her husband, and found her a charming woman."

William asked, "When did the real trouble begin?"

The lawyer frowned. "I should say it started with the white cat."

"White cat?" Ardith echoed.

"Yes," the lawyer said. "The elder Lady Gordon was alive then. And both her sons were at home. The present Sir Douglas had succeeded to the title young because of the early death of his father. And then there was his brother, Henry, the artist. He was still living here, and a wild young man if I may make the observation."

"He's recently returned to live here, hasn't he?" William said.

"He has," Lawyer Macree said grimly. "He's rented a cottage on the outskirts of the village and is living in sin with some barmaid he met in Edinburgh. His brother and Lady Mona are in a dither about it, I can promise you."

"What about the cat?" Ardith said, wanting to bring him back to the main account of the witch business.

"Yes," the lawyer said. "The white cat was a pet of the

elder Lady Gordon. She was very devoted to it. Suddenly it vanished and there was a great to-do about it. But there was more commotion when the poor animal was found, strangled by a scarf bearing the initials of Fanny Bray. The cat's body was in a ditch near Wyndmoor, and on its side there was burned the mark of the Devil's hoof!"

William scowled at this. "It sounds too pat. No doubt somebody who hated the Gordons killed the cat and used the scarf and the Devil's mark to throw suspicion on Fanny Bray and suggest she was a witch."

"Exactly what I thought," the lawyer said. "I don't know how this malicious person could have managed to get the scarf, but no doubt they had the means. One of the servants could have stolen it for a friend. Who knows?"

Ardith listened to the account in horror. She said, "What then?"

Lawyer Macree gave her a knowing look. "With all the gossip there had been, this started a good deal more. People gathered in small groups and whispered ugly things about Wyndmoor and its mistress whom they believed to be a witch."

"Was John Bray aware of this?" William asked.

"He could not help but be," the lawyer said. "But he chose to become indignant and do nothing. All might have ended there if the child hadn't been found throttled in the woods behind Wyndmoor a few weeks later. A twelve-year-old girl found in the deep thicket with the mark of the Devil's hoof crudely cut into the flesh of her cheek. She had also been throttled, although there was no scarf or anything of that sort. Still, the local folk linked the murder of the girl with that of the cat and blamed Fanny Bray."

"They were bound to," Ardith exclaimed. "The plot against her was deliberate."

"No doubt," the lawyer sighed. "Things really became bad. The village was in an uproar. An old woman claiming to have second sight was brought in from the country, and she proclaimed that Fanny Bray was truly a witch. Of course, the majority wanted to believe the ignorant, nearly-blind old woman. Her name is Coline Dougall and she's still alive, though completely blind now. She's ninety or more and lives with a great-grandson down the shore."

William said, "What then?"

The lawyer shook his head. "Things were in an uproar. Coline Dougall said Fanny was a witch and in league with the Devil. The villagers came here to Wyndmoor and stoned the place until more than half the windows were gone. In a rage, John Bray fired a musket into the crowd and injured a couple of them in a minor way. This brought him a rebuke and the threat of imprisonment from Sir Douglas Gordon."

Ardith asked, "Was that when they murdered her?"

"No," the lawyer replied. "I think she still might have lived if an epidemic hadn't hit the village. It was a kind of pneumonia, the ones who got it didn't last more than three or four days. The sexton was busy with burials, and the air was filled with talk of Fanny bringing the epidemic to the village as part of the Devil's work. I came here and warned John about the gossip and begged him to take Fanny away from here. At least for a little while."

"Of course, he refused," Ardith said bitterly.

"You are right," the lawyer replied. "He claimed it was the greatest nonsense to call his wife a witch. Fanny was pale and frightened, but said nothing. In the face of all this, John Bray did a foolish thing. He went off to Edinburgh on business and allowed Fanny to remain here with only his older sister, Mary, for company and protection. Word of his being away got out, and it was then the awful thing happened."

"Go on," she said in a tense voice.

The flat face of the old lawyer showed distress even at this late date after the events which he was relating. He said, "The night after John Bray left, a masked group of men broke into the house and marched upstairs and took Fanny from her bed. They dragged her out to the woods, tied her to a tree, threw pitch over her and burned her to death! It was a mark of shame which Harwick will never lose. The murderers melted away in the darkness, and no one could say who they were. Perhaps the ugliest rumor of all was that they were led by her rejected suitor, James Burnett. One man claimed he knew definitely that the embittered sculptor was the organizer and leader of the murderous gang. It was never proven and he still lives here."

Ardith listened to the account in sheer horror. She knew that in most of its features it resembled the nightmare which had been tormenting her since before she left London. She could only presume that somehow the ghost of the murdered Fanny had been trying to warn her. That the look-alike who had lived here twenty years ago had broken through from the other side to give her a message in her troubled dreams.

William looked troubled by what he'd heard. He asked the lawyer, "Then what?"

"Mary Bray was hysterical with grief and fear. John came back and grimly went about the business of burying the remains of his lovely wife. You can find the grave in the clearing behind the house. Of course, the epidemic ended within a few days; it would have anyway, but those who had blamed it on Fanny continued to do so, and agreed that it was her burning which had freed the village of the plague."

"And John Bray closed the house and he and his sister went to Canada?" William said.

"Yes. John could not bring himself to remain here any longer, or even stay in Scotland. He gave me instructions to sell the property. Every year he sends me the money to pay the taxes on it. But until you came along, I wasn't able to find a buyer, except for Sir Douglas and his offer was ridiculous; all the other prospective buyers heard the history of the place and turned it down because they believed it was cursed."

"It was at this point I came along," William said. "Don't you think you owed it to me to tell me the history of the place when you offered the property to me?"

The lawyer looked uneasy. "I think I did you a favor. You are the owner of a fine property for much less than its true worth. Had I told you the story, I might have stopped you from buying Wyndmoor."

"I think you would have," William agreed. "I'm not a superstitious person, but my wife is not all that well. I'm not sure that a house with a past like this one has is the best place for her to be."

Ardith glanced his way. "Are you going to ask me to stay here?"

"Yes," William said promptly. "We have committed ourselves too far."

She pleaded with him. "You know about the dreams I've had. It is as if she had knowledge of our coming and wanted to warn us off!"

"Nonsense!" William chided her.

Lawyer Macree inquired, "May I ask what Mrs. Davis means?"

"Nothing," William said, almost curtly. "She was referring to another matter."

"Oh?" The lawyer didn't sound convinced.

"I have made up my mind," William went on. "I shall remain here and eventually I'll build myself a good practice. What about Dr. Ivor Carr?"

Lawyer Macree said, "The old man has been more active than usual since hearing you were coming. Before that there were weeks when he didn't show himself and no one could reach him in the house. It was like having no doctor. Now he is making a big show of taking care of everyone."

William smiled grimly. "At least my coming has done that much good."

"He won't last," the lawyer promised. "A little while and he'll begin his drinking again. The people haven't any confidence in him."

"We shall see," William observed dryly. "I shall make a professional courtesy call on him and inform him of my plans to establish an office here. After that, it will be up to him."

"As soon as the word gets around you are here, you'll have patients," the old lawyer said. He reached into his vest and took out his pocket watch to study it. "It is later than I thought," he said, rising. "I must get on my way. I know you are both weary and anxious to get some rest."

"It has been a tiring journey," William agreed, rising.

The old lawyer got to his feet and came around to where Ardith was standing. He bowed to her in his courtly manner and told her, "You must not be afraid of the past. That is all over with."

"I hope so," she said faintly.

"Our good Highland air will do you fine service," Lawyer Macree assured her. "In a short while, your lungs will heal and you will have vigorous health. I have seen this happen to many others."

"Thank you," she said.

The old lawyer seemed reluctant to leave her. He took her hand and kissed it with great chivalry. "Forget the story I told you. Think about the fine future you and your husband are bound to have here." And with a bow, he left her to join William and be accompanied to the front door.

Darkness was at hand, and she watched the two men walk out to the front hall lost in the shadows. Fear tightened its grip around her heart the moment she was left alone. She left the dining room and went across the corridor into the living room. Mrs. MacDonald had seen to it that candles had been lighted at strategic places in the enormous room. Ardith picked up one of the candles in its holder and went over to the portrait of the long-dead Fanny to study it once more.

She was trembling as she studied the face of the dark-haired woman whom she so strangely resembled. It was too much of a coincidence to feel comfortable about. That, along with her series of nightmares, made her believe that strong psychic forces which she did not understand were at work within and around her.

A soft footstep behind her caused her to go taut and turn to see who it might be. It was William. Her husband said, "I had an idea I might find you here."

"I'm sick with terror," she confided to him. "I don't think I can live here!"

"Because of a tragedy that happened twenty years ago?"

"No," she said in a voice with a tremor in it. "Because of what is happening right now. You know the strange dreams I've had. Of being hunted by a group of masked men, taken prisoner in a bedroom and dragged through the woods! It's exactly what that old man said happened here to Fanny Bray!"

William placed a comforting arm around her, his countenance calm in the glow of the candle she was holding. He said, "The story is familiar because it is a common one. As I told you before, I'm sure you must have read it somewhere in one of those too exciting novels."

"No!" she protested.

"As to your looking like this girl in the portrait, that is merely saying you are the same type. I have no doubt we could find dozens of young women who resemble her to such a small degree. We must consider these things sensibly."

"I want to," she said, "but I'm afraid!"

His eyes met hers. "You do want to get well? And you want me to have a successful practice?"

"You know I do," she said plaintively.

"Then have faith in me, believe what I tell you," he said, and he drew her close to kiss her with a gentle ardor.

She shut her eyes as their lips met and fought to hold back her tears. When he released her, she whispered, "I'll try! I really will!"

And she meant to. He saw her up to her bedroom. And Meg, the petite, attractive maid with the straw-colored hair, was there to help her prepare for bed. She dismissed the girl almost at once, as she was used to caring for herself. After she had undressed and put on her nightgown, William came to her from the adjoining room in his dressing gown. He stayed with her a few minutes, saw her to bed and blew out the candle on her bedside table. Then he left her to return to his room.

She was so weary she fell asleep almost at once. She did not know how long she slept, but when she suddenly awakened she felt both chilled and drenched with perspiration. And she was no longer in her own room!

She was seated at the pianoforte in the conservatory with her fingers wildly rambling over the keys!

Chapter Four

Shocked by the discovery of where she was, Ardith lifted her hands from the keyboard and gazed into the shadows around her in the deserted room! She let out an involuntary scream and then pressed her trembling hands to her bosom. She was still seated at the pianoforte when she heard a shuffling sound and then saw the faint glow of a candle approaching the open doorway at the end of the room.

"Who's there?" a frightened female voice asked. It was Mrs. MacDonald in nightgown and cap and with a shawl over her shoulders.

Ardith stood up. "I'm sorry. Did I waken you?"

The woman came closer to her, peering at her anxiously as she held the candle up to study her. "Mrs. Davis!" she gasped. "You're drenched with sweat! What brought you down here?"

"I don't know," she said uncertainly.

"Don't know?"

"No. I only remember going to bed and then waking up here playing the pianoforte."

"And very well you were playing it," the older woman said. "I was about to get into bed when I heard the music. My room is just behind this one. I had to come see what was going on."

"Of course."

Mrs. MacDonald said, "I didn't know what I might find, with all the stories."

"What stories?"

The housekeeper looked uncomfortable. "None that should worry you, ma'am. It's just that some say she comes here of a dark night and sits and plays."

"Who?" she asked tautly, although she really didn't need to.

Mrs. MacDonald sighed. "Her! The one they burned in the woods! Fanny Bray!"

"I'm sorry to have frightened you."

"I was frightened, I can tell you," the older woman said. "I've never heard the ghost music myself, but I know those who swear they have. They used to come by the house when it was locked up and hear the music through the window."

"I'm sure that is an exaggeration," she said.

"No doubt, ma'am," Mrs. MacDonald said, but she did not sound convinced.

"I have no idea how I came down here," she said. "I must have walked in my sleep."

"I had a cousin who almost had to be tied in her bed for two or three years after she went in service," the housekeeper said sympathetically. "The poor girl nearly was dismissed from her job because of it. But the master of the house was a kindly man and brought a doctor in to examine her. He said it was nerves and she'd recover from it in due time. And she did. Has seven healthy children now!"

"Thank you," she said in a wry voice. "You are most comforting."

"You ought to be in your bed, with all that sweat. You'll get a chill, I vow!" the housekeeper worried. And she doffed her shawl and put it around Ardith's shoulders, "Keep that on until you are back in bed."

"I shouldn't take it from you," she said, shivering.

"I don't miss it at all, ma'am," the older woman assured her. "I'll see you safely to your room, and you can give it back to me then."

Ardith shuddered. "I'm being a nuisance."

"Not at all," the older woman said. "I'm glad to be of some service. I heard that your health was frail."

They began walking out of the room in the direction of the stairs as they went on talking in low voices. Ardith said, "I am a consumptive."

"You poor thing!"

"I thought I was cured. Then I had another attack in London. And the doctor suggested I come up here."

"The air here is good for the lungs," Mrs. MacDonald agreed as they started up the stairs.

"I miss my little son, Ian," Ardith lamented. "I had to leave him in Edinburgh for a while with my mother-in-law."

"I'm sure she'll be good to him."

"I know that," Ardith said. "She is a wonderful woman. But I do miss my son."

"That's only natural," the older woman said.

"I take strong medicine three times a day. The last dose before I go to bed at night."

"I know," Mrs. MacDonald said. "The doctor mentioned it to me and gave me the medicine bottle. And I had Meg put the drops in a glass of water and leave it on your bedside table. I do hope you found it."

They were on the landing and she whispered, "Yes, I took the medicine. But now I'm wondering if that medicine, combined with my weariness, didn't cause me to sleepwalk."

"It very well might," the other woman whispered back.

"Since, as I understand it, this sort of thing is all caused by upset nerves."

"I don't want to wake the doctor."

"You're sure you shouldn't?"

"No," she said. "I'll discuss it with him in the morning. He needs his rest badly. He has so much to do now that we are finally here."

"Just as you say, ma'am."

They reached the door of her room, and she saw that it was open. She turned to the housekeeper, "I must have left it open after me."

"Should I lock the door?"

"No. I don't think I'll sleepwalk again tonight," she said. "Thank you for the shawl." And she removed it and gave it back to the worried woman.

"Is there anything else I can do?"

"No. You've been most helpful. Thank you and good night," she whispered. And she went on into her bedroom and shut the door behind her.

She crossed to the bed and rummaged to straighten out the bedclothes and get under them. They were mauled about and she guessed she must have stirred around a good deal before getting up and going downstairs. Only when she was in bed with the clothes tucked around her did she begin to realize the enormity of it all.

She had somehow found her way out of the room and down to the pianoforte, which she had seen only once during the tour of the house in the afternoon. And she had never sleepwalked before in all her life!

How to explain it? She'd been playing the pianoforte very well, according to Mrs. MacDonald. And yet she had no idea of what tune she had chosen or even of playing it. A new feeling of terror surged through her. Perhaps it hadn't been an example of sleepwalking at all, but a case of her body being taken over by an unhappy spirit. The spirit of Fanny Bray!

She had a hard time fighting to control her nerves, to keep from going to the adjoining room where William was sleeping and sob it all out to him. But she did not want to waken him. He would be bound to be irritable and accuse her of having another bad dream. He would somehow make light of her weird beliefs. Better to wait until morning.

If she could!

She stared up into the darkness of the room and wished that there might be at least a single moonbeam to pierce the blackness and make her feel less isolated. Anything to lessen her terror. And now she began to perspire again, and she had the depressed conviction that her health was growing worse rather than better. She would never see Ian again! Never sit him on her lap or run her fingers though his soft, curly hair! How she missed her child!

She would die here in this old mansion with a curse on it. Even now the ghost of Fanny might have taken hold of her. If the unhappy spirit could make her move through the dark house and seat herself at the piano and play, she could well be made to do other things. From now on, whenever her eyes closed in sleep she would know a new fear of what she might do before she wakened.

She wearily went over all this in her mind until at last her eyes closed again in her exhaustion. It was now that she began to have the familiar nightmare once more. The eerie dream in which she was filled with terror, trying to escape a dreadful fate, hunted by the men in black masks. The grim nightmare followed its usual pattern. She fled to her bedroom and the masked men pursued her there and dragged her screaming down the stairway!

With a whimpering sound, she opened her eyes and saw that it was daylight and the little maid, Meg, was standing by her, looking down at her with a rather frightened expression. She at once felt embarrassed and lifted herself on an elbow.

"Was I talking in my sleep?" she asked the girl.

The maid with the straw-colored hair nodded. "Yes, ma'am. You were moaning and acting as if you were in pain."

"I had a bad dream."

"I'm sorry, ma'am. I didn't mean to wake you."

She sat up and ran her fingers through her long raven hair. "It's all right. I'm sure it is time I was up anyway. Is the master about?"

Meg nodded. "Yes, ma'am. He came down to breakfast almost a full hour ago."

"He should have come and wakened me," she said.

"I have hot water for your morning bath and the tub ready," the maid told her.

"Thank you," Ardith said, swinging out of bed.

The tub was a large galvanized one, and when she sat in it the water covered all but her knees. She enjoyed the luxury of this first bath since she'd left Edinburgh. Meg was helpful, hovering by with soap and scrubbing her back for her. The attractive girl had apparently been well trained in her Edinburgh post.

As the maid helped dry her when she stepped from the tub, Ardith said, "You are most helpful. I'm glad Mrs. MacDonald selected you as my personal maid."

Meg blushed with appreciation. She said, "I do my best, ma'am. Tell me if you are not satisfied. Did you get your medicine? I prepared it and left it on your bedside table when I turned down the bed."

"I found it. Please do that every night, otherwise I'm liable to forget it," Ardith said with a smile as she gave the maid the wet towel and crossed to her clothes to begin dressing.

Once again the maid was helpful. And when Ardith was fully dressed, Meg busied herself cleaning up the room. "I will have the water drained and the tub put away while you are down to breakfast," she promised.

"No hurry," Ardith smiled from the door to the hall. And then she went downstairs.

William was crossing the hallway when she appeared at the foot of the stairs. He came to her and embraced her and gave her a brief kiss. "You look very well this morning," he said. "You seemed to be sleeping soundly when I came to your room a while ago. So I decided not to wake you."

"I rested fairly well," she said. "Have you had breakfast?"

"Yes," he said. "But I shall come and have another cup of tea with you."

Not until the maid had finished serving them and they were alone at the breakfast table did she dare to tell him of her strange experience of the previous night. Then she gave him all the details of what had happened. He listened with an almost sullen look on his handsome face.

She said, "You know I have never walked in my sleep before!"

"Not even as a child?" he asked sharply.

"I can't recall any such incident."

Her young doctor husband stared at her. "I'll warrant there were some," was his reply. "Most people who have a history of sleepwalking show first symptoms in childhood. They are often bothered at later intervals in their lives, mostly when they are in a nervous state."

"You think it was just ordinary sleepwalking," she said, placing a strong emphasis on the ordinary.

"I do," he agreed. "Whatever else would you expect me to think?"

Ardith hesitated. "I don't want to make you angry."

"Meaning?"

Again, she hesitated. "Last night I had a recurrence of that nightmare. The one which fits in so well with the tragedy of Fanny Bray."

He spread a hand in a plea for her to be reasonable. "I don't think you should stress that your nightmares are somewhat like what actually took place here years ago. We've been over all that."

"I know and you make nothing of it," she said unhappily. "But think of what I did last night. I went down and played the pianoforte! Mrs. MacDonald found me there!"

"It is embarrassing," William said. "But no more than that."

She put down her empty tea cup and fixed her eyes on his as she said resolutely, "Shall I tell you what I think? I think I may have been taken over by Fanny's spirit. That she somehow entered my body and made me do it!"

"That is sheer nonsense," William said with anger. "I will not listen to such theories."

"You won't even consider the possibility? So we might take steps against it happening again?"

"No. I have no belief in spirits of the sort you are trying to link with last night. You should know that. As your husband, and your doctor, I tell you the sleepwalking was brought on by exhaustion and nervous stress. Try to rid your mind of your unhappy thoughts and I vow you'll sleepwalk no more."

She was hurt by his lack of sensitivity towards her in the

matter, but she knew he was taking this stand for her good and so she did not dare argue with him about it. She still held to her own views, but she realized that it could be a battle she would have to fight alone.

Her young husband broke into her thoughts by saying, "I propose, this morning, to pay a courtesy visit on Dr. Ivor Carr. And I would like you to come along if you will. I'll ask McLeod to have a rig ready for us."

Ardith did not enjoy the prospect of visiting the old drunken doctor whom William had come to rival. But since her husband felt it a necessary duty, she again must give in to him.

She rose from the table. "Very well. How soon do you wish to leave?"

"In a half-hour," William said, also getting up. "I have decided where my office will be."

"Oh?"

"Yes," he went on enthusiastically. "There is a rear parlor behind the drawing room, and it has a door of its own which leads directly to the side lawn. I propose to convert that room into an office and a waiting room. It will require only the raising of one partition and having a doorway made between the two."

"It sounds an excellent idea," she agreed.

"I'm sure of it," he said. "I will have plenty of room for my books and desk, plus an examining table and corner for pharmacy. And yet the area will be shut away from the rest of the house and have its own entrance."

"There is already a door from the back of the parlor to one of the hallways," she recalled.

"Yes," he said. "I shall use that for my own comings and goings between the office and the house. I've asked McLeod to get the work started at once."

She gave him an encouraging smile. "I'm glad it is working out well for you." At the same time she was thinking that it hadn't turned out that ideal for her.

William nodded. "Making good here is extremely important to me," he said. And giving her an anxious glance, he added, "And I want you to regain your health. That is the main purpose for our being here. I have put this above everything. So do ignore the unhappy history of this place and try to keep your thoughts calm and pleasant, conducive to a quick recovery."

"I will try," she said quietly as she left him to go upstairs and dress for the visit to the old doctor.

When she came down again, she was wearing a tiny bonnet of brown and a sober dress to match. She felt it would be an occasion of some solemnity and she had better dress the role of the serious wife of an equally serious, young doctor. Best to make a solid impression, especially with the old doctor and his wife who were almost sure to be super-critical of a new rival in the village.

She went outside as the morning was sunny and pleasant. There was no sign of her husband or the carriage. But she imagined he might be back in the stables talking to Grim McLeod. As she stood there debating whether to go around to the stables or wait by the front door, she was suddenly aware of someone staring at her.

A weird figure emerged from the bushes opposite the house and stood in the clearing of grass, staring at her unashamedly. The intruder was a gnarled-faced old man with long, iron gray hair. He had a kind of squint and he was wearing a faded tam and the traditional Highland kilt though his was so shabby and dirty it was hard to see what clan its plaid might represent.

The old man had a look of fear on his lined face, and he

pointed a knobby finger at her and gasped, " 'Tis you! Come back again!"

His manner upset her. In a taut voice, she said, "Who are you? What are you doing here?"

The intruder went on behaving strangely. He took a step nearer her so that she could clearly see the mad glitter of his watery blue eyes. He gave a rasping chuckle as he said, "Don't tell me you've forgotten Mad Charlie?"

"I've never met you before," she said, standing close to the door as her fears of the strange old man increased.

He chuckled again and came another step closer so that she could see his lined face better and realized that in spite of a stooped back he was taller than she.

He said, "I've seen your ghost by moonlight many a night, Fanny! But this is the first time I've seen ye by daylight! Is it more bold you're getting!"

"You're mad!" she gasped, drawing back.

He grinned at her and showed the rotten fangs of yellow teeth his lips had concealed until this moment. "You're back for revenge, Fanny! I know! I was there hiding in the woods and heard your dying screams! You told them they would pay! And like the witch you are, you're keeping your word!"

"I'm not Fanny!"

"So you say," the old madman chuckled. "But we both know better! You don't like these new people in the house! Nor do I!"

The talk between them was ended by the sound of the carriage approaching. Mad Charlie glanced in the direction from which the sound of creaking wheels on the gravel came and at once darted into the bushes again and was out of sight in a matter of seconds.

She stood there pale and startled as Grim McLeod came

up with the carriage. William was seated beside him. The big man passed the reins to William as the single-horse rig halted before the door where she was waiting. McLeod jumped down and came to her.

The big man stared at her and asked, "Is something wrong, ma'am?"

She gave a sigh. "Not now. There was someone here. He came out of the bushes at me. A strange old man!"

Grim McLeod looked more grim than ever. He asked, "Was he wearing a tam and kilts?"

"Yes. And he called himself Mad Charlie! At least, I think he did."

The big man glared across at the bushes. "He's been skulking about ever since we opened the place. I have a notion he was in here while the house was supposedly closed. Maybe in one of the stables. He has no home that I know of."

"Then he really is named Mad Charlie?"

"All I've ever heard him called," Grim McLeod said darkly. "He's angry because he's been put out of the house. I'll warn him again when I see him not to bother you another time."

"Thank you," she said. "He behaved strangely, seemed to mistake me for Fanny Bray! I can understand now that I know he is mad."

Grim McLeod stared at her. "It is because of your likeness to the poor woman," he said. "No doubt it confused his muddled mind. I'll help ye up in the carriage, if you please."

The big man boosted her up to the seat where William was rather impatiently holding the reins of the brindle horse. He asked, "What was all that long harangue on the steps about?"

"Nothing important."

"It must have had some importance," William protested as he gave the horse lead to be on its way. "You talked long enough!"

The carriage rolled out of the yardway with Grim McLeod staring gloomily after them. She glanced at the bushes which flanked the roadway on either side and wondered if the old madman might suddenly decide to spring out at them.

She said, "An old man apppeared out of the bushes while I was waiting."

"An old man?"

"Yes. A local character from what McLeod told me. He called himself Mad Charlie!"

William was scowling. "You say this madman came and actually bothered you at our front door?"

"Yes. McLeod believes that this Mad Charlie was living in the house before it was opened. That our arrival has driven him away and he resents it! He's been skulking on the grounds ever since."

William fumed as the carriage reached the main roadway. "We'll see to that! I won't be bothered by lunatics! What did he say to you?"

"Nothing important! He was very confused," she replied evasively, knowing if she repeated the old man's words she might only make her husband more angry.

"I would like to hear exactly what he said to you!"

"He said that he knew who I was."

"How could he?"

"He confused me with Fanny Bray. He kept saying that I had returned for revenge. A lot of nonsense talk like that. The man is mad!"

William looked shocked as he drove along through the village. "If there's one thing we don't need it is talk like that!"

William ignored the stares of the few people in the village street, concentrating on this problem which Mad Charlie had brought them.

Trying to placate her disturbed young husband, she said, "He meant no harm, I'm sure. And no one will listen to his comments. He's the town madman!"

"In these places, madmen get more than their share of attention," William grumbled. "They often provide the only entertainment. So people gather around and listen to them. And if his loose talk about your being Fanny returned falls on superstitious ears it could cause some trouble. I'll have enough problem getting patients in any case; I'll get no one if they decide you're a ghost!"

"But they won't!"

"I hope not."

"Do you know where the doctor's house is?" she asked.

"Yes, McLeod gave me directions," William said. "It is on a short street near the cliffs. We'll be coming to it soon. We turn to the right."

They came to a side street, and William directed the rig into it. They'd not driven more than a hundred yards when she saw the black and white sign hanging from a wooden post, reading *Ivor Carr, M.D.* They drove on to the walkway where the sign stood. There was a stone fence around the thatched cottage, but the garden area in front of the place had been neglected and was now thick with weeds. The shutters on the cottage were almost without paint and one of them, at the right window, hung drunkenly from a single hinge.

Ardith confessed, "I'm nervous."

"You mustn't be," William said. "We are doing the proper thing."

"Proper or not, it isn't pleasant," she told him.

They halted the rig and William tied the horse to one of the posts in front of the cottage. Then he helped her down and together they walked up the flagstone walk to the front door of the cottage. At the door they could hear an irritable male voice raised in an angry tirade inside. William gave her a significant glance and then pulled the bell. It rang loudly within and they waited.

There was the sound of slow footsteps approaching the door, and an old woman with a white, frilled cotton cap on her head and a plaid shawl around her shoulders glared out at them.

She said, "I'm not sure the doctor can see you."

William doffed his top hat and said politely, "We will only take a moment of his time."

The dried-up face showed suspicion. "Who is it sick, you or the lass?"

"Neither of us," William said.

"Then what do you want to see the doctor about?"

William said, "I'm the new doctor. I'd like to introduce myself and my wife."

The thin face showed surprise and annoyance. "So you're the one," she said sourly. "The one from London!"

"Yes," William said.

The old woman considered. "I'll tell him you're here and see what he says." And she shut the door and left them standing.

William looked so boyishly unhappy that Ardith found herself feeling sorry for him. She knew her friendly, romantic young husband had expected a quite different welcome. For all his training and hospital experience, he still was less sophisticated in dealing with people than she was. She pressed his hand in hers, and he gave her a look of grim resignation. Neither of them said anything.

The footsteps sounded again and the door opened. The dried-up face studied them with utter contempt, and the old woman opened the door for them to enter. She snapped, "He will see you!"

They entered the cottage which was dark and smelled of the damp of the nearby ocean. A door stood open at the end of a dark hall, and they automatically made their way down to it. They paused at the doorway and saw, seated behind a battered desk covered with musty papers, pill boxes and every sort of odds and ends, a sour-looking, little old man in a wing collar and string black tie. He had a head of white hair which stood up wildly like stiff wire, giving him the peculiar appearance of having just been frightened by something!

But there was no fear in the grim, bony face with the sunken cheeks. He regarded them from under shaggy eyebrows with his small, hard eyes taking in every detail of them. He grunted, "Come in! Come in!"

They entered and William nervously introduced himself and Ardith. The old man accepted the introductions with another grunt as he eyed them with distaste. He did not invite them to seat themselves in the two plain chairs which were part of the furnishings in the untidy office.

"You're one of the banking Stewarts from Edinburgh," the surly Dr. Ivor Carr said.

"Yes," William replied.

"Directly descended from Black Charlie, the highwayman," the old doctor said with a harsh laugh. And at the same time the air became filled with the aroma of Scotch whiskey.

"Not directly," William said. "Though I do not deny he did have a romance with one of my ancestors. They had a son, Billy, who died not too long ago at an advanced age. He left no issue."

"Your grandfather was a doctor in Edinburgh when I was a medical student," Dr. Ivor Carr said. "You know he was suspected of being mixed up with Burke and Hare and those other grave thieves. The resurrectionists! He came near going to jail!"

William's cheeks flamed. "I'm sure if you check the records you'll find my grandfather was absolved of all blame!"

"Naturally," the old doctor said sourly. "In Edinburgh, the Stewarts are sacred cows! But let me warn you, young man, that is not true in Harwick!"

"I have come here as a friend and a fellow professional," William told him. "I wish no quarrel with you!"

Dr. Ivor Carr laughed nastily again, and once more the odor of strong whiskey pervaded the stale air in his office. He said, "You call yourself a fellow professional! I was doing the most complicated surgery long before you were born!"

"I don't deny that, sir," William said, managing to keep himself under control. "But I'm still a doctor like yourself, though not your match in years."

"Nor in experience," the old doctor snapped. "I have heard about you. You've come here directly from Bishop's Hospital in London."

"That is so," her husband agreed.

Dr. Ivor Carr gave him a sarcastic look. "It's seldom a remote country village gets a doctor from a city hospital. When they do, there is usually a reason. Were you running away from a possible draft in the army? From all we hear, there is a great need for smart, young medical officers in the Crimea!"

Once again William showed resentment. He said, "I did

not come here to escape army service. I'm here because of my wife's poor health. I hope the air in this Highland country will do much to restore her."

"Indeed," the old man now turned his attention to her. "You don't look ill, madam."

She said, "I have had consumption."

"You would have done better to have chosen some quieter place if you're looking for rest and recovery," the sour Dr. Ivor Carr said. "Harwick is not the proper spot for you. And Wyndmoor hardly a suitable house. No one has dared live in that place for two decades!"

She said, "It is a fine house."

"Haunted," the old doctor told her. "A place of tragedy. Your husband will have a hard time getting patients to go there. And anyway most of the village people are loyal to me. They have a deep loyalty and affection for me, and they will continue to trust their ills to my care."

William said, "That is probably true. But there are surely some who might like another doctor or even a second opinion. I hope to find myself a place here."

"Don't expect any help from me!" the old doctor warned him.

"I don't," William said. "I would like to feel we were friends. That there is no resentment on your part."

The bony old man stood up behind his desk and said angrily, "We can never be friends! You've chosen to intrude on me here! I do resent it and I will continue to!"

"I'm sorry," William said. "It seems we have nothing more to discuss."

"Nothing!" the veteran doctor said sourly. "You have gained the enmity of Sir Douglas Gordon in buying Wyndmoor; he is the most powerful man in the area. And you have my bad will. I doubt if you last here long."

"We will see," William said.

Just as they turned to leave, the grim Dr. Ivor Carr said, "Madam, has anyone told you that you bear a remarkable resemblance to the former mistress of Wyndmoor?"

"Yes," she said in a small voice.

"Only noticed it now," the ancient doctor said, staring at her strangely. "Odd that this should happen. That after twenty years, you should come to live in the house and look so much like her."

In a small voice, she said, "You see a likeness to her in me."

Dr. Ivor Carr was still staring at her. "A great likeness! Remarkable! I knew her well. I warned she should get away and she didn't listen. I hope your fate will be much different!" And he bowed stiffly to her.

"Thank you," she said quietly and bowed in return.

William bade the old man good day, and they turned and on their own, found their way to the front door. William said not a word until they were out of the house and near the carriage.

Then he stormed. "That was a grand error! How right you were!"

"I'm sorry," she said. "Probably it was just as well for you to talk with him."

"I'm certain of that," her young husband said grimly. "I at least know the kind of unpleasant old fellow he is!" And he helped her step up into the carriage. Then he untied the horse and got into the carriage beside her.

She gave him a wry smile. "At least it's over with!"

William flicked the reins and drove away from the cottage. He was still in a rage. "Talking about the Stewarts as he did! You'd swear there were nothing but rogues and criminals in our past! The Stewarts are one of the most respectable families in all Scotland!"

"You could hardly expect him to be fair!"

"And saying that I came here to escape army service!"

"You can be sure he'll do you whatever harm he can," she said. "But at least you know his attitude. And by the smell of whiskey in that room, he hasn't stopped his drinking."

"I saw a bottle on the floor behind his desk. He thought he'd hidden it out of view, but I caught a glimpse of it. If he keeps at that for the rest of the day he won't see too many patients."

"I'm sure you're needed here," Ardith told her husband.

William went on angrily, "And, of course, he wasn't content to take swipes at me! He had to have his innings with you! I might have known he'd say the house was haunted and bring up the old business of your resembling Fanny Bray!"

"Whatever he said makes no difference," she protested.

"It does, when you already are of the opinion the house is haunted," her young husband said unhappily as they drove along the nearly-deserted main street with its gray houses huddled together. No one could accuse Harwick of being a busy commercial place.

"His saying it is the wrong place for me won't make any difference in the opinion I form," she promised him. "I know his talk is motivated by fear of you. He knows his own failings have brought you here. And now he is afraid you will take his patients from him!"

"It is stupid," William said. "There is room for two doctors in the area. And he is obviously old and not attending to his practice. Why is he so unfair?"

"Because that is the sort of person he is," was her reply. "At least we have tried to let him know we wish to be friendly. Perhaps he will come around in time."

"I much doubt it," was her husband's reply, and he lapsed into a grim silence which lasted most of the rest of the way to Wyndmoor.

She sat quietly beside him, bothered with her own thoughts. It upset her to be continually told that she resembled the late Fanny Bray. Worst of all she knew it was true in at least a small degree. And she worried that perhaps it was the spirit of the murdered woman gradually taking control of her which had caused a physical change in her looks. It had begun with the eerie dreams which had haunted her sleep in London! The dreams which had begun only after William bought the old mansion. And the nightmares were going on, so that now she was finding herself moving about like a phantom in her sleep. William didn't know how she felt about it all in spite of her trying to make him understand!

They drove in the narrow roadway from the main road to Wyndmoor to discover another light carriage in the yard and a tall, well-dressed young man standing by it. As soon as he saw them, he came running forward.

Reaching the carriage breathlessly, he doffed his top hat and asked, "Are you Dr. William Davis?"

"I am," William said, pulling on the reins to keep the horses still.

"I'm John Thatcher, secretary to Sir Douglas Gordon," the good-looking, brown-haired man said. "His only daughter has had a spell, and he sent me over to get you since you are closer to us than Dr. Carr."

"How far is it?" William asked.

"Only a mile or so from here," the young man said. "I've been waiting about ten minutes. His Lordship will be extremely upset. May I lead the way!"

"Very well," William said. "You drive out and I will turn around and follow!"

"Very good, doctor," the young man said, and hurried to the other carriage.

William gave her a meaningful glance as he prepared to turn the carriage and said, "Well, it seems we are to meet all our enemies on this one morning!"

Chapter Five

They followed the other carriage which young John Thatcher drove along at a swift pace. It was evident that the estate of Sir Douglas Gordon was on the other side of Wyndmoor towards the country, rather than between Wyndmoor and the village. This was undoubtedly why, in a crisis, the titled squire of the area had decided to call on William first. Also, there would be the usual problem of whether Dr. Ivor Carr would be sober or not.

William said, "This might prove helpful. If I'm able to do this local tyrant a service he might even be grateful, though I much doubt it."

"At least he has called on you in a professional capacity," she said. "It gives you a trump card."

"My services are as available to him and his family as to anyone else," William said. "But I'm surprised he didn't summon his old friend, Carr."

"Perhaps he doesn't trust him as a doctor."

"I'd have severe doubts about him," William agreed.

They came to the turn-off leading to the estate, and it was almost as broad and well kept as the main roadway. Within a few minutes the huge turreted castle of Sir Douglas came into sight. Ardith, who had thought Wyndmoor large, was overwhelmed by the size of this place.

She said in an awed voice, "It even makes Stormhaven seem small."

"We Stewarts are only bankers and doctors, not titled gents with our estates handed down to us for generations," William said grimly.

The crisis at the castle was clearly still in progress. Servants were gathered at the front entrance, watching for their arrival. And as soon as they came near the entrance, stablemen rushed out to take the horses. John Thatcher came back hurriedly to help Ardith and William down. As William made it a practice to always keep his medical bag with him, he had only to retrieve it from the bottom of the carriage.

"You may as well come along in," he told her as they walked quickly to the imposing entrance of the castle.

John Thatcher led the way. They walked down a long hall to what Ardith took to be a sewing room. There they found a pathetic tableau. Stretched out on the floor and writhing in seeming agony was a girl in her early teens with long, blonde hair. Standing over her was a troubled-looking man of fifty or so, florid and paunchy from good living. Beside him, clutching his arm, was a worried-looking blonde woman who would surely be his wife and the stricken child's mother. She was slim, pale and had the same blonde hair as her little girl.

Kneeling by the child was a troubled-looking woman of late middle years who would be either governess or nanny to the sick girl. William swiftly advanced to the side of the girl and knelt with the woman. His examination was precise, and in a low voice he gave the woman some instructions. She got up and hurried away. Meanwhile, William grimly watched the youngster.

The father and mother of the girl looked on helplessly. After a moment the woman returned carrying a small towel, a pitcher of water and a spoon. She gave all of these to William. He then expertly placed the spoon between the child's grinding teeth. Next he wet the towel and began to bathe her forehead. It was only a matter of a few minutes when the attractive blonde girl's attack began to ease, and she suddenly dropped off into what appeared to be a deep sleep.

William looked up at the parents and said, "She will be all right now. She'll sleep for a while. When she wakes, she will likely have a headache; it may be a bad one or merely slight, in any case she will recover."

Sir Douglas Gordon showed suspicion on his puffy face. "How can you know all that?"

"I have seen cases like your daughter's before," William said, rising. "She should be taken to her bed now."

The middle-aged woman took charge, with Lady Mona hovering by her. Several of the male servants came forward and gently lifted the little girl up, still sleeping, and carried her away. The middle-aged woman followed them out of the room, but both Lady Mona and Sir Douglas remained.

Lady Mona, who seemed near tears, said, "It was good of you to come so quickly, doctor. Whenever we have called on Dr. Carr, it has taken so long for him to get here that her attacks have always been over with before he could examine her."

Sir Douglas silenced his wife with a grim glance and turned to William, saying, "I am Sir Douglas Gordon and this is my wife, Lady Mona."

William bowed, "My privilege to meet you both," he said. "And this is my wife, Ardith; she happened to be in the carriage with me when I was given your message, so I took the liberty of bringing her along."

"I knew you had arrived," the puffy-faced man said. "I'd say this is an ideal opportunity for us all to meet. I suggest we move on to the drawing room and have some sherry."

Sir Douglas led the way to the large, luxuriously furnished room which held a fortune in ornate furniture. Servants quickly appeared to serve the sherry. Sir Douglas saw the ladies seated with himself and William standing between them before they began any general discussion.

Then Sir Douglas turned to William and said, "Dr. Carr has diagnosed my daughter's condition to be fainting spells. He says they are fairly common among girls of her age and she will grow out of them."

William balanced his glass of sherry and stared at it a moment before replying. Then he said, "I understand from what your wife said that Dr. Carr has never actually seen your daughter when she is having one of her convulsions."

"He hasn't," Lady Mona offered seriously. "He has always seen her some hours afterward."

William asked, "Does she have these attacks often?"

The puffy face of the girl's titled father showed uneasiness. "Not too often!"

His wife spoke up. "Be truthful, Douglas. Much more often than we would wish. We have come to fear the spells. They happen every few months."

"And there are signs before the spell comes on?" William suggested.

"Yes," Lady Mona said. "She has complained of numbness in parts of her body and a strange change in taste. Sometimes she says she hears sweet music and the cries of night birds."

"I know," William nodded.

Sir Douglas eyed him worriedly. "What do you know?"

William said, "I'm sorry, sir. But Dr. Carr's diagnosis is not correct. Your daughter is not suffering from mere fainting spells. What I have found her in now was a Grand Mal."

"A Grand Mal?" the older man repeated in a questioning tone. It was evident he had not heard the term before.

William eyed him solemnly. "Yes. I'm sorry to bring you this news. But your daughter is an epileptic."

Lady Mona gasped. "Margaret an epileptic!"

"Yes," William said. "Let me hasten to add she can be treated and made more comfortable. I can give you drugs which may lessen the severity of her seizures. And I can tell you what to do so that she doesn't injure herself during the times when she is in one of these convulsive fits."

"What can be done to cure her?" Sir Douglas demanded with bluff authority.

"I'm sorry, Sir Douglas, there is no cure," William said. "We can only hope that nature intervenes and the seizures become less severe."

"Is her life in danger?" Lady Mona asked, near tears again.

"No," William said. "There is no reason to expect her longevity to be affected. But over a period of years there is the danger that her mind will suffer. Some epileptics become mentally like children before death comes to them."

"Horrible!" Lady Mona gasped. "I don't want to believe it!"

"And I refuse to!" Sir Douglas said in anger. And to William he put the question, "What causes this disease?"

William told the older man, "The cause of epilepsy is unknown. But we are aware that there are hereditary tendencies involved. It often occurs in successive generations of the same family. Or it may show up in a family where there has been evidences of feeble-mindedness or insanity in earlier generations."

Sir Douglas and Lady Mona exchanged a troubled glance. The stout man said, "Your Uncle Graham. And before him, there were others in your family. That is where the bad seed has come from!"

"You can't be certain of that," his wife said unhappily, dabbing at her eyes with a hankie.

The titled man turned to William again and said, "Of course, you could be wrong. Dr. Carr might be right. These attacks could mean nothing!"

"My advice is have a second opinion in Edinburgh if you doubt my word," William told him. "I'm sure I'm right. I have seen enough cases in my time at the hospital in London. But for your own peace of mind, see another doctor."

"You're eliminating Dr. Carr's diagnosis?" Sir Douglas said tartly.

"In this case, yes. Since it appears he never did see the girl in a seizure. If he had, he might have come up with the same opinion I have," William said.

Sir Douglas frowned. "I shall give the matter thought. So you have settled at Wyndmoor?"

"Yes," William said, taking the last of his glass of sherry.

"You paid far too much for the property," the older man snapped.

William shrugged and put his glass down on a nearby table. "I felt it a fair price."

Sir Douglas eyed him accusingly. "I had my eye on that piece of land for years. But I wouldn't pay what they asked. Then you came along and met their price. Someone should have warned you of the evil history of that house."

"I know it and I'm still satisfied with my purchase," William said coolly.

"You may come to regret it," the older man warned him.

"And let me also say I doubt if you'll be successful in establishing a practice here. Dr. Carr is well liked by the local people. They can be hostile to outsiders."

"We will find that out in time," her young husband said.

Sir Douglas gave his attention to her and asked, "How do you like the house, Mrs. Davis. Do you find it gloomy? Forbidding? You know, they claim it is haunted."

She knew she must not show any weakness. She must back up her husband in all that he'd told the hostile Sir Douglas. She said, "I have been in the house too short a time to have any strong feelings one way or the other. I'm used to making my home where my husband has his work."

Sir Douglas Gordon smiled grimly. "You may sing another tune later on."

She said, "We have met your brother, Mr. Henry Gordon. He was on the stage which brought us here."

The titled man's face went cold. "I have no close association with my brother, Mrs. Davis," he said in an icy voice. And turning to William, he added, "You will send me your bill, and I will have a check made out to cover it."

William nodded. "There is no hurry about that. But now we must be going. I'm sure your daughter will be all right. But if there are any problems and you want me, just send word by a servant."

"Thank you," Sir Douglas said brusquely.

Lady Mona rose and crossed to her. "You must come for tea one afternoon and see our gardens. I think they are rather special. And I'd like you to see Margaret when she is herself. She can be a charming child."

"I'm certain of that," she told the blonde woman. "Thank you for the invitation. As soon as we have managed to get properly settled in, I will be pleased to come over."

"Have you any children?" Lady Mona asked.

"One," she said. "I have a three-year-old son who is staying with my mother-in-law in Edinburgh." She paused. "I have had tuberculosis and just now I'm fighting off a second attack. That is why I came up here and why it seemed better to leave my child with someone else for a little."

"How you must miss him," Lady Mona said with sympathy.

"I do," she agreed quietly.

They were seen to the door by Sir Douglas, who mentioned having several times had dinner at Stormhaven when Walter Stewart was the active head of the firm. He said, "I understand he suffered a stroke and is now an invalid."

"Yes," William said. "It is sad."

Their carriage was ready for them. The stableman held the horse's head while they got in it, and then they began the short drive back to Wyndmoor.

When they were underway, William glanced at her and asked, "What did you make of that?"

"A tense experience after just having our interview with Dr. Carr."

"That old incompetent!" William said bitterly. "Not able to recognize the child was an epileptic!"

She said meaningfully, "Could it be that he didn't want to recognize it. He'd know it would upset Sir Douglas and his wife, and he continues on here by toadying to them."

"It might well be the case," William agreed. "But I have an idea he simply missed the important clues which could only lead to his knowing it was epilepsy. He was never there during any of her attacks. So he'd get all the information at second hand."

"You were right about one thing. It was our morning for meeting our enemies."

"Sir Douglas was more frank than I expected," William agreed. "He'll wait and watch now. Hoping we'll either be scared out of Wyndmoor or we won't be able to pick up enough patients to make our stay here worthwhile."

"He's a little uneasy," she said. "He knows you don't have to depend solely on your practice. You can't be starved out. You have the Stewart fortune behind you."

"Not that I care to rely on that," he replied as they turned in their own roadway. "My aim will be to build a sound practice here. The other thing is to see your health improve."

"I want it to so badly," she said. "I can't bear being parted from Ian."

"Mother will bring him here as soon as it seems reasonable."

Her husband's words did little to cheer her. She was thinking of her nightmares and now the sleepwalking. Were these things indications of her health worsening, or did they signify something equally as frightening—was she coming under the spell of a restless spirit who remained in the old mansion seeking revenge after all the years which had passed since that cruel burning at the stake?

She said, "At least Sir Douglas didn't make any comment that I looked like Fanny Bray."

"No," her husband said. "But he may have noticed it. I saw him staring at you several times when he didn't realize I was watching."

So their unusual morning ended. Actually, it marked the start of a pleasant few days and nights in which nothing took place to upset her. She had no bad dreams nor did she do any sleepwalking. She almost began to think the old mansion held no threat for her. And when she paused before the portrait of Fanny and studied it, she decided that the resemblance between herself and the woman in the painting was hardly worth mentioning.

William was busy preparing his office. The carpentry work went ahead as quickly as could be expected, and he had unpacked all his books and equipment in preparation to formally open his practice. In the meanwhile, word had spread of his arrival and he had calls from people with health problems every day. So he began seeing them in the library and used the hall as a waiting room. Several times Ardith came down the stairs to find four or five people waiting in the hall to have their turn in the library.

It was exciting and encouraging. She took a long walk on the cliffs every afternoon when the weather was fine, and she felt that she was growing in strength as the days went by. A letter arrived from Edinburgh in which Ishbel described the fine time Ian was having at Stormhaven. Her young son had become a favorite of the household. She at once wrote a long letter in return and predicted that soon Ishbel could bring the child to her.

One early evening at the start of their second week in Harwick, they had a visitor in the person of the artist, Henry Gordon. He claimed that he had only dropped by to wish them well, but without too much urging he stayed on until late, consuming a quantity of Scotch whiskey as he sat regaling them with his experiences in Italy.

They were seated in the living room as he told them of his studying in Venice with one of the masters. He said, "And would you believe it, I actually lived in one of the palaces in which Byron lived during his stay there years ago."

"I would like to see Venice," Ardith said. "I know little about the Continent beyond Paris. William took me there once."

The stout man showed a knowing smile on his moon

face. "Must do better than that, old man. Take this lovely girl to Italy and let her see one of the historic beauty spots of the world."

William puffed at his pipe. "I expect we'll get around to it one day."

"If I were a Stewart I'd waste no time about it," the artist said with one of his smiles which gave his face a shifty look. "I'm back here in Harwick because I'm almost flat broke, except for a small pittance left me by my father. The rest is held by my brother. And Sir Douglas is not famous for his generosity."

"We have met him, you know," Ardith said.

"You have?" Henry Gordon looked surprised.

"Yes," William said. "It came about by accident." And he went on to tell about Margaret's being stricken and of his going to attend her.

Henry Gordon listened with interest. "Epilepsy!" he said with what almost seemed satisfaction. "And Margaret is their only child. Mona comes from a barren stock; I doubt if they will have another!"

"It's a tragedy," Ardith said.

"Definitely," the artist agreed at once. "Especially if she should develop mental trouble. And even if she doesn't there is the matter of marriage. Is it desirable for an epileptic to marry?"

"The chances are good that a child of hers or even several children might not inherit the disease," William said, his pipe in hand. "But the dark side is that they most likely would pass it on to some future generation."

"So the line of Gordon is in danger," Henry Gordon said. "Perhaps I ought to marry my Jeannie and have a few bairn!"

"Perhaps you should," Ardith agreed. "Is she a pretty girl?"

The artist winked. "One of the best! Not a lady, mind you! But healthy and ready to please! Oh, she can show a bit of temper now and then. But it's soon over with."

"You should have brought her with you," Ardith said.

The artist shook his head. "She'd not enjoy it. She'd not be able to talk at our level, you understand. But when she and I are alone together, we get along well. I like a woman with simple tastes. I developed an affection for peasant women when I was in Europe. Jeannie Truffin is a peasant, though she'd stoutly deny it. Waiting on table in a tavern when I first saw her. Knew at once she'd be the one to bring up here."

Ardith said, "Does she expect that you will one day marry her?"

He shook his head. "I don't think marriage ever crosses her mind. She's known a lot of men. The thing which concerns her most is shelter. Next comes food and a little affection now and then. As I told you, a girl of simple desires."

William smiled grimly at him. "But can such a union last? Won't there come a day when she leaves you, or you find yourself tired of her? Then you'll be alone again and you're getting no younger."

"Don't remind me of that," the artist said with a shudder. "I saw an old artist, French I think he was, ill in a cheap hostel, just skin and bones, without even a decent sheet over him. And he'd done good work in his time, mind you. There he was. Done with and forgotten! No one to care! Wanting to die!"

"Were you able to help him?" Ardith asked.

Henry Gordon shrugged. "The sight of him sent me out on a binge. Lasted for two or three days. When I sobered up I went to him with some food. It was too late. He'd died and the body had been taken away a day before I got there."

William puffed his pipe slowly. "You could avoid any such ending by finding yourself a proper woman of your own class and marrying her. Sir Douglas might even relent, and you'd get some more financial help from him."

The stout artist rose and walked slowly down the length of the living room away from them. Then he turned and with a grim look on his face said, "There was one such woman. A gentlewoman! Down on her luck, but she could have found her place again. She understood me! We had a stupid quarrel and before I could do anything about it she had died."

Ardith said, "I'm sorry."

He nodded. "A lot of me died with her."

William advised him, "You must change your viewpoint. You can't live in the past!"

"Many do!" Henry Gordon said. "Have you met James Burnett?"

"The sculptor who was in love with Fanny Bray?" Ardith said.

"Yes," Henry Gordon said. "Now you can safely say he lives only for the past. He loved Fanny truly. So much that he won't ever leave here, though the place has nothing but bitter memories for him."

"We haven't met him," she said.

The artist came back nearer them again and stood with a smile on his face. "I'll be interested in your opinion of him when you do."

"Does he still turn out work?" William asked.

"Yes," the artist replied. "I know his work is much in demand, and he turns out pieces regularly. He lives in a house not too far from here. But he is a recluse. You might be here a year before you see him."

Ardith asked, "Do you think he lives with regrets? That

he really led the band of masked men who burned Fanny Bray to death in the woods?"

"Folk say he was the one," the artist replied.

"Could his love possibly turn to such hatred?" she asked.

"Love is said to be the closest emotion to hate," was William's contribution to their talk.

"I think that's true," Henry Gordon said.

William stared at him. "You must have been around here in those days. I mean at the time of the murder. And so must your brother."

"We were both here," the artist said. "Douglas had just come into the title, and I was playing the fool with the money I'd inherited. Couldn't spend it fast enough! I was the talk of the countryside. No deviltry I wasn't up to! Then I tired of it all and headed for Europe. I thought my money would last my lifetime. But I soon ran through it."

William said, "Perhaps you should try to be friendly with your brother."

"Not my style," the artist said. He went over to the portrait of Fanny and studied it for several long minutes. Then he turned to her and asked, "Since you arrived here, how many people have told you that you look like Fanny?"

She smiled bleakly. "A few."

"There is a resemblance, you know," the artist said. He eyed the portrait and then her. "I'd say that Fanny in real life was a lot closer to resembling you than the Fanny of that portrait. I don't know who did it. But I could produce a better one from memory."

"Why don't you?" William asked.

"I think as the portrait took shape it would be painful," the artist mused. "I liked Fanny." He turned to Ardith. "But I'll do a study of you any time you'll pose for me."

"Perhaps one day," she said.

"Don't put it off too long," Henry Gordon warned her. "I may take a notion to roam again. Or Jeannie may tire of it here and make me take her back to Edinburgh."

"Would you be able to manage there?" she asked.

The artist showed another of his shifty smiles. "We'd get by some way or other. I guess Jeannie would go back to work." Then he changed the subject and said, "How have you found the house?"

William said, "What do you mean? It's sound enough. We have a good staff."

"I was thinking of something else," the artist said with a strange gleam in his eyes. "I was wondering if you've seen any ghosts? You know Fanny is supposed to haunt the place. That's why it was empty so long."

"We haven't seen anything at all," William said firmly.

"I can't think of her as being evil, either in life or after," Ardith said.

The artist spread his hands. "Yet they burned her because they suspected her of being a witch. And some pretty bad things did happen. And they ended with her death."

"Coincidence," William suggested. "The superstitious accept anything. They are quick to accuse and quick to see signs which mean nothing."

"Too bad you weren't here when the gang came to get her," the artist said. "You'd have been a strong advocate."

"I wish I had been here to save her," William said. "It was a black crime which still shadows the county with disgrace."

"You sound like my brother now," Henry Gordon smirked. He reached in his vest pocket and drew out a huge gold watch and consulted it. "Later than I realized. I have stayed too long."

Ardith protested. "Not at all. We see so few people, we

are grateful for your company."

William said, "When we met in the stage I predicted you would become a staunch friend. And I do not think I was wrong."

"Depend on that," the stout artist said soberly. "I may be a bit of a character, but when I like people I can be loyal. You two have my loyalty."

"We know that," Ardith said, smiling as she rose from her chair.

"I've sent more than one patient to you," Henry Gordon said. "Incidentally, I hear old Dr. Carr is on the whiskey again. He hasn't made any calls for days."

"That perhaps explains why I've been so busy," William said, getting up to see their guest to the door. "If it keeps on as it has been the last day or two I'll have no need to complain."

"It is bound to get better," the artist said. And with one of his sly winks for Ardith, he warned her, "Mind the ghosts."

"I will," she said, managing a thin smile. "And do come soon again. And bring Jeannie with you."

"I'll think about it," the artist said. And he and William went out to the front door.

She remained in the drawing room to make the rounds of the lighted candles and blow them out. When she had extinguished the last one, she went to join William in the hall. Their guest had left and they were alone at last.

They stood at the foot of the stairs in the shadowed hall for a moment. She smiled up at her husband and said, "I find Henry Gordon a strange man."

"But an interesting one," William said. "I think it goes together."

"I doubt if he has any serious intentions about Jeannie."

"He almost said that he didn't," William agreed. "I did not think it good taste for him to discuss this house as he did."

"I think he was really trying to get some information," she reasoned. "I have an idea he believes in the ghostly legends which have grown up around this place."

"He should know better than to bring the subject up," her husband said angrily. "You have been doing well lately. I don't want his silly talk to start you having fantasies again."

"Nothing he said will bother me," she assured him.

"I'd like to believe that," William said earnestly.

"It's true. You know how well I've been. I'm actually beginning to feel at home here, and I didn't think I ever would."

He put his arm around her. "That's the best news I've heard in a long while."

"I see Henry Gordon for what he is. An aging, neurotic artist who is not fond of seeing other people more content than he is himself."

"You've painted a good likeness of him," he said, then he kissed her. "Time for bed."

They went upstairs and talked some more while she sipped the medicine which Meg had left out for her as usual. Then he kissed her again and went on to his own room while she prepared for bed.

When the last candle had been extinguished and she was alone in the darkness of the room, she began to experience the old uneasiness. There was something in the air tonight which she had not known on those good nights. Some subtle threat of ghostly happenings which she'd not been aware of when she'd slept peacefully.

It was almost as if the neurotic Henry Gordon had cast

an evil spell over her and returned her to that state where every shadow upset her. She knew the artist had not done this intentionally; he was their friend. But his talk had rambled over so many grisly subjects it had left her in a nervous state.

In the distance she could hear the wash of the waves on the beach. She tried to block thoughts of the murdered Fanny from her mind but was unable to. The face of the long-dead woman so much like her own came to haunt her. And she had the troubled feeling that this might be a bad night for her again.

She lay very still, and at last she went to sleep. But it was not an easy sleep. Almost at once she fell into the old pattern of her nightmare. She was alone in the house and terrified! She ran up to her bedroom and locked herself in. Then the threatening voices, coming gradually nearer. She ran across the room and huddled in the darkness, hoping not to be seen, praying that they would not find her.

The voices were just outside the door! There was a vicious pounding against its heavy oak frame, and then brute strength was hurled against it so that at last the bolt had to give. The door sprang open and behind it were revealed the masked, menacing faces.

She screamed and there was an ominous growl from the intruders. They came at her and, though she fought hard, they dragged her out of the room and down the stairs. She sobbed for mercy but there was to be no mercy. Relentlessly, they dragged her into the woods. Her flesh and clothing were torn, but she still managed to retain consciousness and beg them to spare her!

All at once the picture changed. She was alone in a vast darkness and there was a great roaring sound which filled her ears! She stood motionless and terrified as she suddenly knew that she was no longer dreaming. She was awake! She had been sleepwalking again and had wandered to this strange place!

She began to tremble as the dampness bit into her. She could see nothing but the blackness. Her bare feet seemed to be on cold stone, so she was sure she was nowhere in the house. Had she wandered to the cellars? If so, what was the meaning of the roaring sound? And where was the cold, swift current of damp air coming from?

Panic forced her to take an awkward step forward. She hesitated and then went a little further. She stretched out her hands and felt rough rock! It was as if she were in some sort of tunnel. But where? She let her hand explore the surface of the tunnel wall. It seemed wet and slimy.

She took another few steps forward and the roaring sound was louder. And now she was able to identify it. It was the crashing of waves on the rocky shore. She was near the shore!

The air in the tunnel seemed fresher as she went on. And then she saw what seemed a core of lighter shadow ahead. It seemed that the darkness thinned out at this point. It became a focal spot for her. She balanced herself by touching a hand out to the rough tunnel wall and using it to steady herself. She was frightened and her head reeling!

The roaring sound now became so loud there seemed to be nothing else. She went on and all at once found herself at the open end of the tunnel. It apparently came out at a point somewhere over the shore. She could see the waves as they came pounding in at this high tide. She could go no further!

Frozen with fear at the thought of going back in the dark unknown or of trying to escape by way of the beach, she stood there unable to make any decision. She could picture herself trying to clamber up or down the rocky face of the cliff and knew it would be beyond her strength or abilities. She leaned against the side of the rough tunnel and moaned in her despair.

She let her eyes drop to the floor of the tunnel and there at the very edge she saw something which struck new terror in her! It was the sight of a hand reaching up. The hand took a firmer grip and came further onto the surface of the tunnel and then another hand came to grasp the edge.

Ardith screamed and stumbled back. As she did so, a head appeared and then broad shoulders. In the near darkness she could not make out who or what it was. But she knew that this other presence would be in the tunnel in a moment and aware of her.

She shrank back against the wall of the tunnel as the huge figure loomed against the entrance and then came slowly towards her.

She screamed, "No!"

The figure halted and she recognized that it was the cold face of Grim McLeod she was staring up at. She cried, "It's you! Grim McLeod!"

"What are you doing here?" he asked in his dour voice.

"I don't know!" she sobbed. "I don't know!"

"Foolish creature!" he said harshly, then he slapped her across the face with his huge hand.

It was too much! She could bear no more. With a choked cry, she pressed her hands to her smarting face and then fell forward in a faint. There was no more sound, no more anything, just the comforting black velvet of unconsciousness.

She reached out and her hand touched something. She lifted her head and she saw that it was the leg of a chair which she had touched. She felt nauseated and she could not remember what had happened or how she had managed to find herself here on the floor.

Slowly, she raised herself and saw she was in her own bedroom. She struggled until she was able to get up and sit in the chair. She held her head and tried to think. Her nightgown felt wet and cold. Her hands smarted as if she had chafed them in some way.

And then it came to her in a frightening flash of memory. The tunnel! She had been in the tunnel by the sea! And out of the darkness McLeod had showed himself in a surly temper. She had pleaded with him for help and he had slapped her face.

She quickly got up from the chair and ran to the door to her husband's room and threw it open. She raced to the bed, ready to pour out her tale of woe to him, only to come to a startled halt when she saw the clothes thrown back and the bed empty.

William was not there!

Panic welled up in her again. She wheeled around to run back to her own bedroom, when she suddenly saw the figure in the doorway. A woman's shadowy figure! In the next moment the face was revealed to her—the glowing face of Fanny Bray!

Chapter Six

The phantom figure with the glowing face came slowly towards her with hands outstretched. The features were so unmistakably those of Fanny Bray that there could be no doubts. It was too much for Ardith in her already shattered state. She tottered back from the approaching ghost, screamed out in terror and then collapsed once again.

"Mrs. Davis!" The worried voice of Mrs. MacDonald came to her through a fog of confusion.

She opened her eyes and looked up at the matronly face of the older woman. In a voice that was almost a whisper, she asked, "Did you see her?"

"See who?"

"The ghost!"

"What ghost, ma'am?" The housekeeper studied her with an odd look.

Ardith sat up. "The ghost of Fanny Bray! She came into this room after me! Her face was glowing as if bathed in flames!"

The housekeeper crossed herself and muttered something which Ardith couldn't make out. Then she said, "I saw nothing, ma'am!"

Ardith struggled up from the floor with the help of the older woman. Mrs. MacDonald had brought a lamp into William's bedroom and placed it on a table near the door. It gave a satisfactory light.

Ardith asked the woman, "Where is my husband?"

"He was called out on an emergency," Mrs. MacDonald said. "One of the fishermen came and roused me. He claimed his young son was suffering severe pain in his side and it seemed to be getting worse. He asked for the doctor. So I came up and told your husband. He dressed at once and went away with the man. That was more than two hours ago. I wasn't able to get to sleep. Then I heard your scream and came back up here."

Ardith listened in a half-dazed state. At least that explained where William was. But it did not tell her anything about her own experiences or the phantom. She said, "I did see something."

"I don't question that, ma'am," Mrs. MacDonald said in a troubled voice. "This is a strange old house." And then she seemed to notice the state of Ardith's nightgown for the first time. She exclaimed, "Your nightgown is torn and soiled. And it's wet! Let me get you another."

Ardith went back into her own bedroom, and Mrs. MacDonald assisted her into another nightgown. By this time the first streaks of dawn were showing. At the housekeeper's insistence, she returned to bed for a little more rest before it was morning. Her sheer exhaustion made sleep easy once she felt the warmth of the bed coverings. She slept on until it was mid-morning.

When she opened her eyes, she discovered the petite Meg seated in a chair by the window. The maid had apparently been waiting for her to wake up.

Ardith sat up and apologetically said, "You ought to have wakened me earlier."

The competent Meg was now standing by the bed. She said, "Mrs. MacDonald said you weren't to be bothered until you came awake on your own."

Ardith saw the sun streaming in the bedroom windows. "It must be close to noon!"

"Yes, ma'am," the girl with the straw-colored hair said.

"Did my husband come home?"

"Yes. Early this morning. He is in his office now."

"I must hurry and get down and see him," she said, turning back the bedclothes.

"Your bath is ready and waiting," the maid told her.

As she was bathing she saw that two of the fingernails on her left hand were broken and there were cuts on both hands—tiny cuts on both palms, as if she had scraped them against some rough surface. She knew she had to tell William about her experiences of the night but couldn't decide how she would begin. It was difficult, since it involved McLeod as well as herself.

Once washed and dressed, she went directly to William's office and found him at his desk studying a large textbook which rested open on the desk before him. As soon as she came into the office he looked up and rose to greet her.

He said, "I heard you had some upset during the night. Mrs. MacDonald mentioned it. I felt you should be allowed to sleep until you were fully rested."

"I slept too long," she said.

"Have you had something to eat?"

"No. I wanted to talk with you first. I think it urgent."

Her husband's young face showed surprise. "That serious?"

"Yes."

"Well, tell me quickly," he said. "I'm in the midst of some important reading. I have a patient with Bright's disease, and I'm looking for help in treating the case."

She said, "And you were out almost all the night!"

He nodded. "Boy with a bad appendix. I had to operate

at once on a kitchen table by lamplight. Happily, these youngsters of the fishermen are a sturdy lot He was doing well when I left him this dawn."

Ardith sank into the chair opposite the desk and clasped her hands in her lap as she gazed up at him unhappily. "I'm sorry to interrupt your work. I know how important it is. But last night I began sleepwalking once again."

Her young husband stood before her grimly. "I know what caused it. Too much talk! That artist dwelt too much on that Fanny Bray business when he was here last night. I was at the point of telling him to drop the subject."

"I don't think it fair to blame him. I think it just happened. I have sleepwalked before."

"Go on," her husband ordered her.

She sighed. "Last night was different and more terrifying. I somehow escaped the house in my sleepwalking, and I wound up waking in a dark, rough tunnel leading out to the beach somewhere."

"A tunnel?" William echoed in a tone of incredulity.

"Yes. I know it sounds strange, but there must be some kind of tunnel attached to the cellars here or perhaps on the grounds with some independent entrance. I only know I found myself in the tunnel."

"You will admit it sounds somewhat far-fetched," her husband said.

"I'm sorry," she replied. "But what I'm telling you did happen."

"Continue," William said, staring at her with concern.

"I can't say how I managed to find the tunnel, unless I was directed by some force outside me," she went on.

"Tell me the facts," her handsome husband spoke impatiently. "We can discuss your theories later!"

She knew what this meant. William had no sympathy

with her feeling that she was being gradually possessed by the avenging phantom of Fanny Bray. And she was more certain than ever that this was the horror she was facing.

With effort she went on, "I wakened in the tunnel and made my way along it. I had no idea where I was or how I had managed to get there. I could hear the angry waves on the beach and guessed the tunnel must open somewhere along the cliffs."

"And?"

"I at last saw the open end of the tunnel and made my way to it. You can see my fingernails are broken and there are tiny scratches on my hands from the rough walls of the tunnel. When I reached the opening, I suddenly saw a hand come over the ledge and then another. A moment later, Grim McLeod dragged himself up into the tunnel."

Her husband looked startled. "Grim McLeod?"

"Yes. He seemed as surprised to see me as I was to see him. He behaved in an angry, strange manner. And in reply to my pleas for help, he slapped me hard across the face. I fainted."

"McLeod struck you?"

"Yes. But that is not the end of it. When I came to, I was no longer in the tunnel. Apparently he had carried me back into the house and up to my bedroom while I was still unconscious."

William looked furious. "If this is true he will answer to me!"

"It is all true," she insisted. "I did not know you had gone out. I rushed to your bedroom to tell you what had gone on and saw that you weren't there. I was standing there, debating what to do next, when I suddenly had the feeling someone was watching me. I turned and saw the shadowy figure and glowing face of Fanny Bray!"

"You saw a ghost?"

"Yes. In the doorway between our rooms. I was in no shape to undergo such an ordeal. I collapsed a second time, and when I next opened my eyes Mrs. MacDonald was bending over me. No doubt she has told you all the rest."

He nodded. "She said something about your being in a badly upset state. That you thought you had seen some phantom."

"I did! The face was recognizable even with the weird blue glow which emanated from it!"

Her husband clasped his hands behind his back and began striding up and down before her, his head bent slightly with concern. He said, "This is a most extraordinary story you've told me! Especially the part about McLeod."

"I knew you should hear it as soon as possible."

He halted and said, "I shall have McLeod come in here and we'll hear his side of it. I'll get Mrs. MacDonald to summon him." And he left the office to do this.

She sat there, filled with despair. In the light of day her story seemed strange and unreal. Yet she knew it to be true.

A few moments later, William came back into the room with a sullen Grim McLeod following him. William took a stand behind his desk, and the big man stood in the middle of the room averting his eyes from her.

William said, "My wife has made certain charges against you, McLeod. I'm going to tell you what they are. And I would like to have your explanation of them." And he went ahead, telling the sullen, big man exactly what she had told him. When he'd finished, he asked, "What is your answer to this scandalous charge, McLeod?"

The big man showed no emotion. His expression was

cold. He said, "I do not like to say this, doctor, but I fear your wife has imagined all this."

"No!" she protested, her cheeks flaming.

"Wait!" William said, lifting a hand to silence her. "I want to hear McLeod out."

Grim McLeod said, "I am ignorant of what Mrs. Davis has said; I know nothing of a tunnel, nor did I ever meet her in one. And if I had I would not have taken the liberty of slapping her face. It is a libel against me, sir. I can only believe your wife had a bad nightmare and it seemed so real to her she has passed it on as truth."

Ardith was on her feet. She told the big man, "The tunnel looked out on the cliffs. And you came clambering in from somewhere below!"

"You are wrong, madam," Grim McLeod said calmly.

"Then you deny the whole episode?" William asked him.

"I do, sir. I'm sorry to dispute Mrs. Davis. But none of this could have happened. I did not leave my bed last night."

William eyed him wearily. "Very well, McLeod. Thank you. I trust you won't hold this against me or my wife. I'm sure Mrs. Davis would not have made such a charge against you unless she was badly confused in her mind."

"I understand, sir," the big man said gravely. "I will forget the matter."

"Thank you," William said. "You may go."

The big man went out, leaving Ardith and William to face each other. She looked at her husband in consternation. "You accepted his word over mine?"

"What else could I do?" her husband said. "You have no proof. I have every reason to think McLeod trustworthy. And you have been having a series of macabre dreams.

What more likely than that you mixed your dream fantasy with fact?"

"I can't believe it!"

William came to her and took her hands in his as he said sympathetically, "You need some food in your stomach and a warm drink. I'm sure you will feel better afterward."

"But you think I experienced all I told you in a nightmare," she went on despairingly. "That is what you think, isn't it?"

"To a point," he said. "I'm sure if you think about it you will discover I'm right. You had a shocking dream, so vivid it made you think it real."

"No!" she protested. "What about the ghost I saw?"

"I'm sorry," he apologized. "Your mentioning it convinces me all the more that you had a vivid, bad dream and collapsed. Then Mrs. MacDonald found you on the floor of the bedroom."

"I couldn't have made all that up!" she pleaded.

"I know it isn't your fault," he said with mild reproof. "But before we act on such flights of fancy again, let us first discuss them in more detail. I did not like McLeod's being dragged into this!"

"What choice did I have?"

"Let us drop the matter for the time being," her husband suggested. "I need to hurry through this article in my textbook, and you need some nourishment." He kissed her lovingly on the cheek and then showed her out.

She was almost unable to accept this unhappy outcome. But she saw that she would have to. Before her husband would listen to her stories she was going to have to produce a lot more substantial proof. And she wasn't at all sure that she could. It was a terrifying position in which she found herself.

Certainly McLeod would hate her for implicating him. But she had only told the truth. She might have known he would deny it. That he had some dark reasons of his own for doing so. It appeared she would have to play the role of detective and find out what they were.

Mrs. MacDonald came to her and insisted that she sit down and have some food. At least William had been right in one thing, she did feel better after she had something in her stomach. She was standing in the living room, staring at the portrait of Fanny Bray, when Mrs. MacDonald came nervously in to her.

"There is a messenger here," the housekeeper said. "He is from the castle. Lady Mona Gordon would like you to come for tea this afternoon."

"All right," she said. "Tell her I will come."

"Very well, ma'am," Mrs. MacDonald said. "The time is four. Will you use your own carriage?"

"Yes," Ardith said. "I think that will be best." She felt that getting away from the shadow of Wyndmoor for even a little while might be good for her. Give her a chance to relax and sort out her troubled thoughts. To fill in the time, she went upstairs and wrote a long letter to her mother-in-law, Ishbel. She also enclosed a note for Ian. Then she took the letter down to have it mailed along with the regular mail which her husband sent out nearly every day.

She left the letter in the dish in the hall in which it had been agreed they would place outgoing mail. Then she stepped inside the living room with the thought of going to speak to her husband before his office was filled with afternoon patients. On her way through the living room she had to pass by the portrait of Fanny. She stopped short in shock when she saw that it had been removed. There was blank space on the wall where it had formerly hung!

She was standing there in confusion when Mrs. MacDonald joined her, and she asked the older woman, "What happened to the portrait?"

The housekeeper looked embarrassed. "The doctor asked that it be removed and placed in the cellar."

"Why?"

"He did not tell me that, ma'am," the housekeeper said.

She was moved by what had happened in a strange way. The action of her husband in this matter made her absolutely furious. It was as if he had taken some personal stand against her. She rushed out of the room and made directly for her husband's office.

She found him escorting the first patient of the day, an old woman in black dress and bonnet with the usual shawl over her shoulders, into the inner office. Angry-eyed, she marched up to the astonished William and declared, "I will have a word with you at once!"

William appeared shocked. He told the old woman to go on inside, and then closed the door after her as he faced a defiant Ardith. He stared at her in amazement. "What is it now?"

"You know very well!"

"I'm sorry," he said. "I do not."

"The portrait! You ordered it taken to the cellar!"

He frowned. "Oh, that! Surely you're not making all this fuss about such a small thing!"

"It is not a small thing!" she cried. "Fanny Bray was the mistress of this house until she was murdered by those scoundrels! How dare you remove her portrait from its rightful place."

He stared at her. "I did it because I felt seeing it so constantly was bad for you. It has become an obsession with you. It might well have been the cause of your nightmares!"

"Ridiculous!"

"Not so," he protested. "I have done what I think best. And I ask you not to make a scene about it. Other patients will be coming. What will they think?"

"I do not care!" she said. "Restore that portrait to its proper place!" The compulsion which made her demand this was strong, and yet she did not fully know why she was so determined. It was as if she were acting for someone else. And this notion suddenly shocked her. Perhaps she was! For the dead girl!

"The fact it means so much to you is not a healthy sign," William told her in a worried voice. "Let us discuss this later. I must go to my patient."

So he left her. She stood alone in the outer office for a long moment and then turned away. Her seething rage had given ground to a surge of depression. It seemed their arguments always ended in this fashion, William summarily dismissing her and going about his own affairs with no thought of the misery in which he might be leaving her. It could not go on! She would tell him so. Meanwhile, he would be occupied all the long afternoon with his patients, and she was to have tea with Lady Mona.

The titled woman greeted her in the garden beside the castle. She had been seated out there waiting for Ardith to arrive. Ardith had been slightly late in getting dressed because of her troubled state of mind. But she had eventually changed into a pale blue checked frock with white ruffles and a lace jabot. She wore a yellow bonnet and carried a yellow parasol to match. The rig was waiting for her, and one of the coachmen drove her to the castle and would wait for her there.

Lady Mona Gordon was wearing white and held a white parasol. The garden with its myriad of colorful flowers provided a lavish background for their meeting. There was a small tea house with lattice-work sides of yellow in which they sat to escape the full strength of the summer afternoon sun.

A maid brought the tea service and Lady Mona poured. The pale blonde woman seemed grateful for Ardith's company, saying, "I was afraid you wouldn't come. I see so few people these days."

"I think it kind of you to have me," Ardith said, taking her cup and the scones on the small plate which her hostess passed to her.

Lady Mona said, "Margaret is most grateful to you and your husband. She is much better since she has been taking the medicine which Dr. Davis sent over."

"He will be glad to hear that."

"Dr. Davis seems a fine man," the other woman went on. "You two must be ideally happy."

Ardith blushed as she thought about the bitter argument she and her husband had just had. She said quietly, "I'm sure we get along as well as most."

"You are fortunate," the older woman assured her. She sighed. "You have met Sir Douglas. He is a good man but not at all tolerant. Not of me nor of anyone else."

She said, "Perhaps it is a matter of personality. He may not mean to create the impression he does."

The blonde woman's worn face brightened. "Now I do believe you have hit on it, my dear. It is his manner which defeats him. He attempts to make himself clear in a civil way and doesn't ever quite succeed. It is tragic. Many people have come to hate him for it."

Ardith said, "He also has a public position in which he

often must take a stand. He cannot always hope to be popular."

"That is also true," Lady Mona agreed. "I won't deny that he is mean about some things. Wyndmoor is an example. He had plenty of opportunities to purchase it at a proper price. But he kept making ridiculous offers. Then he went into a rage when your husband bought the property."

Ardith said, "I would hope he'll get over that."

"I also hope so," Lady Mona sighed. "But Dr. Carr keeps nagging at him about that and other things. You know that old Dr. Carr resents your husband being here, although he is no longer capable of looking after the welfare of the village himself. Your husband takes more patients from him every day."

"The rivalry is unfortunate. But the people are making a free choice."

"That is what I tell Sir Douglas. But he feels he has to offer the old doctor his protection. And I must warn you that Dr. Carr is spreading some scandalous stories about your husband. He is saying that the reason Dr. Davis left London in such a hurry is that he had a bad record as a surgeon. He claims your husband lost an inordinate number of people through clumsy operations."

Ardith was stunned. "That's a lie!" she declared. "William is a most capable surgeon. That is what he did most at Bishop's Hospital."

"I'm sorry, my dear," the other woman said. "I'm simply repeating what that old man is saying. I thought you should know."

"Thank you," she said. "I will tell my husband of this gossip. Though I doubt he will pay any attention to it."

"Yet I think he should know," Lady Mona said. "I feel we are so indebted to him."

"He merely did his duty," Ardith said. "As you know, he is dedicated to his profession. He really enjoys helping people."

"I'm certain he does," Lady Mona said. "And one other word of warning."

"Yes?"

Lady Mona cleared her throat uneasily. "This is most awkward. My husband is aware that you have become friendly with his brother, Mr. Henry Gordon."

She was surprised that the blonde woman would mention this. She said, "Surely that is a personal matter. My husband and I decide who shall be our friends."

"And you have every right to do so," Lady Mona agreed at once. "But I think you should know the sort of person my husband's artist brother is."

"We find him pleasant company. That is all we ask. And he has been a good friend to us."

Lady Mona looked worried. "If I may say so, my husband and I know him better than you do. I doubt if Henry could be a true friend to anyone. He has done some despicable things, and that is why Sir Douglas will not have anything to do with him."

"I know their viewpoints differ."

"There is more than that to it," the other woman said. "Sir Douglas is a hard man and often a mean man. But he is also, within his limits, a man of honor. I cannot say the same of his brother."

"I see. But you understand we have to judge him as we find him."

"I accept that," Lady Mona said. "But I beg you to be wary of him. Especially in any matter of business. Do not lend him money on any account. You will never see him again!"

"Thank you," she said as Lady Mona poured her a second cup of tea. "I'm sure your warning is well meant."

"I promise you it is," her hostess said. "I will say no more on the matter."

Ardith said, "It is hard to form snap judgments about people. We have come here as strangers. It takes a while to know a person."

"It does," Lady Mona said. "How have you managed with your help? Do you find Mrs. MacDonald agreeable?"

"Most agreeable."

"She was once the housekeeper at Wyndmoor when the Brays lived there. She was devoted to Fanny Bray and very shocked when she was murdered."

"It was a foul crime!"

Lady Mona nodded. "The last witch burning in this part of the country. I do not think it would have happened if the epidemic hadn't come along. The villagers are superstitious, and they were really frightened. And someone led them in their madness! The legend is that James Burnett was the one."

"Fanny's rejected suitor. They say he still lives here."

"Yes. Though no one ever sees him. He keeps to himself. They say it is his guilt which makes him act so. He still does his sculptures and goes off to London to sell them. But when he is here he is a recluse."

"I would have thought he would have left here at once if he'd led that gang of murderers," Ardith said. "Staying on as he has doesn't seem the act of a guilty man."

"People behave in different ways under stress."

"I know that is so," Ardith agreed. "Mrs. MacDonald talks very little about the murder. I think she prefers to erase it from her mind."

"She is a good woman," Lady Mona said. "You are

lucky to have her. I hear you also have the girl, Meg Stone, as your maid."

"She is also competent. I understand she was in service in Edinburgh and received her training there."

"Poor little creature!" Lady Mona observed with a sigh. "She has had a hard life. She was illegitimate, you know. And her mother died when she was very young. Her father never showed himself to help her when she was left alone. Her mother's cousin brought her up, and as soon as she was old enough she was sent to Edinburgh to serve in the home of a wealthy family there. However, she became homesick for this village after a while and so she is back. I'm glad you found work for her."

"So am I," Ardith said.

"And your estate manager is Grim McLeod," the other woman said.

"Yes," Ardith replied, nervous at the mention of his name so soon after the startling happenings of the previous night.

"Has he worked out well?"

"My husband thinks so."

"Sir Douglas is very suspicious of McLeod."

"Suspicious?" she said, at once alerted.

"Yes. You know he and his brothers are supposed to be fishermen. But it's not fish that truly interest them. They are smugglers! They meet the ships which come in from France with their cargoes of fine silks and brandy."

"Smugglers?" she gasped, realizing that this might give solidity to her story about the tunnel and the big man's surprising actions there.

"It's common gossip," Lady Mona confided. "Sir Douglas has the constabulary keeping an eye on them. But the McLeods are more than a match for the law. A group of reckless men with Grim McLeod as their leader. That is why Sir Douglas cannot understand his taking over the position of overseer at Wyndmoor."

In a taut voice, she said, "Perhaps it suited him. He had some reason."

"It could be."

"Where does this smuggling go on?"

"Along the coast. No one knows their secret spot for bringing the contraband ashore and storing it. But the fishing is only a cover up, I can promise you!"

Ardith's mind was working rapidly. She thought about the tunnel in the cliffs and the roar of the waves. It was all too likely that in her sleepwalking she had somehow moved from the cellars at Wyndmoor into the tunnel and accidentally happened on the secret rendezvous of the smugglers. No wonder McLeod had been in a rage!

In a small voice, she said, "And Sir Douglas believes that Grim McLeod is the leader of the smugglers?"

"He knows it but he has not been able to prove it. The silks and brandy flow out of here as far as Edinburgh itself. Those fellows are making a fine profit. So why is Grim McLeod content to take a menial post as your overseer?"

"Perhaps to divert suspicion," Ardith suggested. At the same time, she was thinking that he had taken the post because somewhere on the grounds of the estate the tunnel was located. They had been using the property as the headquarters for their smuggling ring. And he had been forced to take the post as overseer to stay at the old mansion.

This also suggested that he would be actively working to get rid of them. Perhaps he was the one who kept the ghostly legends alive and who would cause them as much trouble as he could. They had an enemy in their camp in Grim McLeod. But how to convince William of this.

"It may be that McLeod has reformed, though I doubt it," the other woman said.

"I will tell my husband," Ardith promised. And she meant to. Perhaps this information would help convince him that her story was more than a nightmare. That she had truly had a confrontation with McLeod in that dark tunnel.

Their conversation was interrupted by the entrance of the attractive thirteen-year-old. She looked much different from the day of her illness. She resembled her mother, though she was much more vivacious. It was a pity to think that her ultimate fate might be madness. Now she sat shyly by her mother and joined in the talk when she was spoken to.

The time slipped by quickly, and soon Ardith knew she must leave. Lady Mona and her daughter, Margaret, saw her to the carriage which awaited her.

The blonde girl asked her, "May I come to visit Wyndmoor one day? I have never been there."

Ardith smiled at the girl. "You must do that! Come and bring your mother." Then she bade them good-bye and stepped up into the carriage. They stood waving to her as she was driven away.

It had been an interesting and rewarding afternoon. She liked Lady Mona and knew that anything the titled woman had told her was likely true. She didn't want to offer too much information to her husband at once, yet she felt there were certain things she must convey to him. Old Dr. Carr must be stopped from making the grave accusations he'd been indulging in about William's ability as a surgeon. And she must warn William about lending Henry Gordon any money.

But most important of all, there was the information she'd come by concerning Grim McLeod. She had to present this in the right way and at the proper moment. If William took it into his head to regard the story as nothing but women's idle gossip she would surely be frustrated. She had to make him understand the facts were known.

The carriage was on the main roadway now, and she was so lost in her thoughts that she didn't see the figure spring out from the bushes and begin following the carriage until he began his mad cries.

"Witch! The witch has come back! Curse the witch!"

She gazed down at the hate-distorted face of old Mad Charlie who had suddenly appeared to trail the carriage, all the while pointing an accusing finger at her.

She told the driver. "Please! Can't you get us away from him!"

"I'll try, ma'am," the driver promised, as he flicked the reins and called out to the horses.

Mad Charlie was running now. Breathlessly he shouted, "Vixen! Daughter of the Devil! Returned from the flames!"

The horse was trotting now, and the carriage rolled on at a much faster pace, leaving the mad old man shouting wildly after them. She sank back against the horsehair carriage seat and felt ill. Why had this old man taken such a violent dislike to her? Did he really think she was Fanny returned? Or did he, because of his madness, sense something about her that no one else did? The presence of the spirit of the murdered Fanny!

This last thought increased her feeling of despair. She sat in a miserable state until the carriage came to a halt by the front door. The first person to show himself there was Grim McLeod.

The big man came forward and in an expressionless tone said, "I'll help you down, ma'am."

"Thank you," she said, knowing it would be better not

to refuse his assistance. When she was on the ground, she said, "I hope there are no hard feelings about what happened this morning."

"None, ma'am," the big man said. "I will not ever think of it again."

"That is generous of you, McLeod," she said with irony. "It would seem I was confused." She hoped this would put him off his guard. "I have had many vivid, bad dreams of late."

"I understand, ma'am. You are here to regain your health. You must not think of me as a person who holds grudges."

"That is most kind," she said. And she went inside.

She met Mrs. MacDonald inside and asked her, "Is my husband still in his office?"

"No," the housekeeper said. "He was called away."

"Where?"

"The same fisherman who came for him last night," the older woman said with a worried look. "As I understand it, his son has taken a turn for the worse."

"The lad with the ruptured appendix?"

"Yes, ma'am."

"Then we can't be sure when the doctor will return."

"That is true."

She started to remove her bonnet. She said, "Better to keep dinner waiting until my husband returns."

"I will," Mrs. MacDonald promised.

And a new thought struck her. She said, "Mrs. MacDonald, where is Fanny Bray buried?"

A solemn look came over the woman's face. She said, "The family burial place is out beyond the stables. There's a path leads to it, though the bushes have grown thick now. You can still find it. I was out there not long ago."

"Thank you," she said quietly. And almost as if she were being directed by some other force, she made her way to a side door. She stood for a moment in the setting sun, and then she crossed the yard.

Walking on beyond the stables, she found the path which the housekeeper had mentioned. And true to the woman's account, she had to battle brush to make her way along it. After a few minutes she saw the cleared area ahead and the gravestones.

It took her only another moment to reach the headstone she was searching for. She read the simple inscription on it, *Fanny Bray beloved wife of John Bray.* There were also her birth and death dates listed below. As she stood before the neglected grave with weeds almost covering the stone's inscription, a weird feeling came over her—the sensation that she was gazing down at her own grave!

Chapter Seven

She was lost in this fantasy when suddenly she heard a footstep behind her. She experienced a cold chill of fear, knowing she was alone in this desolate place. Forcing herself to turn around, she saw a bearded man with long shaggy hair and a handsome, weathered face standing regarding her sardonically. He was a tall man and he wore the traditional Highland kilt.

Ardith gasped, "Who are you?"

He said, "Suppose I ask you the same question?"

"I have a right to be here!"

"So have I!"

She stared at him. "I don't know your name, but mine is Ardith Davis. My husband and I own this property!"

"Fanny's grave as well?" the bearded man asked with a mocking smile.

"The grave is part of our land."

"And all that is left of Fanny," the man said wryly. "If you must know my name it is James Burnett!"

Ardith again was shocked. She said, "You are the sculptor? The one who followed her here after she married John Bray."

He moved a few steps nearer and she saw he had a bunch of dainty wildflowers in his hand. He said, "Yes. I was deeply in love with Fanny. The sad thing was that she didn't care all that much for me."

"But you have not forgotten her."

"No," he said, kneeling to place the flowers gently on the grave so that they rested against the headstone. "I have made a habit of coming by regularly when the weather allows and keeping an eye on her grave."

She said, "You continue to live here, though she has been dead more than twenty years."

He stood up and shrugged. "Harwick is as good a place as any to live. The people are no more stupid and cruel than anywhere else. I'm able to do my work here."

Ardith eyed him directly. "I have heard it said that when Fanny rejected you, the love you had turned to hatred. And that when the mob came to burn her as a witch it was you who led them!"

He nodded. "I know the story. Is it possible that any intelligent person could believe it?"

"You say it is not true?"

"I'd prefer to call it a damnable lie," the tall, bearded man said. "I was not even here when it happened. Perhaps I might have prevented the shameful business if I had been around. I'm sure it was Sir Douglas Gordon who started the rumor!"

"Why should he do such a thing?"

"He doesn't like me. I refused to do a sculpture of his father for the lawn at the castle. He's never gotten over it. He is a spiteful man."

"To accuse you of being a party to such a murder suggests more than spite," she said.

"I have gone on living here with one aim," James Burnett said. "To quell that ugly rumor, and to one day find out who was the leader of those cowardly murderers!"

"Have none of their names ever come out?" she asked.

"None. They have a conspiracy of silence. By this time

many of them must be dead. But they died keeping the secret of their shame."

"You still hope to find the man whose crime you have taken the blame for?"

"Yes," the sculptor said. "Sooner or later the truth will come out. If one name is given, others are bound to follow. Once there is a crack in the dam, the truth will burst forth like a torrent."

Ardith said, "I hope you are right."

The bearded man was studying her intently. He asked, "Has anyone told you that you bear some resemblance to Fanny?"

"A number have."

"It is true."

"I wondered that you didn't notice at the start," she said.

"I was intent on making myself understood to you," he said. "I hope you are satisfied I was not her murderer, and I do not pose a threat to you in my visits here."

She said, "I have only your word for all that."

He smiled bleakly. "You had better be satisfied with it. No one else will speak for me."

Ardith gazed at the tombstone again. "I don't know what brought me out here. I had a sudden desire to see the grave. I had never heard of your Fanny Bray until I came here a few weeks ago. Now most of my thoughts are of her and what happened to her."

James Burnett said quietly, "They say her ghost inhabits the house. That she will never leave Wyndmoor and that she will drive away any who come to live here. That is why no one bought the place."

She said, "You know that is only superstitious nonsense."

"I cannot be sure," he said. "You have just told me that you have been overwhelmed by thoughts of Fanny. Isn't that a sort of haunting?"

"If you want to call it that."

"Your husband is a doctor?"

"Yes."

The sculptor said, "Dr. Carr claims he is an incompetent who lost his post in London because of bungled operations."

"Dr. Carr is a drunkard and a liar," was her reply.

"He will make it hard for you here."

"We were prepared for that."

"Your husband is related to the Stewarts of the Edinburgh banking house, isn't he?"

"Yes. His mother is a Stewart."

"I have met Walter Stewart," the sculptor said. "I did a figure for his bank. Perhaps you have seen it?"

"I haven't been in the bank. But likely I will be at some time. I'll look for it."

"It's a study of Robert Bruce. I think it one of my best efforts."

She said, "Walter Stewart is retired now and very ill. He had a stroke."

"There was a Dr. Ian Stewart well known in Edinburgh. He died when I was a boy. I remember seeing his funeral pass by our house."

Ardith said, "His wife, Ann, is alive and in good health. She still lives in their original home. She is my husband's grandmother and Dr. Ian Stewart was his grandfather."

"Interesting. And why did you come to this place?"

"My health. I've suffered with my lungs."

"So you came to sample the Highland air. I wish you well. And I hope you will not object to my coming here to pay tribute once in a while."

Ardith was won over by the bearded man. She said, "I'm sure I don't object, and my husband won't either. Come whenever you like."

The bearded man bowed. "That is kind of you. I hope the house turns out to be less sinister than the stories would have it."

"I think we will live down its evil reputation," she said.

"Good luck and good day," James Burnett said. And he turned and made his way along the path which she had used. After a moment, he was lost in the bushes.

Alone again, she turned to gaze at the worn headstone once more. What had brought on her desire to be there at this time? Had it somehow been worked out that she would meet James Burnett by the grave? Was that what the phantom Fanny wished? Had she followed the nudging of a ghost? It seemed that she might have.

With a sigh, she left the ancient burial ground and made her way along the nearly overgrown path to the stables, then on to the house. When she entered by the side door, she saw William in his office. He was standing by his desk, frowning at an open book which he'd apparently been studying.

She went in to him. "You're back."

"Yes," he said, abandoning the book to join her. "How did it go at the castle?"

"I had a pleasant time," she said. "Lady Mona prepared a lovely tea for me and I met Margaret. She was sweet today. A lovely child."

Her husband sighed. "I'm sure she is. Did they mention the medicine I sent along?"

"Yes. Lady Mona was most appreciative. She claims Margaret has seemed in much better health since taking it."

"It should help," he agreed.

She decided to find out how he'd made out before she went on to divulge the information she'd been given by the titled woman. She said, "I was told by Mrs. MacDonald that you were called out again. It was to see the boy you operated on last night, wasn't it?"

"Yes," her husband said, his handsome face grim. "A bad business. The boy died about an hour ago."

"I'm sorry," she said. She knew how her husband hated to lose a patient.

"Blood poisoning, of course. They didn't call me in until too late. The appendix had already ruptured. I thought I might have managed to get it all cleaned up. But it was hopeless from the start."

"You did your best!"

"They expected more," he said bitterly. "The parents were stunned. They thought after I'd completed the operation he was bound to recover. I couldn't explain to them."

"It is natural they should be shocked," she said.

William gave her a concerned glance. "There was more than that to it. The father of the boy came outside with me and in an almost accusing tone said, 'I hear something like this happened to you many times in London.' I was so taken back I didn't know what to say. He turned his back on me and went on inside again."

Fear and anger welled up in her; fear for her dedicated husband and anger at the drunken doctor who had deliberately spread lies about him in the village. In a taut voice, she said, "You mustn't let it upset you!"

"The boy died and they blame me! It was bad enough to lose the lad, but to be accused of contributing to his death is almost too much!"

"Dr. Carr!" she exclaimed.

His eyebrows raised. "What about Dr. Carr?"

"He's been conducting a campaign of slander against you," she said. "I heard about it from several people today, one of them being Lady Mona Gordon."

William was shocked. "That drunken wretch has actually been going around making up stories about me?"

"Yes. It's his story that you were dismissed from Bishop's Hospital in London because of making errors in surgery. And apparently the people are believing it. That is what the father of the dead boy was referring to."

"I had no idea!" William exclaimed. "What can I do?"

"Very little," she said, "except to prove him wrong by your excellent doctoring, as you have been doing. He's lost patients, or he wouldn't have resorted to this despicable behavior."

"Word will spread that the boy died," her husband said, "and that the father blames me."

"You will live it down," she told him. "You will save others and they'll come to have faith in you."

"What about now?" he demanded.

"It may be difficult," she acknowledged.

"I feel like giving it all up," William said with disgust. "Your health seems to be deteriorating rather than improving. You have let the legend of this house trouble you."

"I'm sorry," she said. "I know I have not helped."

"It's this place," he said, moving a few steps away from her. "I should never have come to Harwick. I should have found a place with no other doctor. Where I would be welcome."

"Welcome or not, you are needed here," she reminded him.

"I wonder," he said bitterly.

"There is more you should know," she went on. "Lady

Mona warned me about her brother-in-law. She says we should not be too friendly with him."

William frowned. "Of course she would say that. You know Sir Douglas and his brother don't get along."

"I think there's more to it than that. She suggested that Henry Gordon is sly and capable of great harm. She warned that we shouldn't lend him money."

"Not that I was ever likely to. I have accepted him as a friend just as he has accepted us. I see nothing wrong in that. Nor do I expect him to approach me for money."

She sighed. "You may be right. There is also something else."

"What?"

She had decided this might be the best time to tell him. Now, when he was weighed down with his other problems, he might give more credence to what she had to say than when he was in another mood. He might accept that there was more going on in the village than he had realized.

She said, "This is about McLeod."

He came back to stand before her. "What about McLeod? I thought we had settled all that."

"This is different."

"Oh?"

"Yes," she said. "Lady Mona swears that McLeod and his brothers are all engaged in smuggling activities. They never have been true fishermen. That is just a screen to cover their real operations."

"McLeod a smuggler?"

"Yes."

"Not while he's here. He is working for us."

"That's just it," she went on to explain. "Lady Mona says Sir Douglas has had the constabulary on the trail of the McLeods, waiting to catch them at their smuggling. So far they have failed, although they know the smuggling is going on. They have found some of the goods but never have been able to catch the gang red-handed."

"I still can't see that it has anything to do with us."

"They suspect that McLeod was using this house or some place on the estate for the headquarters of his smuggling operations. He is the leader. And they believe that the only reason he took the position of overseer with us was so that he could remain here and go on directing the smuggling from this spot."

William stared at her. "Lady Mona told you all that."

"Yes," she said excitedly. "And I at once saw how it all fitted in!"

"In what way?"

"Don't you see yet?" she asked in amazement. "It is all plain enough. In my sleepwalking last night, I must have somehow stumbled onto the tunnel which is the smuggling headquarters. When McLeod saw me there, he had no choice but to knock me unconscious and then bring me back here and pretend it had all been a vivid nightmare on my part!"

William lifted a protesting hand. "Not so fast! You are assuming too much in too short a space."

"But I know I was there in that tunnel leading to the cliffs! McLeod lied today. He had to."

"I don't know," William worried. "It doesn't seem possible."

"Why?"

"How could you have wandered there?"

"I don't know," she admitted. "Sometimes I think that the ghost of Fanny has truly taken me over. Perhaps she was my guide. Just now I wandered to the cemetery where her grave is. I couldn't resist going there. And when I was there

James Burnett came. We met each other. And somehow I feel that is what she wanted."

"Burnett was here?"

"Yes. I'm impressed by him. He seemed very nice. He did a sculpture for Uncle Walter. And he remembered your grandfather's funeral."

"Where is he now?"

"He left. He brought some wildflowers for her grave. It was very touching. He claims he never stopped loving her and the stories they spread about him leading the band who burned her were lies."

William looked bitter. "That doesn't surprise me in this place!"

"He asked if he might visit the grave occasionally, and I said he could."

"I hope you didn't make a mistake," her husband said. "Things have been happening far too fast for my liking." With a weary sigh, he went to his desk and, sinking into the chair there, leaned his elbows on the desk and covered his face with his hands.

She came to him and placed a placating hand on his shoulder. "I'm sure we will somehow come out of this victorious if we don't become confused and lose hope."

He removed his hands from his face and gazed up at her earnestly. "Tell me what you had in mind."

"We must find out if McLeod is really deceiving us. If he is truly a smuggler. And prove that I did meet him in that tunnel."

Her husband said, "I've already taken his side in that. Now you're asking me to change my opinion because of some gossip offered you by Lady Mona. I'm not sure it's enough."

"I somehow found that tunnel when I was sleepwalking.

We should be able to find it now. But we mustn't let McLeod suspect we're searching for it or that we know about him."

"We don't know about him until he's proven guilty," he reminded her. "And just where do you suggest we start looking for this tunnel?"

She said, "It has to lead from the cellars or from under one of the other outbuildings. Since I reached it so easily, I'd say we should search in the cellar. If we don't find the tunnel opening there we can move on to the other buildings until they are eliminated."

"If what you say about McLeod is true he is a scoundrel," William said.

"And he's likely interested in having us leave the house and Harwick."

"No question of that."

"So he may have arranged some of the ghostly happenings to scare us. I did see something last night. A glowing face resembling Fanny's. It was either her ghost or a clever effigy enough like her to terrify me."

William rose to his feet with a knowing look. "I can tell you who could easily come up with a death mask. Your new friend, James Burnett! Don't forget, he's a sculptor and one of those closest to Fanny!"

"Why would he want to frighten us away?"

"He could be in league with the smugglers," William said.

It was a new idea and she realized how many possibilities there were. She said, "I hadn't thought of that."

"In our position, it might be wise to think of everything," he said. "I'll encourage you to the extent of making a search of the cellar. When shall we do it?"

"Tonight," she said. "McLeod usually goes to the tavern

in the village in the evening. Or at least he leaves here. Better to do it when he isn't around."

"All right," he said. "It's not likely I'll be occupied with patients with the rumors that are going around."

"You can win out," she assured him.

"I wonder," was his bleak reply.

She had never seen her young husband in such a desolate mood. Usually he was the one with the enthusiasm and optimism. But now he was in a valley of depression. She suddenly realized that it was she who must spearhead their battle for a change. And she hoped she was equal to it.

Dinner was a tense meal. They talked little at the table. When it was over they went to the drawing room and waited. It was more than a half-hour before they saw McLeod riding out from the stables on a brown mare he favored. He was away on one of his nightly excursions to the village tavern.

Ardith stepped back from the window, letting the curtain drop back in place. "He's gone. Now is the time."

Her husband nodded. "I hope we aren't going to find ourselves wasting time for nothing."

"I say it's a good gamble," she told him.

They secured a lamp from Mrs. MacDonald and made the excuse they were going to the cellar to see if there might be any pieces of furniture still in storage down there. The housekeeper made no comment, but she showed a doubting look on her matronly face.

William, the lighted lamp in hand, led the way into the deep cellar. When they were out of earshot of Mrs. MacDonald, he said, "I'd wager she didn't believe us."

"Let her think what she likes," Ardith said tensely. "We have our opportunity to search the cellars."

They went all the way down and stood on the earthen

floor taking in their surroundings. The cellar had been partitioned off at several points. Near the foot of the stairs was the wine cellar with its rows of shelves and dusty bottles.

William held up the lamp to examine the wine cellar to more advantage. He said, "We seem to have bought ourselves an ample store of wine along with the property."

At his side, she said, "Who knows what else we'll find down here?"

The cellar was damp and the main area filled with things thrown there haphazardly. There were chairs with a leg broken, and a table of such huge proportions that it seemed to be there only because it was too large for even the big dining room upstairs. There were tables with missing legs or scratched tops and a trunk which was not locked.

"Let me look in this," she said, going to the trunk and lifting the lid.

Her husband held the lamp for her and said impatiently, "It was my understanding that you came down here to look for a tunnel opening, not to dig in old trunks!"

"This one looks interesting," she said. And she rummaged through some ancient dresses and frock coats which smelled of mold to finally find a wooden box carefully hidden near the bottom. She dragged it out from under the clothing with an air of triumph.

"What is that?"

She said, "I'll know in a moment." And she looked to see how the box of highly polished pink wood was going to open. She suddenly found a hidden spring and the top popped up. It was filled with letters and when she raised one of them to her nostrils she could still smell the faint fragrance of perfume.

He said, "Just a lot of old letters!"

She shook her head as she opened the envelope and

studied the letter. "Not just old letters! These are letters sent to Fanny Bray! And I'd be willing to bet there are some of her own letters, written by her, in this box. I must take it up with me and read everything in it!"

William said, "All right. Have your letters. Bring the box along. But let us start searching for that tunnel!"

Ardith closed the trunk top and held the small box with the letters in it under her arm. With William leading the way, they began exploring every room and wall of the cellar with a view to finding some hint of the tunnel opening. It was a long, tedious job as the cellar was a large one.

Their search brought them back to the wine cellar. Her husband gave her an exasperated look. "Just as I expected," he said. "Nothing. I don't think there is any tunnel. It's just a part of your nightmare. I doubt that McLeod is a smuggler, that is more of Harwick's false gossip!"

"You give up easily," she told him. "There are the other buildings."

"We'll not explore them tonight," William said. "I want to think about this. I'm not at all sure there is anything in this theory of yours."

She saw that it had come to a point where it was useless to try and press him further. She would have to wait until he was in a mood to try again. So she said, "Very well. At least we found these letters."

"What value will they have?" he asked.

"I can't say until I've read them," was her reply. "They may not be worth anything, but hopefully they will tell us a few things about the people who once lived here."

He held the lamp for her to start up the steps. "I think this house is making you morbid," he complained.

As she started up the steps, she suddenly saw the portrait of Fanny which had been removed from the drawing room leaning against a packing case. She halted and asked, "Aren't you going to let that be hung where it belongs?"

"No," he said. "Let's not discuss it!"

She sighed and went on up the steps, leaving the lovely Fanny's portrait to rest forlornly in the cellar. But she had not given up hope. She was determined to make William change his mind at some future time.

When they reached the upper hallway, Mrs. MacDonald came to greet them. The housekeeper said, "You have a caller. Lawyer Macree."

William gave the housekeeper the lamp and said, "I'll see him."

The box of letters still clutched under her arm, she asked, "What do you suppose he wants?"

"I can't imagine," William said grimly.

"I'll take these up to my room and then come back down," she told him.

As she mounted the stairway to her bedroom she again knew that strange feeling of exaltation she had experienced several times since coming under the spell of the old mansion. It was as if she had done something right and was proud of it. Almost as if that other voice was congratulating her and giving her directions what to do.

Reaching her room, she opened a lower dresser drawer and carefully placed the wooden box with its letters inside it. She promised herself that as soon as she had time the following morning she would go thoroughly through the contents of the box.

Meg had already turned down her bed, placed a lighted candle on her bedside table and put her glass of medicine and water beside the candle. She noted these details and smiled with appreciation. In spite of all the other problems of Wyndmoor, she at least was blessed with a perfect maid in the petite girl with the straw-colored hair.

When she returned downstairs she found her husband and Lawyer Macree in the library in the midst of a sober discussion. The flat-faced lawyer with the gray side-whiskers rose as she entered the room and respectfully bowed to her.

William brought her a chair and said, "Sit down, my dear. Lawyer Macree has news for us."

"What sort of news?" she asked.

William smiled at her as he stood by her chair. "He has come with an offer for our property."

She gasped and looked at the old lawyer who was seated in a chair opposite. "You must be joking!"

"No, he isn't," William said. "It seems that after being wanted by no one for two decades Wyndmoor is suddenly in demand."

Ardith said, "Please explain."

Lawyer Macree cleared his throat. "The fact is, Mrs. Davis, my firm has received an offer from a party in Edinburgh who wishes to buy Wyndmoor and will pay you what you paid John Bray for it plus a five hundred pound bonus."

William gave her a wise look. "What do you say to that?"

She said, "I'd say it was Sir Douglas Gordon trying to get the property away from us and not wanting to show his hand."

William nodded. "I agree."

The old lawyer shook his head. "No, I don't think it can be Sir Douglas. I know his lawyers in Edinburgh and this is a different firm."

She said, "Probably he hired them especially for this purpose."

Lawyer Macree said, "I hardly would believe that. Sir Douglas is a strange man. He is not the sort to change his legal representatives, even for deception."

She said, "Then if it is not Sir Douglas, who can it be?"

"I can't hazard a guess," the lawyer said. "I had no choice but to bring you the offer. I realize it is not apt to interest you."

William said, "We will consider it."

Ardith looked up at him in dismay. "You're not ready to give up so easily?"

William spread his hands. "I must admit I no longer find Harwick as appealing as I did at the start."

"Because someone is deliberately trying to discourage us," she told him.

"Maybe," he said.

Lawyer Macree looked at them nervously. "I can write this firm in Edinburgh and say you have the matter under serious consideration."

"And ask if they can't make a better offer," William said. "We bought the property cheaply. It should be worth at least an extra thousand pounds if this party really wants the place."

Lawyer Macree seemed to understand this. "Yes," he said. "I will also add that a higher offer might make the transaction more interesting to you."

"Do that," William agreed.

The old lawyer stood up. "I shall compose the letter the first thing in the morning."

Ardith was on her feet and she said indignantly, "If it were up to me I'd say that we wouldn't sell at any price."

William said, "You are all at once strangely attached to this place. I don't understand it."

She blushed. "I do not like to be the victim of a conspiracy." But she knew it was more than that. The phantom which had invaded her was making her take this stand, forcing her to say these things without her really understanding why she was saying them.

Later, after the old lawyer had left, William saw her up to her room. He remained with her a long while as they discussed all that the day had brought them. He still hinted strongly that he might decide to sell the property. She was just as strong in her wish not to give in to the pressure which had been brought to bear on them. It ended with nothing settled. He kissed her good night and then went on to his own room.

Left alone, she took her medicine. She had a sudden impulse to get the box from the dresser and read the letters in it. But after taking her medicine she became so light-headed and drowsy that she decided it would be best to leave this task until the morning when her mind was clear.

She extinguished the candle and almost immediately fell asleep. And soon after she began to dream. In her dream she relived the adventure in the tunnel the previous night with all the terror it had brought her. Then a new face suddenly intruded in her dream, the face of James Burnett; she was again standing talking with him in the cemetery.

As they talked her tension grew. And then she saw that behind him, hidden in the shadows of the tall trees, there were a group of masked men! She cried out and tried to warn him, but he paid no attention to her, going on talking as if nothing were wrong. The masked men began advancing towards them and this time she not only cried out a warning but turned and ran straight into the woods!

The masked men called out threats and came trampling through the dry bush after her. She ran aimlessly, not knowing where she was heading, simply intent in escaping that masked gang! She reached a small downgrade and suddenly she tripped over a tree root thrust across her path.

She screamed as she went tumbling headlong, and before she could lift herself from the ground she heard the voices of her pursuers. A moment later they were upon her, seizing her with rough hands before she could escape them!

"No!" she cried plaintively.

And then she awoke. She was standing in the darkness and not in her own room. It took her a moment to realize that she had made her way down the stairs and to the music room. Once again she was standing by the long-neglected pianoforte. She gazed down at it and began to tremble!

Her sleepwalking had become a thing of terror. She did not know where it might lead her next. She had come to fear sleep. It seemed that once she surrendered to sleep this phantom force took hold of her. Fanny's restless spirit guided her in paths which she would never have otherwise taken.

Even in the daytime when she was fully awake she found herself succumbing to sudden, strange impulses such as the one which had led her to the cemetery and the meeting with James Burnett! Was she gradually falling under the spell of the murdered Fanny?

Perhaps she should not argue with William if he wished to sell the property and leave Harwick. It might be best. Why not take the mysterious offer and get away from all the tension and mystery? Yet she did not like to have them accept defeat. And it would be a defeat. Her husband had come to Harwick full of high hopes of the climate restoring her health and his being able to bring new standards of medicine to the isolated community. Their leaving would be an admission that they had failed.

She felt the chill in the after-midnight atmosphere of the strange old mansion and decided that she should return to her bed. In the morning she would report this latest incident of sleepwalking to her husband, though she doubted that he would pay much attention to her. He had not in the past.

She returned to her room without any unpleasant happening and soon was asleep again. When she awoke in the morning she saw it was a dull, rainy day. Meg was on hand as usual to help her bathe and dress.

When she went downstairs she came upon her husband and Mrs. MacDonald in serious conversation in the front hall. When William saw her, he left the housekeeper and came over to her.

He said, "I've been waiting for you to come down."

"Oh?" she said, sensing by his clouded face that he was upset about something.

"Did you sleep well last night?" he asked.

"I walked in my sleep again," she said.

"Again!"

"Yes. But I only went as far as the music room. When I woke I decided to go straight back to bed. And I slept soundly for the balance of the night."

"That's strange," her husband said, his eyes meeting hers in a grim fashion.

"I know," she said. "The sleepwalking has me badly worried. I never know when it will happen."

"I was thinking of something else," William said. "Come into the drawing room with me." And he led the way.

She followed him, noticing that Mrs. MacDonald was staring at her in an odd way. She went into the big room after William and at once saw what he had been talking about. The portrait of Fanny had been returned to its place on the wall!

Standing by the portrait, her husband said, "Not only is the portrait back in place, but you will see some of the furniture in here has been moved. Mrs. MacDonald claims the pieces have been changed to the spots they occupied when Fanny was mistress of the house!"

Chapter Eight

Ardith glanced around her and saw that some of the chairs in the drawing room, and at least one of the tables, had been moved. She frowned and said, "I don't understand it!"

"Nor do I," William said crisply.

"Did all this happen during the night?"

"Yes," he said, coming a step nearer to her. "I have it on Mrs. MacDonald's word that everything was in order when she came to extinguish the lamps here last night. All this must have been done between midnight and this morning."

"Who would do such a thing?" Ardith wondered.

"Any number of people, I suppose," her husband said with some annoyance. "But I'm thinking about your strong interest in having the portrait hung again. Also, there is the fact that you walked in your sleep again last night. Could it add up?"

"To what?"

"To your retrieving the portrait from the cellar where you saw it and changing the furniture around," William said, watching her with sharp eyes as he made the charge.

Her mouth opened in surprise. Then she said, "I know nothing about it!"

"You wouldn't if you did it in your sleep," was his suggestion.

"No! I wandered to the music room! I woke up there!"

"But perhaps you were in here first."

She stared at him in dismay. "You really think I might have done all this while I was sleepwalking?"

"I know you were determined the portrait should be restored here," he said. "Your subconscious may have goaded you to these acts."

She sank into the nearest chair and placed her hands over her face, trying to straighten out her thoughts. She could not swear she wasn't responsible for what happened. She might have done exactly what William was saying. But if she had gone to the cellar and brought up the portrait and then changed the furniture to the pattern it had been in during Fanny's time at Wyndmoor she believed she must have done so under the guidance of Fanny's spirit!

Lowering her hands, she looked up at her troubled young husband and asked, "If I moved the furniture how would I know the arrangement of it when Fanny lived here? The only one now in the house who could possibly know that is Mrs. MacDonald."

"She didn't do it! She brought it to my attention," he said.

"Then you'll have to blame it on a ghost," she said in a grim tone. "Either Fanny's ghost doing it directly or guiding me to do it."

William waved an impatient hand. "You know I refuse to accept the existence of ghosts."

"You may have to change your mind," she warned him.

"I think not," he said. "At any rate, you deny having knowingly done this?"

"Yes."

"I'll let it drop at that," he said. "I merely wanted to question you. Think no more about it."

She said, "Are you going to leave the portrait and furniture as they are?"

"Yes," he said. "I think I will. I'm sure you have no objections."

"I thought it was silly of you to move the portrait in the first place."

"It was your obsession with it that made me do it," he said. "I see that it didn't help much."

"If you think it was only the portrait which upset me you are wrong," she said. "It is the house and everything about it. This place is still under the shadow of that woman's murder. Perhaps it always will be."

"Perhaps," he said. "I'll be going out directly on the rounds of my patients. I will return for office hours and luncheon."

She stood up. "You're not angry with me?"

"No," he said, his manner changing and becoming more that of a considerate husband than of a questioning medical man. "I'm not angry with you. If you did this it was the result of your overwrought nerves. You can't be blamed for that." And he drew her close and kissed her in an understanding manner.

Still she was not satisfied. She knew he was bothered and that in his mind she was to blame for the weird incidents of the night. Later, after he had driven off in his carriage, she stared out at the rainy morning and pondered on who else might have been responsible. And the name she came up with was that of the person she most suspected of wishing to get them away from Wyndmoor. It could well be Grim McLeod.

He was in the house and no doubt at some time Mrs. MacDonald might have mentioned in passing the different arrangement of furniture. And while she might have forgotten about it, the wily McLeod might have noted it for his own future use. It was a possibility.

Her chief fear was that her original theory was the solution to the mystery. She was gradually becoming more and more of a puppet directed by the spirit of the murdered young woman whom she resembled. And etched on her mind was the encounter with the shadowy figure and the glowing face!

She was standing there lost in thought when Mrs. MacDonald came into the room. In her nervous fashion the older woman said, "You have a visitor. She came in by the back way."

Ardith was surprised. "Who is it?"

"I don't know the young lady," the housekeeper said with what could have been a look of disapproval on her lined face. "I had her wait in the music room."

"Thank you," Ardith said. "I'll go to her."

Puzzled as to who it might be, she made her way along the dark hallway to the music room. Mrs. MacDonald knew almost everyone in the village; it was strange that she had not recognized her visitor.

Entering the music room, she saw a young woman in a cheap, low-cut dress standing idly playing with the keyboard of the pianoforte. On hearing her enter, the girl looked up and Ardith saw that she had a coarse attractiveness about her. Her best features were her large brown eyes which now fixed on her with interest.

"You wished to see me?" she asked.

The girl nodded and Ardith saw that her shoulder-length brown hair was matted from the rain. The girl held up a small square wrapped in brown paper. "I have a gift for you."

"A gift?"

The girl's full red lips twisted in a smile. "A gift from Mr. Henry Gordon!" And she came to her and gave her the parcel.

She took it. "Yes. I know Mr. Gordon. Why didn't he bring this himself?"

The girl pursed her mouth in disgust. "Laid up! Has the gout! Gets it every now and then!"

"That's too bad. I hope he recovers soon."

"He's better today," the girl said. "But he didn't want to wait to send you this. He did it while he was laid up."

"I see. It's a work of art."

"He thinks so," the girl said. "You've got a regular castle here!"

"I'm glad you like it," Ardith said with a smile, as the girl moved about admiring the room. She was a thoroughly uninhibited creature and she talked with a slum accent. "You must be Jeannie Truffin?"

The girl paused in admiring a silver bowl which she had picked up from one of the tables to turn to her and nod. "That's right! I'm Jeannie. He told you about me?"

"Yes," she said, rather embarrassed. "I must open his gift." And she quickly untied the string and opened the brown paper to reveal a white square of tile with a pen and ink sketch of herself, head and shoulders, adorning it. The likeness was excellent and she gasped with pleasure. "It's very good!"

Jeannie put down the bowl and moved across the room to stand before her. "Looks like you!" she commented.

"Yes. Tell Mr. Gordon I'm very pleased."

"I will," the girl said. And then in a slightly disdainful fashion, she said, "He's done sketches of me. Dozens of them. He says I'm his best model!"

"You are attractive," Ardith agreed. "I'm sure he must get inspiration from you."

Jeannie stared at her in a way which indicated she was not sure what inspiration meant. The former bar girl went on, "He's done me with my clothes on and without a stitch. It's all alike to me."

Ardith felt her cheeks warm. "I'm satisfied with this study," she said. "But I realize as a model you would have to be depicted in all moods."

The girl stared at her wide-eyed. "You talk funny!"

"Do I?"

"Doesn't matter," Jeannie said with a snap of her fingers. She moved away to admire the furnishings of the room again. "He will be glad to know you're pleased."

"Be sure and tell him I'm delighted!"

Jeannie smiled wryly. "I've never been inside a house like this. I guess there aren't that many of them."

"More than you'd think," Ardith said. "This is modest by the standards of some. Would you like to see the drawing room?"

"Yes," the girl said.

Ardith took her in and Jeannie was sufficiently awed to move about the wealth of fine furnishings in silence. It was not until she all at once found herself standing before the painting of Fanny Bray that she halted and spoke out.

In an accusing tone, she exclaimed, "He'd already done your portrait!"

Ardith went to stand beside the girl who was still staring at the painting. She explained, "No. That wasn't done by Henry Gordon and it isn't of me. Someone painted it long ago. It's a likeness of the woman who once lived here. Her name was Fanny Bray."

The girl turned to stare at her in amazement. "The one who was murdered for being a witch?"

"Yes," she said.

"She looks uncommon like you, or you like her," Jeannie said, glancing at the portrait again. "That's real strange!"

"I know," she said. "Many people say we look a lot alike."

Jeannie again turned to her. "You're no relation to her?"

"No," she said.

"Gives me a chill down my back," Jeannie said.

Ardith managed a smile. "I've sort of become used to it, I try not to dwell on it."

"I guess I'd feel the same way," the girl said. Then abruptly, "I have to be going!"

She said, "Have you no shawl? Nothing to protect you from the rain?"

"No. I don't mind it."

"You'll be drenched by the time you get back to the cottage."

"I'm drenched now," the girl said. "It won't hurt me. When I get back to the cottage I'll strip and dry off before the fireplace."

"You won't take a shawl from me?"

"No. Henry would say I was accepting charity and he'd be angry," the brown-eyed girl said. Then she paused and stared hard at her again. "You do look like her!" And with that she left the room. She insisted on leaving by the back door by which she had come.

Ardith had been amused by the girl's frankness, and she knew that Jeannie had been shocked that she so resembled the murdered Fanny. Her reaction had been interesting. Ardith then took the tile upstairs to her bedroom.

Meg was just leaving the room; she curtsied and said, "Everything is done, ma'am. I've just finished with the cleaning and the bed."

"That's good, Meg," she said. She was grateful to be having the room to herself since she wanted to sit down and read the letters she'd found in the wooden box in the cellar.

Entering the bedroom, she placed the tile on the dresser top and then she bent and opened the drawer in which she'd put the small, wooden box. It was still there. Her inner excitement rising, she took it out and went over to a table by the window and began to tremble as she played with the hidden lock which finally allowed the lid to spring open.

The first letters were from a girlhood friend of Fanny's, married and living in Glasgow. There were references to their schooldays and the other young woman wrote that she was the mother of two.

All the letters smelled faintly of that long-ago perfume which Fanny must have used. From the tone of some of the letters, Ardith gradually formed a picture of a Fanny who was not all that happy in Wyndmoor. In the letters of her correspondents there were mentions of her telling them that she was lonely and frightened.

Ardith read on. Going through every letter and then carefully placing it back in its envelope and putting it to one side. A letter which Fanny had received from an aunt in Edinburgh was rather severe and reprimanding in tone. It said in part:

The complaints of fear and homesickness in your last letter were not at all mature. You should be grateful to have a wealthy husband such as John Bray, and even if his sister, Mary, is stern towards you, you must look at it from her side. She sees you not as her brother's beloved wife but as an intruder. She is an older woman and versed in the running of a fine mansion. You will do well to be patient with her and model yourself after her. There are dark nights and high, wailing winds here in Edinburgh! You would not escape such minor annoy-

ances by returning here.

Ardith frowned at this letter. It was clear that Fanny had sensed the growing hatred of the villagers towards her and had tried to convey this to her aunt without making any impression on her. Fanny had been lonely and terrified long before they had come to burn her as a witch! How unfortunate she hadn't gone to pay a visit to Edinburgh. She might have escaped the dreadful fate which overtook her in the woods of Harwick.

There was another later series of letters from the girl in Glasgow. And this was in a happier vein. It seemed that she and Fanny were proposing to gather together all the best recipes they could find and issue them as a joint effort. They would call the cookbook, "To Sup In The Highlands." The girl's husband in Glasgow was the proprietor of a printing press and would have it printed.

Ardith felt herself caught up in the enthusiasm of the two. And in the bottom of the box she found pitiful witness to the plan—a number of recipes written on various slips of paper in Fanny's own hand. There were at least forty or fifty of them. She lifted out these slips and, to her dismay, found she had come to the bottom of the box. There was nothing more in it.

It left her with a definite feeling of frustration. She had learned a great deal about Fanny, but not nearly enough. She fervently wished there might be more letters to read, but there were only the few which she had gone over. Slowly she placed both the slips of papers and the letters in the box again and closed it. Then she put it back in her dresser drawer.

She crossed over to the window and stared out at the heavy downpour of rain. Of course, the cookbook had never been published. Before Fanny had been able to continue with the project she had become embroiled in the superstitions of the villagers. They had decided she was a witch and the cowardly band who attacked the house had murdered her.

What about John Bray's sister, Mary? Why had she not tried to help? Surely she could have done something to aid her brother's lovely wife as she was being dragged off to be murdered in the woods. Why had she not raised an alarm? Called on someone for help? Or had she been too terrified? Mary Bray had gone to Canada with her brother after the tragedy. Presumably she was still with him. The answers to all the many questions of that dreadful night were lost in the haze of the past.

In the next several days, things went badly for the new owners of Wyndmoor. Apparently the death of the boy on whom William had operated had been used to good advantage by the evil old Dr. Carr. His gossiping that William had fled London because of his many surgical errors had been taken as the truth by the ignorant villagers.

The stream of patients dropped off to only one or two a day. William became morose and spent a lot of his time alone in his study poring over his textbooks. Ardith knew how unhappy he was but could do little to help him.

Worse, she was having her own problems. Twice again she walked in her sleep. The first time she came awake in the kitchen of the old mansion after giving the cook a terrible fright. That good woman had taken her for a ghost. And the second time she came to herself at dawn on the lawn just outside the front door of Wyndmoor.

There was another unpleasant incident when she went out for a stroll along the cliffs. Old Mad Charlie appeared and resumed his weird antics, following after her and accusing her of being Fanny's ghost. She hurried back to the house and he followed her. As she hastily entered the front door, he stood on the lawn shouting after her.

"Daughter of Satan! Go back to your grave, Fanny Bray!" he cried loudly.

Both McLeod and Mrs. MacDonald were there to see her shocked behavior and it was McLeod who went out and drove the mad old man away. He came back inside where she was waiting with the housekeeper.

"Did he do you any harm, ma'am?" McLeod asked.

"No," she said. "Nothing beyond shouting at me as you heard him just now."

"The constabulary should be told!" Mrs. MacDonald said indignantly.

Grim McLeod shrugged his broad shoulders. "You know well he'll pay no heed to the constables. I think I put the fear in him. I told him I'd shoot him if he trespassed here again. He ran quick when I said that."

"Thank you," she told the big man, the one she suspected of being a smuggler.

"No more than my duty, ma'am," McLeod said, and he went off to the rear of the house.

Ardith went upstairs, still trembling from the unhappy experience. She knew that McLeod kept a more restrained manner than normal in her presence since the time she'd accused him of meeting her in the cave and slapping her so that she fainted. William had promised to keep a close watch on the overseer, but with all the other problems which had come along she did not think her husband was giving this much thought.

The weather had become warm, much warmer than it normally was in summer. And with the hot August nights she felt there was a brooding threat in the air. She could not explain why she felt this way, but she knew it was so. She had asked William if she might write Ishbel and ask her to bring Ian up for a week or two.

William had not taken kindly to the idea. He'd said, "No. I do not want the boy here now. We are in too much of a state of unrest."

"Is it liable to be different?"

"Perhaps not. We'd best wait and see if Lawyer Macree gets a reply to our offer to that law firm in Edinburgh. We may be selling."

"Why not let your mother and the boy come for a week? A single week! I miss him so!" she'd pleaded.

"And so do I," William had said. "But I do not consider it a proper time to have them here."

So she let it go at that. The slight argument with her handsome husband upset her all over again. And that night the dream which she feared so much came back, and when she wakened from it she stared into the darkness of the warm night and saw a shadow at the foot of her bed.

At first she thought it was William, unable to sleep. He had come to her the night before after some restless hours of being awake in his own room.

Plaintively, she said, "Is that you, William?"

Her answer came quickly. The figure turned and she saw the glowing face of Fanny which had so terrified her once before. The phosphorescent face so much like her own in feature!

"No!" she screamed, drawing back against the head of her bed.

The shadow moved and the face vanished. At the same time, Ardith cried out for help, "William! William!" The door between the two rooms opened and her husband came hurrying in. He crossed to her bedside and asked, "What is it?"

"The ghost!" she sobbed. "I saw it just now!"

"In here?"

"Yes!"

He got up and, lighting the candle by her bedside, made a search of the room and the hallway outside. He finally came back to her with a resigned look on his tired, young face. He said, "You must have had another of your nightmares!"

"I saw the face of Fanny! Glowing in the dark!"

"I've searched thoroughly," he said. "There's no one. You mustn't go on like this. Try to get back to sleep."

"I'm afraid," she said.

"I'll stay with you," he said. And he did.

But if the night was bad it was only a prelude to the grimness of the following morning. They had barely finished breakfast and were about to go their different ways when a carriage came rolling into the driveway. William went to see who it might be. It was the elegant carriage which was a showpiece of Sir Douglas Gordon. And the corpulent squire of Harwick descended from the vehicle and came striding purposefully to the front door.

He saw them standing in the doorway and with a look of anger mixed with concern on his bloated red face he asked, "Have you seen my daughter?"

William was first to reply, "No. Why should we have?"

Sir Douglas stood there defiantly in his blue frock coat and matching top hat. He said sternly, "Margaret has often spoken of coming to visit you. Last night she vanished."

"Vanished?" Ardith echoed the stout nobleman.

"That is what I said," Sir Douglas continued grimly. "She must have left the house some time in the night."

William said, "What would make you think she would come here?"

"I have called on other places," the stout man said, in a voice which held a tremor in it. "You people are my last hope. You're sure she isn't here?"

"No. I only wish she were," Ardith said.

Sir Douglas looked at her with grim dismay. "She wanted to come here. I refused her permission. Sometimes she takes matters into her own hands. Is it possible she is here somewhere without your knowing?"

"I'll see a thorough search is made," she said. "Won't you come in for a sherry while you are waiting?"

"Please hurry, madam," Sir Douglas said, removing his hat and coming inside.

William served him sherry while Ardith, with the help of Mrs. MacDonald and McLeod saw that a search was made of the house and even the stables. There was no Margaret in hiding. She was forced to bring this unhappy news to the girl's father.

Sir Douglas slammed on his top hat and strode to the door. "I must continue looking for her," were his parting words.

They watched as the carriage was driven off. William came in after closing the door and gave her a questioning glance. "What do you make of that?"

"I don't like it," she said.

"Nor do I."

She gave him a worried look. "The girl is an epileptic. Suppose she left the house for some reason and then, while she was out alone, had one of her fits."

"It could happen," William agreed. "A stressful period sometimes is the forerunner of such attacks."

"She and her father might have quarreled."

William gave her a significant look. "He admitted that he refused to allow her to visit us as she wanted."

"Poor dear!" Ardith said. "And Lady Mona would not dare take her side."

"The father is in a bad state."

"You can't blame him for that," she said.

"I don't," William agreed. "But I do hope she turns up quickly and in good health."

"She could be in one of their own barns, dead from choking during a sudden spell," Ardith said. "Do you suppose her father realizes that?"

"I can't say," William sighed. "He is an unreasonable man much of the time."

"There is so little we can do," she worried.

"I know," her husband said.

The ghost scare of the night before was forgotten in this new crisis. William drove into the village in the afternoon to see if there was any word. She waited at home, seated on a side verandah.

Because it was warm she remained outside a long while waiting for William to return. And it was while she was on the verandah that she saw the tall, bearded James Burnett come out from behind the stables and start across the lawn. She at once guessed that he had been visiting Fanny's grave again and called out to him.

He halted and shaded his eyes with his hands. When he saw it was her, he came over to the verandah. He said, "I didn't recognize your voice."

"I suppose you've been visiting the cemetery," she said.

The lean face was bleak of expression. "I have no other purpose in coming here."

She said, "I'm waiting for my husband to return. Have you heard about Sir Douglas Gordon's daughter being missing?"

"No," he said. "When did that happen?"

She told him as much about Margaret's vanishing as Sir Douglas had confided to them. She ended with, "The girl is an epileptic, although her father refuses to admit it. We are afraid she may have taken a spell and died without aid in some lonely place."

"That would be too bad," the sculptor said.

"Harwick seems to be a place for tragedy."

"Some people think that," the bearded man said.

She said, "I came upon some letters sent to Fanny, which she had stored away in a box. And also some recipes she had collected and written down."

He at once showed interest. The sharp eyes under the bushy brows fixed on her. "You found some of Fanny's letters?"

"Not her letters. But letters sent to her by others. Her aunt and a friend of her schoolgirl days. A young woman married and living in Glasgow who seemed to be her best friend."

"Jean," he said tautly.

"Yes," Ardith remembered. "That was the name signed to the letters. You knew her?"

"I knew her."

"I have a strange feeling from the tone of the letters. I don't think Fanny was happy here. I'm sure she wrote that to Jean and her aunt."

"No doubt."

Ardith studied the face of the bearded man. "Did you know that she was homesick and frightened?"

"Yes," he said. "I begged her to leave with me and she refused. She felt she could not betray such a fine man as John Bray. Yet he deserted her!"

"Not really. He merely went away on a business trip. What happened was not his fault."

"I blame him," the bearded sculptor said angrily. "He could have taken her with him. He knew the high fever of superstitious fear here. He should not have left her for a moment!"

"She was not alone. His sister was here."

"Much good she was! Taking hysterics and not trying to send word to anyone!" James Burnett said with disgust. "It was your Mrs. MacDonald who brought the news to me. By that time it was too late!"

"I can understand how you feel," she said.

"You think so?" the sculptor said derisively.

"Of course not truly," she hastened to say. "Yet I do know how you suffered."

"The worst was when they first told me what had happened to her. And then when the word spread that I had been the one who led the gang."

Ardith asked, "Who do you think started the rumor?"

"I can only guess," he said bitterly. "I think it was Sir Douglas."

"Why would he do such a thing?"

"Someone had to be blamed. I was an outsider."

"But there were many local men involved in the attack on Fanny."

"You could not find a single one to admit it. By the next morning they were all ready to swear they were as innocent as the sheep in the fields. But the shame of what they did will shadow this village for all time."

"Without a doubt," she said.

He seemed about to go on his way when he hesitated and turned to ask her, "Can I look at those letters one day?"

"Yes."

"I would like to read them," he said.

"Did Fanny tell you why she was so unhappy?"

"She was afraid of the stories going around that she was a witch," he said. "And she was also afraid of this house!"

"Afraid of Wyndmoor?"

He smiled knowingly. "Do you find that so strange?"

"No," she said. "No, I don't."

As she finished speaking, there was the sound of a carriage coming in the driveway. She rose and saw that it was William back. She stepped down from the verandah to greet him.

The sculptor said, "I will be leaving, now."

"Wait a moment," she said. "You have not met William. He'd be interested in meeting you."

"I have to be on my way," the bearded man said with a firm harshness. "We can meet later!" And he walked quickly away and vanished in the bushes before William drove up.

William got down from the carriage as one of the stable boys led the horse and vehicle away. He asked her, "Who was that?"

"James Burnett, the sculptor."

"The one who followed Fanny here and whom they claim may have been the one who led her murderers?" William asked, glancing in the direction in which the bearded man had vanished.

"Yes."

"He moved fast when he saw me drive in."

"I asked him to wait."

"What did he say?"

"That he couldn't. He'd meet you later."

William frowned. "Odd way to act!"

She said, "He is strange. But you know he has gone through a lot."

"I'm not anxious to have a fellow like that on the

grounds. He could be more of a menace than Mad Charlie."

"I wouldn't say so," she said. "Any news?"

"None," her young husband said grimly.

"That's awful!"

"I know," he agreed, placing an arm around her as they stepped up onto the verandah and sat on the wicker love seat there.

"Her father must be frantic."

"I didn't see him," William said, frowning at the gray planks of the verandah floor. "I understand he is leading a search party in the woods."

"Do you think she might be lost there?"

"It's a possibility. There is also a search party doing the cliffs and the shore. Dr. Carr is very prominent in it all. He is assisting Sir Douglas in organizing the searchers."

She nodded. "You were not needed."

"He made that plain," William said with a sigh. "And he even hinted that my medicine may have made the child's condition worse."

"Never mind."

"I don't," he said. "I know it's untrue and that's enough. There was something else going on which upset me."

She stared at him. "What?"

"That crazy old man!"

"Mad Charlie?"

"Yes," William said. "He's running around saying you are a witch! Fanny come back to torment the village! He is blaming you for Margaret's disappearance!"

She said incredulously, "No one pays any attention to him!"

"Not normally," William agreed. "But today it was a little different. I actually think some of them believe him!"

"No!" she protested.

"I'm afraid so," her young husband went on. "I heard two of the villagers talking after he went by. And one of them said that Coline Dougall ought to be brought into the village."

"Coline Dougall?"

He gave her a worried look. "You must recall the name. She is the old woman who declared Fanny was a witch and started all the trouble. She's blind and about ninety now. The villagers regard her as a mystic! Blessed with special powers!"

"It's nonsense talk," she said lamely, though his words made her uneasy.

"Probably," he agreed, as he rose to go inside. "Just the same, I'd be a lot happier if that girl had been found safe and alive."

"She still may be."

"With every passing hour the chances are less," was his troubled reply.

It was well after dinner when their visitor arrived. He came on foot so they did not have any warning of his approach. They were in the drawing room talking in low voices about the disappearance of Margaret when Mrs. MacDonald let their caller in. It was Henry Gordon, artist brother of Sir Douglas.

He stood in the double doorway of the drawing room mopping his brow with a soiled white handkerchief. "I'm a little winded," he gasped. "Long walk! Just over the gout!"

Ardith and William both came forward to greet him. Ardith begged him, "Do sit down, Mr. Gordon."

William said, "I'll fetch you a drink." And he hurried to the sideboard to get it.

The paunchy Henry Gordon sank into the nearest easy

chair. He said, "I had to bring you the news!"

Ardith gazed down at him and saw that his mood was grim. Tautly, she asked, "What is the news?"

He shook his head. "Bad!"

Chapter Nine

William brought the artist a glass of sherry and then handed a glass to her. He said, "Don't keep us in suspense. Did they find the girl?"

Henry Gordon gulped the sherry down and then gave them a grave look. He said, "Yes. In the woods. She was dead when they reached her."

Ardith touched a hand to her temple. "I was afraid this was how it would be!"

William, more professional, asked, "What were the circumstances of her death?"

The artist spoke dully, "A sad business. She left home in the middle of the night and wandered into the woods. They found her body in a shallow pond. But she didn't die from drowning. She'd been throttled first!"

"Then it was murder!" William said, shocked.

"Yes," the stout man in the chair said. "And something more than that."

"What?" William demanded.

"There was the mark of the Devil's hoof scratched on her cheek," Henry Gordon said, disgust on his oval face.

William stared at him. Then he said, "Echoes of the Fanny Bray case. Does this mean there's supposed to be another witch in the area?"

"I don't know what it means," Henry Gordon said

wearily. "I'm giving you the facts. May I have another drink? I'd prefer whiskey if you have it."

William nodded and took his glass from him as he went out to get the whiskey. Ardith was left alone with the shabby brother of Sir Douglas Gordon. She stood in a kind of daze with her sherry untouched.

She said, "Who would do such a monstrous thing?"

"I don't know," he said. "My brother will have all the constabulary in the country out to try and solve the crime. He is almost out of his mind with grief."

"Have you spoken with him?"

"He won't speak to me. But I did manage to see Mona for a few minutes. I don't think she's realized what has happened. She is in a shocked state."

"Nature can be kind. Shock will ward off the blow until she can tolerate it," Ardith said.

"If Douglas had been more understanding of the child she wouldn't have been straying out of the house in the night," the man in the chair said angrily. "He is partly responsible."

"I'm sure he won't think so."

"He never will take blame. But, more often than not, he is in the wrong."

William came back with the artist's whiskey and brought the bottle he'd poured it from as well. He handed him the whiskey as he said, "I don't like the sound of any of it. That was how the trouble began here before. A child was murdered and there was the Devil's mark on her cheek."

"That's right," Henry Gordon said.

"I'd say whoever was responsible for those murders of twenty years ago is to blame for what happened last night," William said.

Henry Gordon gave him a knowing glance. "You forget

that a witch took the blame for those murders, and she was murdered."

"I don't think Fanny Bray killed anyone nor was she a witch," Ardith said, taking a chair near the artist.

"You interest me in your defence of her," Henry Gordon said, his half-empty whiskey glass in hand. "I had no idea you felt such sympathy for your predecessor at Wyndmoor."

She felt her cheeks burn. "I have no reason to take sides. I'm telling you what I honestly believe."

William said, "At this moment I have a strong desire to get away from Harwick and everything in it." He asked the artist, "Did you know we have had an offer for the property?"

"No," Henry Gordon said. "My brother?"

"A law firm in Edinburgh," William said. "Lawyer Macree seems to be certain it is not your brother. But we don't know yet who the principals interested in Wyndmoor may be."

The artist said, "Regardless of what Macree thinks, I'd be willing to place a wager that it is Douglas who is trying to get this place without your knowing."

"It may be," William said. "The way I feel right now, I'm not liable to stand in his way long."

Henry Gordon pointed out, "Margaret's murder may change everything. He may lose his interest in acquiring more land in the village. He's liable to be bitter and move away from here."

"I wouldn't blame him," Ardith said.

William gave the artist a wary look. "May I ask if you heard any ghost talk in the village? Any reference to the possibility that the ghost of Fanny Bray had come back and committed this crime?"

Henry Gordon hunched uneasily in his chair. "There is always a certain amount of loose talk going the rounds. You know that."

"What did you hear?" William's tone was sharp.

"Nothing important," the artist said, reluctant to discuss it further.

"I might have a different opinion," her husband said. "I'd like to hear anything you heard in the village."

The paunchy man gave her a worried glance. "I don't want to upset your wife."

Ardith spoke up, "Don't hold back anything on my account. I'd rather hear the truth."

"You see," William nudged him.

Henry Gordon rubbed the stubble of gray beard on his chin and seemed to be considering his words. He took a deep breath and then said, "I heard talk of Wyndmoor being haunted. That a witch had returned. You know that people have noticed your wife looks like Fanny. Some say that Fanny has come back in her body."

"Superstitious fools!" William said with contempt.

"Granted," the artist said. "But remember, it was a group of those same superstitious fools who, twenty years ago, brought about Fanny's murder."

William turned to her. "Maybe we should leave here at once."

She could not believe what she heard herself saying, as she told him, "No. I mean to stay here and see this nasty business through."

The artist gave her an anxious look. "You're a plucky young woman, but the doctor may be right. Harwick may be a dangerous place for you."

"I will stay," she said firmly, again feeling as if she were speaking for someone else. It was uncanny. "People will soon realize the child's death was brought about by some vile murderer and not by witchcraft."

"You could be right," Henry Gordon said quietly. "At the moment there is just no telling."

William was staring at her. "I don't understand you, Ardith. When I was anxious to stay here you talked of leaving. Now that I'm willing to go you suddenly decide you want to remain."

Her eyes met his. "It is because I don't think this is a thing we should run away from. If we do we will leave under a shadow of guilt."

"I hadn't thought of that," her husband said in mild surprise. "You do have a point."

She said, "We would likely regret our action for the rest of our lives."

William sighed. "So it seems we're trapped. At least until the real murderer is found."

The stout Henry Gordon raised himself out of his chair. "And let us pray that will be soon."

"If Sir Douglas alerts all the constabulary they should come up with something," William said.

"The murderer must be sly," the artist said. "It won't be easy. I must get back to Jeannie. She is afraid to stay alone in the cottage. She'll be worse now."

She was on her feet. "How good you were to walk this long way to tell us."

He said, "You two are my friends."

William said, "I can't let you walk all the way back in the dark. I'll have a carriage made ready and drive you back myself."

"No need!" the artist protested.

"I would enjoy doing it," William said. "I'm too restless to sleep, and some night air would do me good."

Henry Gordon nodded towards her. "There is your wife to consider. Do you dare leave her here alone?"

"I won't be alone," she said. "Mrs. MacDonald and all the other servants are here. I don't mind William driving you."

"That settles it then," her husband said. "I'll go out to the stables. As soon as the carriage is ready, I'll drive around to the front."

"It's very good of you," the artist said gratefully. "My Jeannie will thank you for getting me home quickly."

William went on out and she was left alone with the artist. All at once she felt uneasy. She found herself unable to carry on a casual conversation. She hesitated, searching for the right thing to say.

It was he who broke the silence. He said, "The longer you remain in this house the more I see Fanny in you."

She blushed. "You only imagine that!"

"It's a fact," he insisted. "When you talked about remaining here just now it might have been Fanny speaking. Is it possible she is trying to return through you?"

She stood facing him with an almost guilty feeling. She knew she had asked herself this question enough and had not been able to come up with any certain answer. But she did not dare let him know how weak her position was. That at this very moment she felt she was struggling with a dual personality.

She said, "Aren't you too intelligent to ask such a question?"

The artist said, "Intelligence can mislead us. As an artist I find it more practical to trust my emotions and my instincts. And my feeling about this is that there is something going on which we don't quite understand. A riddle of the occult which intelligence will never solve."

"You're saying you believe in ghosts," she said, trying to keep her voice calm.

"I'm saying there are forces we don't know about. And Fanny may have finally found a way to return."

"I'd rather not discuss it!" she protested.

"Sorry," he said. "I am your friend. Remember that. If you need someone to talk to at any time . . . I mean, if you have something to tell which you'd find difficult to say to the doctor, you can come to me."

"That is generous of you."

"No," he said. "I want to help." He gave her a strangely knowing look. "And I have an idea you may need help."

The sound of the carriage coming around to the front door was a welcome relief at this tense moment. She said, "That will be my husband."

"Yes," Henry Gordon said, starting for the door. On the way out he paused to turn and say, "Remember my offer." Then he left.

She stood there watching after him, hearing his and William's voices, and then the carriage drove off. She remained there rigid, conscious of the heat of the night. She remembered the artist's words with growing panic. He must suspect her of being possessed! And, for all she knew, she might be!

So much had happened. Her sleepwalking and the strange things she did while in this state! She had played Fanny's favorite ballad on the piano one night, a melody which she could not recall knowing before. She had wandered to the cave, although McLeod chose to deny it. And then there was the weird business of the portrait being returned to its place and the furniture being moved. Some guiding word from Fanny may have made her do these things.

She was mentally confused. At one moment she was completely rational and in the next she discovered herself speaking words which were not her own. It was as if an internal battle were taking place within her, in which she was sometimes the victor and then the loser. A seesaw kind of game!

She had prided herself on not being a creature of impulse, but now she found herself taking on activity which was completely foreign to her. An example being the way she had been directed to visit the cemetery. Another, her feeling that the trunk contained something she should see. This had resulted in her finding the box with the letters.

The further she delved in all this the more she was aware of her becoming involved with the interests of the woman who had been burned as a witch!

She heard a floorboard creak in the hallway behind her. It brought her out of her reverie, and she turned to see a frightened looking Mrs. MacDonald standing there.

Ardith said, "I was just going to call you. There is bad news. You can pass it on to the other members of the household staff." And she briefly gave an account of Margaret being found murdered in the woods.

Mrs. MacDonald was shocked. "I can't believe it!"

"It is hard to accept that anyone would do such a thing," she agreed.

"And that mark on the child's cheek," the housekeeper lamented. "It was just such a witchcraft sign which brought them here against poor Mistress Fanny!"

"I know," she said.

"It is like it's all happening again!"

Ardith said, "Perhaps this will bring out the truth of who the murderer is. I'd say the same person who killed Margaret was responsible for those other witchcraft killings twenty years ago."

Mrs. MacDonald nodded. "I never doubted that Mistress Fanny was innocent."

"I'm certain she was," Ardith said. "I, for one, would like to see her name cleared."

"So would I, ma'am," Mrs. MacDonald said. "Is there anything you want?"

"Not just now."

"Then if you'll excuse me, ma'am, I'll go and break the sad news to the others," the older woman said. And she hurried back down the hall.

Ardith felt the need for some fresh air, so she opened the front door and went out to stand on the stone steps. It was a lovely night, the sky filled with stars. So placid. It seemed out of keeping with the tragic news of the night. As if these happenings among humans were at odds with nature. She found it easy to believe that this could be the case.

Without warning, a hand reached out and touched her on the arm. She drew back with a small cry!

Then the bearded face of James Burnett peered at her from the shadows. He whispered, "It's all right!"

"You terrified me!"

"Sorry," the sculptor said. "I wanted to speak to you, and I didn't want to make a loud cry about being here."

In a near whisper, she asked, "What are you doing here at this hour? What do you want?"

He said, "I heard about the murder of that poor girl."

"Well?"

"I have some things to tell you," he went on in the same low voice. "I didn't think there would be any need before. But now I have an idea you should know."

"Know what?"

"What is going on here."

"Don't speak in riddles," she said desperately. "If you have something to tell me, go on with it!"

He said, "I think this murder may be part of a scheme to scare you away. To make you give up Wyndmoor."

She whispered, "Sir Douglas was the one who most wanted this place. He wouldn't murder his daughter to get it!"

The bearded man said, "He's not the only one with an interest in Wyndmoor. There are others."

"Who?"

"The McLeod brothers."

Tensely, she asked, "You know something!"

"I know a lot!"

"Go on!"

"The McLeods have been making themselves rich with their smuggling silk and brandy from France and all the while playing the part of poor fishermen."

"Grim McLeod is their leader, isn't he?"

"Yes," James Burnett said. "That is why he took the job here as overseer. He didn't dare leave the place. By being here he's able to protect his smuggling operation."

"There is a cave, isn't there?" she asked excitedly.

"How did you know?" he said, surprised.

"I found my way there when I walked in my sleep one night," she said. "I don't know where it is. Grim McLeod appeared and slapped my face. I fainted and when I came to I was in my room. I had William question him the next day, and he contended that it was all a nightmare on my part! But I knew different!"

The bearded man said, "The entrance to the tunnel is directly under the cellar stairs. You can't see the trap door for the shadow of the stairs."

"That's why William and I couldn't find it when we made a search of the cellar," she said excitedly.

"No doubt," he said. "And when you came upon it in your sleepwalking it was because McLeod had likely left the trap door open. You simply descended the second flight of stone stairs, though why you didn't break your neck I'll never guess. That set of steps to the tunnel is steep!"

She said, "I seem to have some strange guidance when I sleepwalk. Something seems to protect me from harm."

"I hope it goes on doing it," he told her. "I think McLeod may have come upon that child during one of his midnight exploits and murdered her. Then he put the Devil's mark on her cheek to rouse up the old superstitions."

"And cast suspicion on me," she said bitterly. "I know many of the villagers already think I'm a reincarnation of Fanny."

"By doing all this he is reasonably sure you'll have to leave Harwick and Wyndmoor. And he'll be free to carry on his smuggling without fear of exposure."

She hesitated, that odd feeling of some soft whisper echoing in her mind once again. "There is one thing which spoils your story. I don't believe McLeod is the sort of man who would murder a child."

The bearded man stared at her. "Why not?"

"I have no reason. It is the way I feel. Even though he may break the law as a smuggler, I think he is essentially an honorable man."

"I wouldn't be too sure," the sculptor said. "And if not McLeod himself, why not one of his gang?"

"Because they would take orders from him. And I don't think he'd give such an order."

"Think it over," the man in the shadows urged her. "I warn you, you could be in the same kind of danger as

Fanny. Rumors about you are spreading in the village."

"There must be some other answer," she said. "Some other suspect."

The silence of the night was broken by the sound of William returning with the carriage. She turned to tell the bearded man this and, to her amazement, he had vanished just as silently as he'd appeared. The carriage drew nearer and she took a few steps out on the grass to see if she could see any sign of the missing sculptor. It was hopeless! He had melted into the shadows. It was apparent he had no desire to talk with anyone but her.

William came driving up and she went out to the carriage. She said, "I've been waiting for you!"

"Anything happen while I was gone?" he asked.

"Hurry and take the carriage to the stable. I'll be in the hall. I have a lot to tell you!"

"I won't be more than a minute or two," he promised, and drove quickly on to the stables.

She went back inside, and it was truly only a moment before he joined her. She said, "I had a visitor while you were gone, James Burnett!"

"That fellow again," William said with annoyance. "What did he want?"

"He'd heard about the murder. He also knows there is a lot of unpleasant talk about me and my being a witch," she said. "And because of his love for Fanny he wanted to try and help me."

"Go on," her husband said in a cynical tone.

"I think he truly does want to befriend us," she said. "He knows about McLeod and the smuggling."

"We've heard all that gossip!"

She said, "It's more than gossip. It's true. There is a tunnel!"

William's eyebrows lifted. "He claims that?"

"Yes."

"We couldn't find one."

"No. We missed it. He told me where the entrance is. Under the cellar stairway."

William frowned. "I guess we didn't look there."

"Of course we didn't. There is a trap door and it leads to a second stairway down to the tunnel. And the tunnel leads to the cliffs where they bring their smuggled goods from the shore."

"Burnett told you all this?"

"Yes. He says Grim McLeod is the leader and he wants us away from here. Burnett thinks McLeod murdered the child as part of the scheme. I don't agree."

"Nor do I," William said. "But he may know who did kill the girl."

"Burnett also said that."

"Frightening us off in this fashion would benefit the McLeods more than anybody else," her husband said grimly. "We have to keep that in mind."

William asked her, "Where is McLeod now?"

"I don't know," she said.

"I'll go out back and ask," he said. "The other servants will know if he's in his room."

"Then what?" she asked.

"I don't know," he said. "Wait here a few minutes."

She did. She heard the clock in the drawing room strike the hour of midnight. It was later than she'd thought. The shattering events of the night had made the hours pass swiftly. And now it seemed very likely that a great deal more might happen.

Her young husband came striding back up the hall with a grim expression on his handsome face. "He's not in his room, and no one has seen him since around eight o'clock. They say it's his habit to go off to the village in the evening."

She said, "He leaves here but I can't agree that he goes to the village. He most likely is busy with his smuggling."

William gave her an odd look. "Come to my office with me," he said.

He picked up a lighted lamp on the way and carried it in his left hand. When they reached his office he put the lamp down on his desk and, going to his bookcase, he pulled two thick volumes from the top shelf and reached in behind them. He drew out a businesslike-looking pistol and showed it to her.

"I always have it here ready and loaded," he said, rising. "And we're very liable to need it tonight."

She gave him a frightened look. "What are you going to do?"

"Take a look at that tunnel!"

"No!" she said. "It's the job of the constabulary!"

"They're too busy looking for Margaret's killer."

She said promptly, "If you're going to risk your life I'm coming along."

"There's no need!" he protested.

"It was my story-telling made you decide on this," she said. "And my place is with you!"

William's face shadowed. "It could be dangerous. And I only want to confirm the story. To take a look at the tunnel."

"Then it needn't be dangerous," she argued. "And you need me to show you where it is."

He hesitated. "I want your promise that you'll keep your distance behind me, and if there's any sign of danger you'll run back up here for help."

"I promise," she said, knowing she had to pretend to accept his terms or give up hope of accompanying him. He could be stubborn.

"All right," he said, with a sigh. "Let's go to the cellar. We'll have to make do with candle light and you can carry it."

She found a suitably large candle and lit it. Then they made their way to the cellar stairs and down into the dark depths. This time they turned and searched under the stairs for the trap door. It was easy to find. William lifted it up by the metal ring attached to it, and the stairway was revealed.

He whispered, "I'll go on down. You wait until I reach the bottom, then follow."

She leaned over the opening, holding the candle to give him the best possible light. When he reached the floor of the tunnel he waved up to her. She followed him and found it a precarious descent with the candle in her hand. She tripped on the last steps and he deftly caught her and saved her from a fall.

"Not a woman's work!" he whispered.

"I can manage," she told him.

"We'll see," he said. And he started on ahead, crouching slightly, as the tunnel was low at this point.

She held the candle carefully and tried to recall her surroundings from the night of her sleepwalking. The sides of the tunnel looked familiar enough with their roughness. The floor was also uneven and every so often it dropped a few inches. She had to watch constantly so that she did not stumble again.

In the distance she could hear the rumbling of the waves on the rocky beach. She assumed that the tunnel must run all the way from the main house and across the lawns to the cliffs, a distance of perhaps a hundred and fifty yards.

There could be no other secret passage to the beach like it. No wonder the McLeods prized the place and had made good use of the tunnel from their point of view.

The sound of the waves grew louder. William halted to tell her, "We must be close to the cliff face now."

"I remember," she said. "It's not far!"

They moved on a little and then he stopped again briefly to say, "I see the opening ahead."

They continued their cautious progress, and within a few minutes they were close to the tunnel opening. And it was there that they came upon a rich cargo of colorful bales of silk piled high against the cave wall. And there were wooden cases filled with bottles, dozens of cases stacked along the tunnel's sides, which were bound to contain the best French brandy!

William stood staring at the rich find. He told her, "They must have just had a shipment arrive!"

"And not been able to move it out of here," she agreed.

"They likely do that a little at a time," William said. "I have an idea there's another opening in the top of the tunnel which leads directly to outside. They probably keep it hidden with a huge boulder or two rolled over it when they're not using it."

"In that way they wouldn't have to bring this through the house," she said.

"They'd never risk it with us living there. In the years when Wyndmoor was empty they no doubt used it for storage as well."

She held the candle so it would not blow out in the draft from the mouth of the tunnel. "What are we going to do?"

"Wait a little."

Uneasiness surged through her. She knew this could be a dangerous business. She said, "You promised me you'd go back after you had a look around."

"I didn't expect such a find!"

"No matter," she said. "This is a job for the constabulary!"

"We'll just wait a few minutes," he said. "I have an idea we might hear or see something to our advantage." And he raised the pistol in readiness as he gazed at the tunnel mouth.

She said, "You wouldn't try to settle with them on your own! It would be a foolhardy thing to attempt!" And she touched his free arm.

"Wait!" he said. "Don't say anything. Stand back in the shadows so the candle light won't be seen. That way they won't see either of us if they should appear on the beach."

She reluctantly took a few steps back and sat forlornly on one of the brandy cases. She placed the candle and holder on the floor by her feet. Then she crossed her arms on her knees and sat there waiting tensely.

The minutes went slowly by. She could hear nothing but the pounding of the waves as the tide washed in. William stood there motionless like a kind of sculptured figure with the pistol in his hand.

She thought of James Burnett and again wondered about him. He had given her all this information, yet he behaved so strangely that she was not sure that they could consider him their friend. Perhaps he had sent them after the smugglers to divert them from suspecting the true criminal.

He could be the killer! The claim that he had been driven mad with jealousy of Fanny could be true. He might have been the leader of the group who burned her to death as a witch. And perhaps her likeness to Fanny had maddened him and he was again planning a series of diabolical murders which would end with her own death! It was an unsettling idea and she felt a cold chill race down her spine as she considered it.

Suddenly she was alerted by what she thought were distant male voices shouting to each other on the beach. She quickly reached for the candle and stood up. At the same instant William turned to give her a sign to be quiet and stay where she was.

Now she was filled with overwhelming panic. She began to tremble and her teeth were chattering, tears brimming in her eyes. She felt helpless and trapped, and she had the strong premonition that something frightening was going to happen.

William took a step back, and then she heard a scraping sound from the mouth of the tunnel. And as her eyes riveted on the tunnel ledge, she saw hands appear and grasp the ledge just as she had the other night. And in another second the head and shoulders of Grim McLeod appeared. He saw William and quickly dodged down just as William fired at him!

The flash of the pistol's shot brightened the tunnel for a moment. Then there was a return shot from outside, and she watched in frozen horror as she saw William raise a hand to his temple and stagger back! The pistol dropped from his other hand as he fell to the floor of the tunnel.

She came to life in the moment that he fell. She plunged forward and grasped the pistol he'd dropped. Without hesitating she took a stand above his body to defend him. She heard shouts from outside again, and this time they seemed to be moving further away. She stood there waiting for the attack. But it didn't come! The smugglers had fled!

Not able to believe this good fortune, she moved warily to the tunnel mouth. And she saw a half-dozen men racing along the beach to a spot where another waited with a large boat. She leaned weakly against the wall of the tunnel and realized that the smugglers must have thought there were more than just William in the tunnel. They apparently felt the constabulary had gathered there, and they were not waiting to make a stand against the authorities.

This immediate risk over, she turned and gazed at her fallen husband. She felt her head reel as she saw that his face was bloodied. And now she put down the pistol and went over to him. She took a hankie from her pocket and began to try and clear the blood.

"William!" she cried plaintively.

He showed no sign of regaining consciousness. She fetched the candle nearer and tried to see the extent of the wound. It seemed to her that the bullet had grazed his temple and cut through some of his hair at the back of his head, but it had not buried itself in the skull. So the wound seemed not fatal though serious enough to render him unconscious.

She felt she dared not leave him. And now a new concern began to nag at her. Suppose the ugly crew on the beach decided there were only the two of them in the cave. They could well come to this conclusion since they hadn't been pursued by anyone as surely would have been the case had the constables been there. If the smugglers grew confident they had only a wounded man and a lone woman to deal with they might well return.

What to do?

She took off the white scarf she was wearing around her neck and tore it in two. One section she kept for future use and the other she tied around the wound on her husband's head. His face was very calm and his breathing was gentle enough, but she still could not rouse him so they might make their way back to the house.

Then she thought she heard voices again. She got up and went back to the mouth of the tunnel and her worst fears were confirmed. Several of the men were still by the boat, but the others were slowly making their way back along the rocky shore. They were gaining courage and without question would keep on approaching and try entering the tunnel once again.

She rushed back to her husband and shook him. "Hear me!" she pleaded.

But he did not stir. Then her eyes wandered to the wooden cases of brandy. And a new thought came to her. She left William's side to go over to the nearest case and lift out one of the dust-colored bottles. The bottle seemed all too well sealed and so she made a quick decision. She went to the wall of the tunnel, and holding the bottle by the bottom, deliberately struck its neck against the sharp rocks.

The neck broke off midway and the amber liquid began spilling out. She quickly turned the bottle upright and went back to where her husband lay motionless. Now she took the other piece of her scarf and saturated it with the brandy, and then she began applying the brandy-soaked scarf to his lips.

She was careful just to touch his lips with the wet cloth. She could not chance the liquid going in his mouth and perhaps choking him. And as she frantically continued these efforts to revive him she clearly heard Grim McLeod shouting exhortations to his companions to join him in an assault on the tunnel once again!

Chapter Ten

She had given up hope when suddenly William opened his eyes and stared up at her blankly. And then almost immediately recognition came, and her husband struggled weakly to a sitting position.

She said, "They're coming! We must get out of here! Can you walk?"

"I don't know," he said in a thick voice. "My head is dizzy and paining!"

"McLeod shot you, but I don't think it's a bad wound!"

The voices outside came clearly now between the regular roar of the waves. She frantically tugged at his arm and helped him get to his feet. He stood there swaying slightly.

"We must try to get back to the house!" Ardith implored him. At the same time she bent down and swooped up the pistol.

"I'll try," William said in a dazed fashion. Leaning heavily on her, he began taking awkward steps. Their progress was slow, but fortunately the turn in the tunnel was not far away, and by the time they heard the smugglers clambering up into the tunnel again they were beyond being seen.

"Move as quickly as you can," she told him, at the same time taking the main weight of him.

He made no reply, but he kept on moving which was as much as she could expect under the circumstances. She was gambling that as long as they were out of sight the smugglers would concentrate on removing their loot from the tunnel and saving it rather than coming after them! McLeod was too sage to waste time in a pointless revenge on them and risk the constabulary arriving before he could remove the cargo of silks and brandy.

Her guess proved correct. The smugglers did not follow them, and slowly they made their way back to the steps which led to the cellars of Wyndmoor. She thought William would not be able to manage the stairway, it was so steep and uneven. But though their progress became slower, he did make his way up it. And with her almost dragging him, he finished the second flight. When he reached the safety of the hallway, he collapsed again.

She called Mrs. MacDonald who summoned two of the male servants to carry the unconscious William up to his bedroom. When he was safely in bed, she and Mrs. MacDonald carefully washed the wound and bound it with a clean cloth.

The housekeeper asked, "Should we send for Dr. Carr?"

The temptation was great. But Ardith did not want to find herself relying on the drunken old doctor who had so libelled her husband with his gossip. She said, "No. We will wait. I'm sure he will be all right. It's no more than a flesh wound."

"And you say McLeod shot him?" Mrs. MacDonald asked.

"Yes. I think he fired without knowing who he was shooting at. William surprised him by firing at him first, but he missed. McLeod's return shot came almost instantly!"

Mrs. MacDonald shook her head with grim indignation. "So it is true, after all! McLeod and his brothers are smugglers. He denied it to me."

"There's no question," she said. "The tunnel from here was filled with goods. I have an idea they won't take long removing it all."

"And McLeod will not dare show his face here!"

"I think not," she said. "Unless he has a great deal more gall than I give him credit for." She looked down at her still unconscious husband. "He doesn't know whether his shot killed my husband or not."

"We all wondered why he would come here as overseer," the housekeeper said. "Especially as he had never been in service before."

"Now you know," she said grimly.

"We do, indeed!"

Ardith moved away from her husband's bedside with a troubled expression on her lovely face. "My husband will have to be watched the entire night. I will be here, but I may need you to spell me if I get very sleepy."

"Of course."

She frowned. "If there is any change, I will have to swallow my pride and call for the dubious help of Dr. Carr. I pray it won't be necessary."

"One of the lads can always take a message," Mrs. MacDonald said.

This reminded her of something else and she said, "I will write a note now and you will have it delivered to the Chief Constable. I want him to come here. I mean to lay charges against McLeod, for using our property for smuggling and for shooting William."

"Yes, ma'am," the other woman said. "I expect the constabulary are still out searching for the killer of that poor child."

Ardith gave her a significant glance. "It may be that McLeod knows something about that. Fetch me notepaper and a pen, and I will write the letter while I'm keeping watch up here."

"Yes, ma'am," Mrs. MacDonald said, and she went off to secure the writing materials.

Ardith returned to her chair by her husband's bedside. She leaned close to hear his breathing. It seemed easy enough, and so she hoped there were no complications. His eyes were closed and his face pale, but that was to be expected. He had lost some blood and suffered shock from the wound, and the effort of escaping from the smugglers had used up his last ounce of energy.

She would outline all that had happened in her note to the Chief Constable. And she would ask that he come immediately, since she had an idea Grim McLeod might know about more than the smuggling. She hoped the Chief Constable would respond to her plea and she would get some action.

Mrs. MacDonald returned with pen, ink and notepaper. She wrote the note, sealed and addressed it and passed it to the housekeeper to see that it was delivered. Then she resumed her vigil at William's bedside.

She was beginning to feel extremely weary, and she wondered how much these unhappy experiences would set her health back. This reminded her of her midnight medicine. It was bound to be in her room, and she had not taken it. She left her husband to go into her own room and saw that Meg had, as usual, left out the glass of water with the potent drops in it. She took the medicine, draining the glass, and returned to the other bedroom.

She did not know when she fell asleep. But the dream she had was vivid enough. It was a repeat of the nightmare which had first bothered her before she left London. But what turned out to be the most dreadful part of it all was when she came to.

She was no longer by William's bedside!

She opened her eyes to find herself standing in a clearing in the woods. It took her a moment to orient herself to her surroundings. She felt strangely dizzy, and everything was distorted in an odd way. As if she were looking at things with glasses which were not properly in focus. Her mouth was dry and yet she was drenched in perspiration!

Worst of all, she knew she had wandered in her sleep and left William unattended! She would never be able to forgive herself if anything went wrong in her absence. She looked around her and blinked impatiently as she tried to make her eyes picture things properly!

There were stars and a moon. And the moonlight was streaking down between the tall evergreens so that she now began to make out different objects. To her horror she saw that she had sleepwalked to the cemetery where Fanny was buried. And before her, brilliant in a shaft of moonlight, the murdered woman's headstone stood out.

Could there be any doubt that Fanny was using her? That she had come here under the guidance of that avenging spirit? Even if she hadn't thought so before, she was certain of it now. But why? What was the long-dead Fanny trying to use her for? To prove her innocence was the most likely answer. But how?

She gazed at the tombstone in the spotlight of the moonbeam. And she gasped! For there was a huddled, dark thing stretched across the grave mound which she was sure had to be a body!

Barely had she made this discovery than she was shocked by a second one. From out of the woods on the other side of the cemetery there came a figure. It was the ghost of Fanny! The glowing face stood out against the darkness!

It was too much! On the verge of hysteria, Ardith gave a wild cry and plunged towards the path which led to the stables and eventually the house. She paid no attention to the bushes which had edged onto the path, allowing them to brush across her face and sting her with their sharp branches. She was racing in full panic from the cemetery and the horror which it held!

She ran past the stables and into the house. There was no one in sight downstairs! It was very late and the servants would have all gone to bed, except for Mrs. MacDonald and the lad sent to the village as a messenger. She reached the stairway in breathless dismay and, clutching the railing, made her way up.

Mrs. MacDonald was seated by William's bedside when the shattered Ardith appeared in the room. The housekeeper got up and came over to her, to ask in a taut whisper, "I wondered where you'd gone! I came up and no one was here!"

Ardith nodded as she caught her breath. "I had one of my sleepwalking spells!"

"Dear me," the housekeeper sympathized.

She sank into a chair. "It was horrible!"

"Can I get you anything?" the housekeeper worried.

"No. My head is gradually clearing. Did you send the lad to the Chief Constable?"

"Yes. He's been gone a while."

Ardith gave her a significant look. "It seems to me we may need him more than ever."

"Why do you say that, ma'am?" the older woman asked, staring at her with concern.

"In my sleepwalking I wandered out to the cemetery."

"The cemetery!"

"Yes," she said, her voice taut. "And I saw Fanny's

ghost! She came out of the woods, her face glowing with that eerie blue light!"

"Lord save us all!" the older woman said in pious horror.

"You may well say that," Ardith told her soberly. "For at the same time I saw a crumpled body on her grave. Unless I was hallucinating, there's very likely been another murder!"

"Another?" Mrs. MacDonald gasped.

"That is why it is most important the Chief Constable be asked to come here," she said.

Mrs. MacDonald's matronly face was agitated. "Should I rouse one of the coachmen and send them out to look?"

"No. I think we should wait," Ardith said, making the decision without quite knowing why she made it.

"I shan't sleep a wink this night!" the housekeeper said, twisting her apron in her hands.

"I doubt that we will have the opportunity," she said, and she moved to her husband's bedside to resume her night watch.

The lad who had been sent with the message for the Chief Constable returned about an hour later. He informed them that he hadn't been able to speak with the Chief Constable but had left the note with his wife. And she had promised to give it to him as soon as he returned home. So it was unlikely their suspense concerning the body in the woods had any chance of being ended until the police official arrived sometime in the morning.

Around four o'clock William stirred in bed and opened his eyes. He gazed up at her and in a low voice said, "My throat is parched!"

She was jubilant that he had come out of his second collapse. But she made no show of her relief. Instead she busied herself getting him a glass of water and helping him as he greedily drank it.

He lay back with a sigh. "Good!" he said. Then he shut his eyes and drifted off into a natural sleep.

Mrs. MacDonald had fallen asleep in the chair by the door, but wakened on hearing William speak. Now she stood in the middle of the room, and whispered to Ardith, "He is going to be all right."

"I felt he would be."

"No need for Dr. Carr now," the older woman said.

"Just a matter of watching him carefully," Ardith said. "By morning he should be able to take some food and drink."

Her prediction proved right. Shortly after dawn he woke again, and this time he sat up on his own. He stared at her in the chair and recalled, "We managed to get out of the tunnel."

"Yes, dear," she said. "How does your head feel?"

"Sore!" He reached up and touched the bandage.

"McLeod was a better shot than you!"

"Don't remind me," he winced at the memory. "You were right. I was foolish to try and take them all on."

"I tried to make you see that."

"How did I get up here in bed?"

"The servants," she said. "You were unconscious for a long while."

"I'm hungry," he said.

She smiled and rose. "I thought you might be. I'll let Mrs. MacDonald know and she'll have a tray sent up."

"No," he protested. "I'm well enough to go downstairs."

"Not yet," Ardith said. "Let us see how you feel after you've eaten."

"I'll feel better," he predicted.

And he did. In fact, he insisted on dressing as soon as he'd finished breakfast. Ardith helped him and noticed that he was still not too steady on his legs. Meg came to make their beds and seemed amazed by the strange events of the night.

"You won't be wanting your morning bath, ma'am?" the petite blonde girl worried.

"No," Ardith said as she stood with her arm linked in William's in preparation to helping him go downstairs. "I'll rest and bathe later."

William smiled grimly for Ardith's benefit as they left the maid making the beds. "I don't think Meg approves of anything which upsets her routine."

"I'm sure she doesn't," Ardith agreed as she and William descended the stairs. "She seemed appalled at the sight of your bandaged head."

"All in a stalwart undertaking, however misguided on my part," he said. "What are we going to do about the McLeods?"

"I've already done it," she said. "Sent a note to the Chief Constable asking him to come here. I want him to see the tunnel and hear our story."

"I wouldn't have believed it if I hadn't been there," he said. "And there were hundreds of pounds worth of contraband piled up against the tunnel wall."

"All moved by now," she guessed.

She waited to tell him about her later sleepwalking adventure after they were seated in the drawing room waiting for the Chief Constable to arrive.

William eyed her bleakly from the easy chair in which he sat. "That sleepwalking is a damnable business. Hard to explain to laymen."

"I know," she said with cynicism. "The popular view is that I'm Fanny reincarnated or at the very least a puppet guided by her avenging spirit!"

"Why else would you have gone to that cemetery?" he asked wearily.

"It's hard to say. I'd been there before. And I was very upset." She glanced at the portrait of the handsome dark woman so like herself. "Perhaps she is behind what I'm doing."

"Don't even talk about that!" he moaned. "It's bad enough for the ignorant villagers to have it on their tongues!"

She said, "I'm mostly concerned about the body I saw stretched out on Fanny's grave."

"If there is actually such a body. You may have been mistaken. It might have been a shadow! Or perhaps just your imagination! You had to be very upset at that moment!"

"Seeing the ghost assured that!"

"Someone is playing ghost here to scare us away," he said angrily. "And why should McLeod continue to play such games when he knows we're on to him."

"It could be all the more reason for him to have someone act as the ghost to frighten us away. His last hope! And he may be guilty of the murder as well!"

William drew his watch from his vest pocket and looked at it. "Seven-thirty! If the Chief Constable isn't here by eight I shall call some of the stable lads and go out and explore the cemetery on my own!"

"You're not well enough," she said.

"I'm much stronger than you think. It was only a small wound on my temple."

"Bad enough to make you collapse twice."

"I'm over it now," he said. "You tell me these stories of ghosts and dead bodies and expect me to be patient!"

"We will wait," she said placatingly. "It will be better if

the Chief Constable investigates the cemetery."

William asked her, "How are you going to explain that you know about a possible body being there?"

"I'll have to tell the truth," she replied. "That I sleepwalked and found myself out there."

Her handsome young husband warned her, "Don't think he's all that much smarter than the other villagers. When he hears that story from you he's liable to also wind up thinking you're a witch!"

"I'll have to chance that," she said.

Their ordeal of waiting ended at about ten minutes after eight when a carriage came rapidly in the driveway. A constable jumped down from beside the driver and opened the door of the carriage for the Chief Constable. There was a moment before this champion of the law appeared. Then he thrust his head out like a cautious tortoise and after that his unwieldy body emerged. The constable assisted his nearly three-hundred-pound superior to the gravel walk.

Chief Constable Jonas Neal had a scowl on his broad face. He was resplendent in a crimson frock coat, a yellow vest, tight gray trousers and knee-high gaiters. He had an enormous stomach and when he walked it somehow wobbled in front of him. Now he strode importantly to the front door as Ardith came and opened it to him and the constable, a meek looking man in drab gray who stood respectfully behind him.

The Chief Constable's eyes were bloodshot, and his face with its several chins sagged with weariness. "You sent for me, madam?" he barked in a harsh, nasal voice.

"Yes. I'm sorry to trouble you, since I know how busy you must be!"

"I have been out all the night in an attempt to track down the murderer of Sir Douglas Gordon's child," he said.

"I trust what you have to convey is of importance."

"I think it is," she said quietly. "My husband awaits you in the drawing room. He would have personally come to greet you at the door, but he was shot and wounded by smugglers here last night!"

The fat Chief Constable's eyebrows lifted and his chins rippled as he exclaimed, "Smugglers? Did you say smugglers, madam?"

"Yes."

The fat man's face had gone purple. "So the scoundrels have been at work again. Take me to your husband!"

She led the big man inside and his constable followed with quiet respect and stood a distance from him. The Chief Constable marched in to where William was standing and demanded loudly, "Tell me all that happened here last night! And tell it quickly!"

"I shall do my best," William said. And he proceeded to tell him about their discovery of the cave and of the melée with the smugglers.

Chief Constable Jonas Neal slapped a fat hand in the palm of his other one. "I've suspected those McLeods all along! Damn! Why did it have to happen at this time, when I am so occupied with this murder?"

"It is possible the smugglers may have some bearing on the murder," William pointed out. "We believe they are attempting to scare us away and make us uncomfortable by throwing suspicion of wrongdoing on our part."

The fat face puckered in puzzlement. "I fear I do not follow you, sir?"

"There is more," she said. And she took it on herself to tell him of her sleepwalking, of seeing Fanny's ghost and of her apprehensions that there might be another murder victim in the cemetery!

The Chief Constable looked shocked. "I have never heard such an incredible story!"

"I'm telling it exactly as it happened," she said.

"Are you given to this sleepwalking?" the Chief Constable asked suspiciously.

William spoke up, "My wife came here in ill health. She has not much improved. She has already had consumption and is fighting off the disease again. It is not uncommon for such patients to display unusual symptoms such as sleepwalking!"

The Chief Constable looked surly. "I know you are a licensed medical man, Dr. Davis. But will you tell me if such patients are also given to seeing ghosts?"

"They have been known to hallucinate," William said quietly.

"It will be better for you and your wife if all she experienced in the cemetery turns out to be an hallucination," the Chief Constable said sternly. "I will ask that you supply my constable and me with a guide to this cemetery and that you wait here for my return."

"We have been waiting for you all morning," Ardith quietly reminded him.

William glanced at her, "Have Mrs. MacDonald fetch a stable boy and show these two gentlemen to the cemetery."

"I will," she said.

Within a few minutes the Chief Constable and his assistant were being led to the cemetery, and Ardith and William found themselves alone in the drawing room once more. William watched out a side window where the men had vanished. She came up to him and smiled grimly.

She said, "Your predictions about the Chief Constable were all too correct."

"I know the type," William said unhappily. "I told you

he would react badly. Be suspicious of you."

"It doesn't bother me anymore," she sighed. "One extra isn't important with the entire village seemingly thinking I'm a witch!"

"It does when the extra one happens to be the Chief Constable," her young husband said. "We need him on our side if we're to come out of this unscathed."

She indicated the bandage on his head. "You've spoiled any chance of that."

"I swear he's more annoyed about learning the McLeods are smugglers than if we hadn't told him anything. He doesn't want the diversion of going after them while he's occupied with the murder!"

"You can hardly blame him. But he is stupid not to realize that McLeod or some one of his gang could also be the murderer he is looking for."

"I doubt if he'll ever see any link between the crimes," William said. "You have him badly mixed up already. I hesitate to think what conclusion he'll come to if he does find a body out there."

"We'll soon know," she said, tugging at his arm as she gazed out the window. "They're coming back now!"

Following her glance, William said, "It doesn't look too good! He's walking slow! As if he's had some sort of shock."

"I'll open the door for him," she said, and she hurried to the front door again.

The Chief Constable approached the door with a grim expression on his fat face. He halted on the step and said, "You were right, madam. There is a body on the grave!"

She was not surprised. She had been certain of it. But she was curious as to whom it might be. "Who?" she asked.

His small, red-streaked eyes fixed on her balefully. "The murdered man is Mad Charlie! Stabbed in the chest!"

"Mad Charlie?" she gasped.

"Yes, madam. And most interesting of all, he has a Devil's hoof scratched on his cheek. Just the same as that poor girl!"

William had also come to the door in time to hear these last answers. He placed his arm around Ardith and said, "We are both deeply shocked!"

"Are you, sir?" The Chief Constable said, a hint of derision in his tone.

"Do you now wish to see the tunnel and find out what the smugglers may have left?" Ardith wanted to know.

The fat man's face went purplish. He cried, "I have no time for smugglers, damn! I have a second murder to solve! And I mean that it shall be solved."

William asked, "What can we do to help?"

The Chief Constable told him, "I shall be asking you and your wife a number of questions. Also, my constable will summon extra help to move the body of Mad Charlie and take it to the jail building. There will be a complete investigation into this affair!"

The big man strongly hinted that they were both under suspicion. And his manner during the period of their being questioned also underlined this. Ardith felt he was treating them as if they were confessed murderers. It was evident that the village of Harwick was not fond of outsiders. And they were outsiders under a shadow.

When the Chief Constable finished with his questioning, he said, "You will kindly inform me if you indulge in any more sleepwalking, madam."

"Very well," she said.

William protested. "I don't see that my wife's sleepwalking is any of your business."

"Doctor, you are not investigating this murder," the fat

man said. And he turned to her again and asked, "Madam, when you have these sleepwalking periods, do you have any recollection of your activity from the moment you fall asleep until you wake up somewhere?"

She stared at him uneasily. "No," she said. "I have no recollection of what I do. None at all. I'm in a kind of dream state until I wake."

"So you might do anything in this trance-like state and not remember it later?" the Chief Constable suggested.

"True," she said nervously.

William said with annoyance, "I think this a harassment of my wife."

"I think not," the fat man said.

"We have volunteered all this information," her husband went on angrily. "Given it to you by our own choice. And part of it you won't even act on. You are content to let the smugglers who shot me go scot-free!"

"I'm putting their case aside until I have finished what I have in hand," Chief Constable Neal said.

"What do you expect to prove by harping on this business of her sleepwalking?" William wanted to know.

The fat man gave him a sneering look. "Don't tell me you haven't followed my logic, Dr. Davis. Your wife is given to sleepwalking, she can't remember her actions while she is in this state and she wakens last night to discover a stabbed Mad Charlie. We know that Mad Charlie has annoyed her with his calling her a witch. Who can tell whether or not she murdered him in her sleep?"

"I didn't!" she cried out in dismay.

"How can you be sure?" the fat man asked glibly. "You don't remember anything about that time?"

William frowned. "We are wasting time discussing this with you. It is clear you can't tell a criminal when you see one. If you could, you'd know my wife is not the sort of person to kill anyone."

"That remains to be proven, Dr. Davis," the Chief Constable said smoothly. "I will not place a charge against her yet. But I will advise both of you to remain within the limits of the village."

Having delivered himself of this, the fat man waddled back to his carriage with dignity and the constable helped him inside. Then he listened to some message from his superior through the open window of the carriage and nodded. After that he jumped up onto the seat beside the driver and passed along his instructions. The driver jogged the reins and the big carriage with its span of gray horses rolled away in the direction of the main road.

Ardith and William were left in consternation. They had expected to be commended and instead they found themselves regarded as chief suspects for a crime of which they knew nothing.

She closed the door and exchanged glances with her husband in the hallway. She thought he looked more doleful than ever, and this effect was heightened by his bandaged head.

She said, "He was even worse than you expected."

"He's a stupid idiot!" William complained. "And to make it worse, Sir Douglas Gordon is the judge here. If we are charged with anything I cannot see us getting a fair trial!"

"I don't think it has come to that yet," she said.

"We may not be far from it," he warned her.

She looked up at him with troubled eyes. "You don't look as well as when you first came down this morning. I say you should return to bed. You need a lot more rest than you have had."

He moved away from her impatiently and touched his hand to the bandage. "I'm all right. I cannot go back to bed with things going against us in this way!"

She said, "What can we do?"

"Try and find out who murdered Mad Charlie and the girl."

"How can we?"

William came back to her suddenly, a new light of excitement in his eyes. He said, "I think we've been blind to the obvious right along!"

"Why do you say that?"

"We've closed our eyes to the person who must be the chief suspect!"

"Go on!" she urged him.

"Who frequents that cemetery more than any other living person?"

Ardith hesitated. Then she said, "James Burnett! He goes to pay homage to Fanny!"

"So he says," William exclaimed. "It seems to me more likely he goes there to expiate the guilt he feels for leading that gang of witch hunters who burned her to death twenty years ago."

"He swore he is innocent!"

"Of course he did. But that doesn't mean he is. And he was here last night."

"Yes."

"And when I came he slunk away as if he had guilt on his conscience. He has never wanted to face me!"

She protested, "There could be other reasons than guilt for that. He is a recluse! A sensitive man!"

"He is strange in his behavior," William said, carried away with his certainty of the sculptor's guilt.

"No more than many artists. And he has had a tragic experience. Losing Fanny broke his heart."

"I wonder," her husband said. "I say he is our murderer, just as he was the murderer years ago. And his purpose now is to have you branded as a witch, just as Fanny was."

"Why should he do that to me?"

"He's mad. He doesn't need a reason. Possibly because you are living in this house! And because you look like her!"

"You're jumping into this too fast!" she protested.

"I want to talk to him," William said firmly.

She sighed. "All right. I'll send him a message."

"He won't come here at your bidding."

"Why not?"

"Because of what he's done," William said. "He's likely the one behind the ghost business. Perhaps he's created a glowing mask of Fanny and dons it himself to play the ghost. In the darkness, with a cloak, the ghost could be a man!"

She listened, knowing that all he said was right. And despite the fact that she had liked James Burnett and had been willing to believe his claims of innocence, she found her faith in him wavering. Wavering as perhaps Fanny's faith in him had wavered in him long ago, and so she had run off and married John Bray. William had made a strong case against the aloof, bearded sculptor.

Resignedly, she asked her husband, "What do you propose to do?"

"I'm going to see him! Now!"

"No! You can't! You're not well enough!" she argued.

"I have to go find him," William said.

"If he should be guilty you're not fit to protect yourself," she warned him.

"There's the pistol! You said you brought it back last

night. I'll take it with me."

She shook her head. "You didn't have so much luck with it last night."

"It will be different today," he insisted.

"You cannot go alone!"

"Then you can come with me and drive the carriage," he said.

In the end she knew it was the best compromise she could hope for. And so she gave in to his plan. He went to his office and hastily reloaded the pistol while the carriage was being made ready. Ardith explained their errand to a nonplussed Mrs. MacDonald, and then she and William began the grim journey to the cottage of James Burnett.

The cottage was set deep among a host of tall evergreens. It was the house of a man who wanted no company. Only a little ground was cleared around it, and the road in to it was little better than a widened path. There was no sign of life about the place as she and William got down and advanced to its door.

No one answered their knocking. After a wait, William gave her a meaningful glance and tried the door. It opened easily and he led the way in. Ardith followed and saw they were in what appeared to be the studio of the sculptor. On a table in the center of the room was a figure in clay only partly finished. It was a study of a man's head and shoulders, but the face was not complete, giving the sculpture a strange air of death and decay!

There were many other finished items on various shelves and some larger pieces of sculpture standing on the wide-board floor of the room. She saw William halt before a shelf and then he motioned her over. She knew by his expression he had come upon a find.

"What did I tell you?" he asked, and he pointed to the shelf.

She stared at it in a stunned state. Side by side on this shelf were a half-dozen death masks of the murdered Fanny Bray!

Chapter Eleven

William picked up one of the sculptured death masks. He held it before her so she could study it more closely. "Just as I suspected. He's obsessed with his memories of Fanny."

She stared at the placid face carved from the cold, gray marble. "That doesn't mean he murdered her. He was in love with her."

"I say it's a dead Fanny which fascinates him," her husband said, placing the mask down by the others on the shelf again. "And that makes me suspicious of him in the extreme. And you will agree he could easily devise some sort of face mask by making an impression of these with plaster or with some other such material."

"I can't deny that," she admitted in a small voice. But she still did not see James Burnett as a killer, although she knew she could be wrong.

Glancing around him, William wondered, "Where do you suppose he is?"

"He often goes away."

"With so much happening in the village," her husband said critically, "I'd expect him to have enough interest to remain here. After all, it was he who tipped you off about the McLeods and the tunnel."

"I can't answer for him."

William gave her a penetrating look. "But you won't agree with me that he had been acting strangely?"

"No," she said. "He has always kept to himself. Why should he change now?"

William shrugged. "Think what you like," he said. "I'm going to take a look around at the rest of the cottage and outside."

While he made a general search for the missing sculptor, Ardith remained in the studio admiring the bearded man's work. Even the few pieces which remained there showed him to be a man of outstanding ability. She paused by a figure of a deer and was enchanted by the charm and graceful lines of the sculpture.

It seemed to her that one who had such a sensitive appreciation of beauty could not possibly be the murderer of the fragile, blonde child. And yet there were always such contradictions, so that one couldn't be positive. The James Burnett she had known this far had been a kind, understanding person. His reluctance to meet her husband might only be the natural reticence of a shy man who disliked too many contacts with strangers.

The door from outside opened and William came back into the studio to join her. He said, "No sign of him anywhere. It is my opinion he's fled."

"I don't think so. He may only be out strolling or in the village. The cottage wasn't locked."

"Has he any need to lock it in this isolated spot? No one here would be interested in his sculptures, and I doubt if there is anything else of value here."

"Perhaps we'll meet him on the drive back," she said.

"I doubt it," he said. "But at least we know where the glowing ghost face you've been seeing may have originated."

"Yes," she was forced to agree. Although she was now asking herself if the ghostly apparition she'd seen more than once were not the real thing? What if the murdered Fanny had not only managed to take possession of her at times, but also occasionally materialized to test her.

Her young doctor husband said, "We may as well leave here. He won't be back."

She did not agree, but at the same time she didn't offer any argument. As a result they returned to the carriage and began the drive back to Wyndmoor. When they neared the village they saw Lawyer Macree and the tavern owner standing outside the gray building talking. There was also another group of men and women gathered not far from the two. The second group seemed to be circled around someone who was addressing them.

William said, "I think I'll stop for a moment and see if Lawyer Macree has any word from Edinburgh."

"Isn't it almost too soon?" she asked.

"It might be," he admitted. "But we can stop long enough to ask him, in any case."

As they came up by the lawyer and the tavern keeper, he brought the wagon to a halt. He passed the reins to her while he stepped down onto the ground to chat with the two men. Ardith saw that the tall, flat-faced lawyer looked more nervous than normally. And it also struck her that the expression on the face of the tavern keeper was not all that genial. They surely had heard about the murder of Mad Charlie on the grounds of Wyndmoor and this was responsible for the new attitude they were showing.

She held the reins tight to keep the horse under control. Another carriage rolled by on its way out of the village, and its wheels raised huge billows of dust which floated in the air in its wake. Ardith pressed a hankie to her mouth and nose to strain the dust since she still coughed easily, and once she began it was difficult for her to stop.

William approached the two men he knew, ignoring the other group of villagers who were a few yards distant. She could easily overhear anything William might have to say.

He approached Lawyer Macree first and said, “Have we had a second offer from Edinburgh?”

“No,” the thin lawyer said. “But I look for it to be in the mail before the week is out.”

“I trust it will arrive soon,” William said, very business-like. “I have to make up my mind about Wyndmoor very shortly.”

“I understand,” the flat-faced man said, and he raised his hat to her in the carriage.

The innkeeper next spoke, asking William, “Is it true the ghost has shown itself at Wyndmoor? Several of the servants have been in here and claimed they’ve seen the phantom figure of Fanny Bray.”

“I have nothing to say to you on the matter,” William said, his handsome face pale and strained.

The innkeeper grew bolder. “I would not think you’d get many patients out there with these ghost stories making the rounds. I hear it was old Mad Charlie whom the constabulary found dead on Fanny’s grave last night.”

“I’m not prepared to enter into such a discussion,” was William’s firm reply, and he turned and started back to jump into the driver’s seat of the carriage.

But before he could do this, a shrill cry went up from someone in the group standing close by. The shriek was so frightening it gave the horse a start, and Ardith had a bad time keeping him reined and at a snorting, uneasy stand-still.

The shriek was not the end of it. The circle of people opened and from their midst there came a bent old crone in near rags, leaning on a hickory cane. A thick, gray shawl covered her head and was tied or pinned at her throat. Her face was a weathered brown and puckered with wrinkles, and she held one hand out before her as she took a few steps like a person who could not see.

"I smell a witch!" the old crone whined as she reached out with her thin, claw-like hand. "There is a witch here! Coline Dougall can not be tricked by the Devil!"

William stood between the old woman and the carriage and he demanded angrily, "What kind of nonsense is this?"

"No nonsense, good sir," the ancient blind woman shrilled out. "I named that vixen as a witch before, and I name this one as her servant now!" As she said this she pointed up at Ardith, still seated in the carriage, and there was an angry murmuring from the group of people who now had formed again behind the crone.

William exclaimed, "I do not know what your ravings are intended to mean, old woman! And I ask you not to point your finger at me or my wife!"

Having said this, he wheeled around and jumped up into the carriage and drove on. The old woman took a faltering step nearer the carriage as it rolled away and shrieked some new indictment after them. Ardith glanced over her shoulder with a frightened look on her face and had a glimpse of the old woman waving her cane high in the air as if to chase them off, the crowd near her looking surly and Lawyer Macree standing open-mouthed and with an unhappy expression on his flat face. The innkeeper seemed to be excitedly shouting something to him!

Then the dust rolled up in a high curtain behind them, blotting out the eerie scene. She turned to her angry husband who was giving his full attention to driving and, in a shocked voice, said, "That must be the same old woman who years ago called Fanny a witch! Now they've brought her in to the village to cry out imprecations against me!"

"We must not pay any attention to any of it!" William said grimly.

"But where will it end? They seem to think the murder of Mad Charlie last night proves I'm somehow linked with Fanny and the witchcraft!"

"If the constabulary are not asleep they should soon find that the man they want is James Burnett! I think he is mad and the evil figure behind all this!"

"I wish I could be as certain," she worried. "I think the constabulary will act slowly and that grave injustice could be done before the truth comes out. And everyone appears to have forgotten about the McLeods and their villainy."

William said, "That's because many of the villagers are sympathetic to them. They've known about the smuggling all along and looked the other way."

"So they don't appreciate outsiders coming here and exposing the game," she said.

"That's about it," he said as they drove on. "So we can't look for much action there either."

They reached the entrance to Wyndmoor and Mrs. MacDonald came out to greet them. She said, "You have a visitor. Mr. Henry Gordon is here."

Still seated in the carriage, Ardith sighed and confessed to her husband, "I do not feel up to entertaining."

William said, "We must try to receive him graciously. Who knows? He may have some good news for us."

"If only that might be true," she said with another sigh. She felt like going to her room and resting.

Her husband helped her down from the carriage and they went inside. She removed her bonnet in the hall and they went on to the living room where they found Henry Gordon seated, reading a newspaper.

He rose at their entrance and said, "I have just received my copy of the Edinburgh *Gazette*. The news from the Crimea is not good. Lord Lucan is the only one with the expeditionary force who has had any real military experience and that was all of twenty years ago in the Balkans. Lord Cardigan and the rest should have been retired. I'd hate to be there, I can tell you. I agree with the editor of the *Gazette*, when he says we have gone into this, 'ill prepared and ill advised!' A nasty business!" He folded the small paper and put it in a side pocket of his shabby brown frock coat.

William said, "I must confess I've forgotten all about that distant war with all the troubles we've had here."

"It was picking up the paper at the post office which brought it all so vividly to me," Henry Gordon said. "It was only a few months ago that my brother and the recruiting officer were stoned by an angry mob here. So the war has reached us."

"I heard about that," Ardith said as she sat in a high-backed chair. "And I must say Harwick seems to be given to angry mobs. They are common enough here!"

The artist stared at her with a show of amazement. "May I ask what you mean by that, Mrs. Davis?"

William replied for her, "We have just come from the village now. The word that Mad Charlie was found here last night with the Devil's mark scratched on his cheek has the villagers up in arms. Someone found old Coline Dougall and brought her to the tavern. She pointed Ardith out as a witch before a group of people gathered there!"

Henry Gordon gasped. "I can't believe it. They did not learn their lesson years ago. This is exactly how the muttering and murmuring against poor Fanny began. And it ended, as you know, in the violence which has been our shame over the past two decades!"

Ardith smiled wanly. "I have been indicted as a witch, and I wonder what they will do next."

"Nothing," William said. "No one will pay serious attention to that mad old woman!"

"They did once before," she reminded him.

"I agree with Dr. Davis," Henry Gordon said. "I do not think there is any danger of history repeating itself. Though, I must say, the murders of my niece and of Mad Charlie have the village in an uproar."

She asked, "How is Lady Mona making out? Is she dealing well with her grief?"

"I talked to her for a few minutes this morning," the artist said. "I have to wait until Sir Douglas is out on some business or other until I dare venture into the castle. I have a friend who is a manservant there, and I wait in the servant's quarters until I dare present myself to her Ladyship."

William frowned, standing by her chair, one hand on the back of it as he faced the stout man who had taken a stand by the fireplace. He said, "Your brother still carries on his feud with you?"

"Yes," the artist said with a sad look on his oval face. "But I do all I can to comfort his wife. I think she has now resigned herself to Margaret's murder. She knows that if the girl had lived she would have eventually lost her mind. So at least she was saved from that."

"I'm glad she has that small satisfaction to cling to," William said. "They did not like to hear the grim truth when I told it to them. And I hated to have to be the one to warn them of her likelihood to deteriorate mentally. But now it does give them a tiny amount of comfort."

"Exactly," Henry Gordon said. "The fact she was their only daughter is especially unfortunate. And Lady Mona says she is not able to bear my brother another child."

Ardith said, "Which places you next in line for the title."

"Unhappily, that is true," Henry Gordon agreed. His blue eyes clouded. "Not that I shall ever live to receive it. My health is much poorer than my brother's, even though he is a good deal older. And I, in turn, have no children. So the likelihood is that the family fortune and title will go to a distant cousin living in Leeds. Someone we have not seen in years and barely know."

William said, "You cannot predict who will live or die. Sir Douglas could have an accident tomorrow, and you might find that in spite of indifferent health you are destined to go on living to a truly old age. Many with ill health survive the fittest by years!"

Henry Gordon looked brighter. "I must tell my Jeannie that. I swear if I should inherit the title I'd throw my objections to marriage away and make an honest woman of her. Can you picture her as Lady Jeannie?"

"Why not?" Ardith asked. "She is pretty enough in her way."

"And she is devoted to you," William added.

"The most devoted female I have ever known," the stout man in the shabby brown coat and fawn pants said. "But not a lady as you have seen and not anxious to be one. That's my main reason for liking her." Then, abruptly changing the subject, he went on to ask, "What about Dr. Carr? Has he bothered you lately?"

"I almost called him in when McLeod shot William in the head," Ardith admitted. "But I managed without him."

William touched the small bandage still covering the wound. "I imagine he's doing his share of talking against us. The last I heard, he was telling of my muddling cases in London. He claims my poor surgical record had me thrown off the staff of Bishop's Hospital!"

"You can easily prove him wrong, I'm sure," Henry Gordon said, studying him intently.

William shook his head. "Not all that easily. Rumors are hard to put to rest. Like all doctors, I had my cases of failure. He claims to have had a letter from a former colleague of mine in London listing many such incidents."

"Obviously trying to hold on to his dwindling practice," the artist commented bitterly.

William said, "It appears all the patients have returned to him. I have only had a small dribble of people these last few days, and today there are none. People not only have lost confidence in me, but they have become afraid of Wyndmoor."

"You had the constabulary here?" the artist said.

"Yes, the Chief Constable himself was on the scene. He questioned us and removed the body."

Henry Gordon nodded solemnly. "I can't think why they haven't gone after the man who is most likely to be guilty. You two both know who I mean."

William said, "James Burnett."

"Yes," the artist agreed.

Ardith shook her head. "I'm not all that sure. Why not blame the McLeods? They have the most to gain by placing us in a position where we have to leave here and of wanting to scare others from the place."

Henry Gordon proved more amenable to her theory than she had thought he would be. He nodded and said, "You may be right. Unhappily the locals, even the constabulary, think of the McLeods as lawbreakers only in their smuggling. They cannot see them doing other criminal things, though it is well enough known that one criminal activity can soon lead to another."

"That is well said," Ardith agreed with him, encouraged

by his reasonableness. "Surely Sir Douglas is a man with enough sophistication to understand this danger."

"He should be," Henry Gordon agreed. "Just now I think he is too shattered by his daughter's murder to think clearly. He is rushing around and accomplishing little. And the constabulary look to him for advice and leadership."

"So there is not too much hope," William said. "We have had an offer for Wyndmoor, and it may well be that we'll accept it."

"Have you talked about this to my brother?" Henry Gordon wanted to know.

"No," William said.

"You ought to," the other man said. "He has long wanted Wyndmoor. I know he lost it through his mean offers, but now that it has passed to your hands he might be willing to pay you as well as anyone else."

"I rather doubt it," William said. "In any event, I have to wait until I hear from the legal firm in Edinburgh representing the would-be purchaser to learn the exact amount this party is willing to pay."

Henry Gordon said, "As a member of the Stewart banking family, you should be able to get any information you wish about the legal firm and whom they represent."

"I have not gone deeply into it," her husband admitted. "Things have been happening too quickly here."

"Without a question," Henry Gordon said. "Well, I have had my chat with you two. I must be getting back to my Jeannie."

Ardith rose, relieved that he was about to go, but feeling she must invite him to stay, "Won't you remain and have some food with us?"

"No, thank you, Mrs. Davis," the stout man said with a

smile on his beard-stubbled face. "Though I do appreciate your generous offer."

William said, "If you hear anything you think we should know please come and tell us."

"Depend on that," the artist said.

"We are cut off a good deal from the village," she said. "So we need friends like you more than ever."

"You must lock up securely at night," the artist warned. "I don't believe there will be any violence, but it's better to be on the safe side."

Her eyes widened in fear. "Are you suggesting some of that suspicious crowd might come out here?"

"I hope not," the artist said. "But you can't be sure what they'll do."

"I fully agree," William said. "I intend to alert the servants and take every precaution."

It was a grim note on which their conversation ended. They saw Henry Gordon to the door with the feeling that they were saying good-bye to one of the few, true friends they had made since coming to Harwick. And because of his own instability he was not too much use to them. The people of the village looked on him as something between a mad artist without morals, and a drunken, inferior version of his titled brother.

William went to the table in the hall when they were alone and sorted out the mail which the servants had put there when they were out. He held up a letter, saying, "Here's one from Mother!"

Ardith rushed to his side eagerly. "What does she have to say?"

He tore open the envelope and scanned the letter. She says, "Edinburgh is suddenly caught up in the war fever. A regiment is being formed there and Uncle Ernest has made himself unpopular with his speeches against the war!"

"Never mind the war!" she protested. "What about Ian?"

"Flora has a new pony and cart and she and Ian go driving in it every day," he read. "He is healthy and has a good appetite, but he is beginning to ask about his mother and you. I think he is lonesome for you and perhaps it would be a good idea if I brought him to Harwick for at least a short stay." William paused with the letter and glanced at her. "Bring him here! Impossible!"

"Then we should go to Edinburgh," Ardith said, her eyes moist with repressed tears. "I miss my boy and I'm not gaining anything in health here."

"Let me think about it overnight," William said. And then he read the balance of the letter to her. When he finished she went upstairs with the idea of resting, but she found herself too upset to settle down.

She paced by the window, pausing to glance out now and then. And all the while there was something nagging at her, that ghostly voice which came at intervals to whisper in her mind. Now it was telling her not to forget about the box. The box of Fanny's letters which she had found. But she did not think it was of any importance to look at the contents of the wooden box again.

The letters had been pathetic and harmless. They had told her very little, except that Fanny had been happy in her marriage and frightened of the house for some reason. There had been no references to James Burnett in any of the letters, but this was not too strange. By the time of their writing Fanny had jilted the sculptor for John Bray.

Still the nagging persisted. Look at the letters! She could not get the thought out of her head. And so, at last, she went to the dresser and found the ornate box. Then she went to the bed with it and sat there as she reached for the secret spring which opened it. The hinged top sprang up to reveal the stack of ancient letters tied with a rose ribbon and smelling of that perfume of another day. She lifted out the letters and the slips of paper with the recipes Fanny had collected.

She and her friend had planned to publish a cookbook, but tragedy had overtaken her before that had happened. Ardith looked in the box again to see if she'd missed any of the recipe slips, and she was at once struck by a strangeness in the pattern of the wood in the bottom of the box. It was fitted together in an intricate fashion with a square of wood in the middle. Once again, the voice in her mind directed her actions. It told her to press on the square. And she did. To her amazement the square depressed and the entire bottom came out of the box. But what was most startling was that it was a false bottom with a space between its two layers. And slipped in this space was a sealed envelope.

Trembling at her discovery, she slid the envelope out and tore it open. It smelled of the same perfume as the letters. And inside in a handwriting she hadn't seen before was a long note. She found her excitement growing as she began reading it.

To Whomever May Find This:

I am writing this message and placing it here in the false bottom of my letter box in the hope it will be found. At this moment I feel I am in dreadful danger, and I despair of living. I have been accused of being a witch, and the present plague in the village has raised the people there against me. I cannot blame the poor souls for being afraid with them dying like flies, but why must they blame the epidemic on me and my witchcraft!

I know now how this all came about, but I'm afraid to tell anyone, even my good husband, John Bray, because I fear to cause him pain. Some time soon he must know, but until I decide it is the right moment I must hug my terrible secret close to me.

My being accused of witchcraft began when the elderly Lady Gordon's pet cat was found strangled on her lawn with one of my initialed scarves used to throttle the poor beast. I knew nothing of the wicked deed, but Lady Gordon blamed me and raised a great clamor against me.

I had done some innocent fortune-telling with tea leaves and now this became a subject of whispering. It was said I had made predictions of deaths and other happenings and that I was a witch. I had killed the cat as part of some ritual associated with witchcraft! There was an outline of a Devil's hoof mark on the cat's side.

The local people called on old Coline Dougall who is almost blind and who claims to have a special power for telling the future. She fed their anger by agreeing that I was a witch and that she had seen me flying about over the harbor on a stormy night! The old woman is either mad or enjoys the attention these wild statements get her.

It was shortly after that the daughter of the miller was found strangled out back of Wyndmoor. There was nothing to identify me with the crime, but because it happened here and also because there was a Devil's hoof scratched on the child's cheek, the murder was linked with me.

Now the epidemic has come. John is away until Monday next. And I have been told that the villagers are talking of coming for me because they blame me for the plague.

The only one I have to turn to is my sister-in-law, Mary. Mary, who before my advent ran Wyndmoor for John. I took her place here so I have never been a favorite of hers. She is a plain girl with a temper and so, despite the fact she has an excellent dowry, we have long despaired that she will ever be asked to marry.

James Burnett came to see me, and the poor fellow is not at all like the man I knew in the city. My jilting him hit him hard. However, I told him I loved John Bray and there was no hope of my leaving him. James begged me to run off with him. I told him I would not see him again if he continued to press the subject. So now when he calls we talk of other things and have become quite good friends!

He is worried about me, and today he told me he thinks I'm in great danger. The people are convinced I'm a witch and that I brought the plague to torture them. I did not dare tell him the discovery I made only yesterday. I'm waiting until John returns and I will try and convince him.

Mary has been going to one of the attic rooms a good deal, supposedly to store items which we have discarded as no longer being useful. She has regularly kept the door to the storage room locked. But yesterday she came down and forgot to lock it. Later she went out for a stroll in the cemetery; she takes a great interest in the cemetery and keeping it in good condition. I have always felt this morbid, but then she has a morbid nature.

I was upstairs on another errand and saw the door was not locked. It occurred to me to take a look inside and see what she had put in there and if the room were nearly filled.

The moment I touched the doorknob I had a sensation of evil within that room. I became terrified without, as yet, any reason. When I opened the door and went in, I found the room so dark I couldn't see anything. I found the window and moved away the blind which had been pulled down to blot out the light, and to my horror I saw a black magic altar erected in the room.

Before it there were an incense burner, the skeletons of two small animals, the scattered feathers of birds and several wicked-looking knives. There was also a kind of log book in which my sister-in-law, Mary, had written her thoughts at various times. I took the journal to the window and went over several pages of her crabbed handwriting!

I did not read much, but I learned enough. In that vile place she regularly worshipped the Devil. She offered prayers to Satan and set up evil spells against me, and many others in the village. There was a mention of her killing both the cat and the little girl, and also a notation of causing the death by drowning of a young boy. She had held him under the water until the life was gone from him! And that crime had not been connected with anyone but put down as an accident!

My sister-in-law, Mary, is mad! There can be no doubt about that. And it is she who has had me branded as a witch! She shows concern for me, but it is all a fake. She hates me in her madness, and she is probably waiting for the villagers to do me some violence so that she may again become the mistress of Wyndmoor!

John will be here soon, and I will somehow brave myself to tell him and show him the room. I left it quickly and did not let Mary know I had gone in and found her terrible secret. I noticed that later, after she returned from the cemetery, she went up and locked the room again. It has been locked ever since.

So now I'm counting the hours I pass with this mad woman! John will soon be here, and then we shall have a settling of this grim affair. He will be grieved but not as grieved as if anything happened to me. I can be comforted by that thought. Because I cannot confide this to anyone as yet, I'm writing it to get some relief. I will place it in my letter box. And one day I will read it again and think about the ordeal which I endured.

Mary must go to an asylum. She must remain there until she recovers. And John must let the villagers know it was she, and not I, who was responsible for those macabre crimes.

Fanny Bray

Ardith's head was reeling with excitement. She stared at the letter after she'd finished reading it and realized the discovery she'd made. She left the box and the other letters scattered on the bed and rushed out the door and downstairs. She found William in his office and thrust the letter before him.

"I've found something of great value," she said breathlessly. "Read this!"

He frowned and glanced at the signature on the second page of the letter and said, "Fanny Bray?"

"Read it!" she insisted.

William read the letter while she stood by watching over his shoulder. When he had finished, he said, "Where did you find this?"

She told him about the secret compartment in the box. And she said, "It must have been written the night before they took her out and burned her as a witch! The letter and its secret have lain in that box all those years!"

Her young husband stood up. "This is a grim business. As far as I know, Mary Bray left here with her brother. She is now living with him in Canada."

"I'm sure Lawyer Macree said that."

"And if this is so, he is harboring a madwoman who may have since committed many other crimes," William said.

"Or could be contemplating some murder now!"

William frowned. "We must turn this letter over to Lawyer Macree and have him send it on to John Bray in Canada. It is most urgent."

"I agree," she said. "I knew she wasn't a witch! That she hadn't done any of those things!" Her voice was triumphant and her eyes bright as she stared up at her young husband.

William took her by the arms and in a serious voice said, "What made you look for that letter?"

She hesitated. "I don't know. It was as if a voice was whispering to me. Telling me to look for it. I've had those strange moments ever since I came to Wyndmoor." She paused and then told him, "I think maybe she has somehow used me. Made me do this for her."

William eyed her strangely. He said in a quiet voice, "I have always disparaged anything you've said along this line. Normally, I'm not inclined to believe in ghosts or their powers. But this has almost convinced me!"

"William!" she said, her voice choked with emotion.

"We will see this through," he told her, taking her in his arms and kissing her. "And then we'll go back to Edinburgh and see our son!"

"What will we do first?" she asked.

"I'm going to attach a note of my own with this and have one of the lads take it in to Lawyer Macree in the village," he said. "I'm sure he will act on it right away."

"The room," she said. "The room where she had her altar to Satan. Do you think we can find it?"

"We can try," he said. "But first let me get this ready and on its way."

After he'd given the letter to the stable boy and sent him to Lawyer Macree's house, they went to Mrs. MacDonald and from her secured the keys to the house. In the attic they tried each door and were able to unlock every one of them with a single exception. This was a small room at the end of the attic overlooking the stables and the cemetery.

"There is no key for this lock," William said, giving her a meaningful look.

"Mary probably kept it when she left here," she said.

"There ought to have been more than one key for it."

"Not if she had some dreadful secret to hide in there," Ardith said.

William touched the ancient, rusted lock and in a taut voice said, "Well, that leaves us only one way to find out what's in there. Break the lock!"

She nodded as they stood there in the shadowed attic hall. And she knew that the truth of the letter she'd discovered might depend on what they found in there. What if it were empty, or merely filled with innocent items of storage?

Chapter Twelve

William found a long iron bar, and she stood by tensely as he forced the door lock of the secret room. As the bolts gave way with a shudder he glanced at her significantly and opened the door. The stench of decay, dampness and dust came out of the darkness. Her husband groped his way across the room and, finding the covering which blocked out all window light, he tore it down.

Light from outside flooded the room, and from the doorway Ardith saw the makeshift altar on a dresser by the wall. The mirror of the dresser had been decorated with various black magic signs and the top of the dresser had been covered in black velvet now thick with dust. On the covering there were two tiny skulls, suggestive of small animals, and a pattern of bones. Everything else had been removed, no doubt by the insane Mary, before John Bray had her leave Wyndmoor with him.

The journal which the madwoman had kept was either with her in Canada or destroyed. But enough remained of the macabre altar to Satan to confirm what Fanny had written.

William studied the altar with the dust and cobwebs of twenty years and said, "This proves that Fanny wrote the truth."

"I didn't doubt it," she said.

"We'll leave everything just as it is," her husband said.

"It must be shown to Lawyer Macree and the constabulary. I wonder what the Chief Constable will say to this?"

"It has been a long while," she said with a sigh. "But finally Fanny's name should be cleared. I'm glad to be having a part in it."

Her husband gave her a troubled look. "Just now it is your name I'm anxious to see protected."

"I'm only suspected of being a witch through the link with Fanny," she said. "Once it is proven that Fanny was no witch, I will automatically be out of trouble."

"I hope so," her husband said cautiously.

They closed the door of the room and went downstairs again. By this time their messenger had returned with news that Lawyer Macree had been away, but that his wife took the letters to give to him on his return. He was expected back in the early evening. So it appeared they would learn nothing more until later in the evening or the next morning.

The events of the long day had left Ardith in a nervous, excited state. The hours went by quickly and soon it was dusk. She and William were taking a stroll on the lawn outside the front door of Wyndmoor when a carriage came up the driveway. It was a troubled Lawyer Macree who had received the letters.

He joined them on the lawn and said, "I'm most shocked by this revelation. Do you think that Fanny was writing the truth?"

"No question of it," William said. "We have found the room and forced the door open. The altar is there. Mary Bray was a madwoman and responsible for the crimes blamed on Fanny."

"Dreadful," the thin man with the side-whiskers said. "As I understood it, John Bray's sister was still with him when he last wrote me a few weeks ago. After the sale of the property to you people."

Ardith said, "He ought to be warned that she is capable of great evil."

Lawyer Macree said, "Without question. I shall send a message to Edinburg tomorrow and have a cable sent to Canada with this new information you've turned up. I shall ask John Bray to cable a reply back. So we should know within a few days or a week what has happened to her."

Ardith said, "It places everything in a new light."

"I'm well aware of that," Lawyer Macree said. "May I see this room?"

They led him upstairs and, as darkness had come, they used candles in the attic area. The room by candlelight looked even more menacing than it had in the sunlight. Ardith pictured the grim madwoman up there alone in the shadows, kneeling before the altar dedicated to the Devil and whispering incantations against poor Fanny and anyone else she thought might be her enemy. And the unfortunate John Bray was still at the mercy of this mad Mary wherever they were in Canada. Who could guess what other crimes she had committed?

When they came back down again, Mrs. MacDonald had set out lamps in all the rooms. They stood in the front hall discussing the situation in the village.

Lawyer Macree told Ardith, "I was very distressed by the behavior of those people in front of the tavern. That old woman is mad and they have been using her in a vile fashion to amuse themselves. They want another witch hunt!"

"With my wife as their victim," William said bitterly.

"Most unfortunate," the lawyer said. "I took it upon myself to report what took place there today to both the Chief

Constable and Sir Douglas Gordon."

"What was their reaction?" her husband asked.

The lawyer said, "The Chief Constable promised to keep a sharp eye on the troublemakers, but Sir Douglas was haughty and unsympathetic. He is still badly hurt by the loss of his daughter."

"I do not expect any understanding from him," she said.

"You should be careful for the next few nights," Lawyer Macree went on. "I would have someone you can trust sit up and keep watch. And I would leave all the lamps on that are lighted now. Have lights blazing from every window of the house if possible."

William's eyebrows lifted. "You think the house may be attacked."

"They came before without warning," Lawyer Macree reminded him. "It only takes a few hot-heads to stir up a mob. I don't think you should take chances."

Ardith heard his words with a rising panic. "You actually believe they are ready to burn me as a witch as they did poor Fanny?"

"There are some here who would be capable of it," Lawyer Macree said. "You should be prepared."

"They couldn't be that mad and superstitious," William protested, but behind the protest there was a hint of fear in his tone.

"I'm telling you what I honestly think about this unhappy business," the old lawyer said. "Once we are able to get the word around that Mary Bray was the villainess of twenty years ago, we can stop this new fever of madness. But until then your wife is surely in danger."

It was nearly ten o'clock when the lawyer left. And it was a tense house which he drove away from. William at once informed Mrs. MacDonald that the lamps in the various rooms were to burn all night. He next rounded up several of the stable lads and recruited them to act as guards and alert him if anyone came in the driveway. He personally loaded his pistol and poked it through his belt ready to be used.

The reactions to these preparations were many. Meg and the other maids glided silently about their duties with wan, frightened faces. Mrs. MacDonald fussed and rearranged the position of the lamps to show to the best advantage outside. The lads assigned to the guarding of the driveway stood in the darkness like sentries and boasted about what they would do if any witch hunting villagers turned up.

Ardith, caught up in all this now, knew in real life the fear she had experienced in her nightmares so many times. She knew what it felt like to be hated and wait for an attack from unknowns out of the darkness. She prayed that there would be no trouble and begged her husband not to upset the household too much with his efforts to prepare against a surprise visit by the ignorant villagers.

"I think Lawyer Macree exaggerated," she protested. "There won't be any trouble!"

William stood in the hallway looking pale and worried. "He is closer to the villagers than we are. He knows more about them."

"When are you coming up to bed?"

"Not for a while."

"Then I shall remain here with you."

"No," he said. "Better for you to go to your room and try and get some rest."

She gave him a wry look. "In the midst of all this? A house poised for attack?"

"Simple precautions," he said, kissing her. "Go to bed!"

Ardith did as he asked her. When she reached her room, Meg was just finishing turning down the bed and setting her medicine out. Ardith said, "You have heard what is going on?"

Meg came to stand with her. The petite, straw-haired girl looked frightened. "Do you think the villagers will try to raid the house?"

"I hope not. But they did it once before."

"That was long ago," Meg said. "And Fanny Bray was a witch. You have done no one any harm."

"The murder of Mad Charlie in the cemetery here last night has given them the idea I'm Fanny back again," she said bitterly.

The maid said, "It is so stupid of them! Is there anything else, ma'am?"

"No," she said. "I see you have my medicine ready as usual."

"I always prepare it as soon as I come upstairs," Meg said.

The maid finished her duties in the room and left. Ardith prepared for bed and went to the window in her nightgown to look out. It was a black night, grim and forbidding, with not even a star showing. And it was strangely silent, almost weirdly so. Even the waves on the shore seemed subdued. A night of brooding evil, she worried.

Crossing to her bedside table, she began sipping her medicine. She worried whether all this medication was doing her any good. She really felt no different than when she had first arrived in Harwick. If anything, she was more nervous because of the ordeals she'd undergone. And nervous tension could not be good for her lung condition and general health.

When she finished the medicine, she slipped between the sheets and tried to summon sleep. But sleep was not to come easily. She was far too frightened for that. It must have been nearly thirty minutes before her eyes closed and she slept lightly.

It was not surprising that she again had the nightmare which had haunted her from the start of her coming to Wyndmoor. She tossed and turned in the bed, uttering small moaning sounds, as she raced and hid from her pursuers, rushed upstairs to an upper bedroom and again sought to hide before she was overtaken by the angry, masked men and dragged out into the woods!

When she opened her eyes she was not in her bed. She was in a hallway of the upper attic, her bare feet cold on the hardwood floor. She stood there dazed for a moment before she realized she'd been sleepwalking again!

Her head was reeling and she could not imagine why she had made this strange pilgrimage to the attic. She was standing close by the door of the room where the mad Mary had practiced her Satanism. She tried to collect her shattered nerves and turned to start down the stairway to the floor below. She had barely reached her own floor when she heard a rock crash through a window downstairs. There was a crash, the tinkling of glass and then a loud, angry roar from outside!

They had arrived! The lawyer had been right!

In terror, she descended the stairway to where William stood in the hallway close to the front door. Mrs. MacDonald stood behind him, her face twisted with fear and her hands clasping and unclasping.

The older woman saw Ardith and exclaimed, "You oughn't to be down here!"

William turned sternly and ordered her, "Back to your room; we'll look after this!"

Before she could reply, there was another crash of a rock going through a living room window. This was followed closely by another rock smashing a window in the same area. More angry shouts could be heard from the outside darkness.

William said, “If they come near the door I’ll open it and fire at them.”

“And then what?” Ardith demanded. “They’ll rush you and overpower you and kill the rest of us! Don’t start any violence.”

“We can’t let them gradually wreck the place,” he shouted, as a window in the dining room splintered from a neatly directed rock.

Ardith was going to reply to this when something quite unexpected happened. There were a series of shots outside and screams of terror and panic. The shots came again, and then there were the sounds of running feet and angry shouts gradually fading in the distance. All this loud commotion was followed by an eerie silence.

William turned to her in amazement. “Did you take note of all that?”

“Yes,” she said. “It sounds as if someone came to our aid. Probably the constabulary.”

Her husband, the pistol in hand, nodded, “Yes. Macree said he had spoken to them.”

Mrs. MacDonald spoke up nervously. “They didn’t get here a minute too soon. I’ll go make sure everything is all right out back.” And she turned and hurried along the rear hall to the servant’s quarters.

William was by the door. “I think I’ll take a look out there and thank our rescuers.”

“Be careful,” she said.

“The villagers have fled,” he assured her. “You could hear them running away.”

“You need to be sure!”

"There's only one way to find out," he told her. And he slid the bolt from the door and opened it.

She was at the door with him. "Do you see anyone?"

"No," he said. "No one!"

"Strange," she replied. They both stepped out on the steps and gazed into the shadows.

From the darkness behind them came a sharp command, "Up with your hands, Dr. Davis, and you, too, ma'am!"

An agonized expression came to William's face as he dropped the pistol and slowly raised his hands. "Sorry, my dear," he said to her. "I've been a fool again!"

"No matter!" she murmured grimly, her own hands raised.

The voice with the thick burr said, "You feel the cold steel of our guns against your backs. So be wise! Don't try to move!"

There was a movement in the shadows nearby, and as they stood there with the cold muzzles of the guns pressed against them the figure materialized of a tall man in a cape and mask. When he spoke, Ardith at once recognized him.

He said, "You can be thankful to me and my brothers for your safety tonight, Dr. Davis!" It was Grim McLeod who told them this derisively.

"You back!" William said angrily.

"And thankful you should be for it," McLeod said in mocking fashion. "Otherwise your good lady might now be on her way through the woods to a burning!"

Ardith asked him, "Why did you do it?"

"To let you know I'm not the blackguard you've painted me," McLeod said. "It happens we have still a deal of cargo stored in various parts of the grounds. Tonight we were here to move some more of it, and we were able to drive off those villagers at the same time."

William said, "So your good deed was accidental!" And he made a movement to lower his hands.

"Up with those hands! My brothers are better shots than I. And they can't miss with their guns at your backs."

"What do you want from us?" William demanded.

McLeod chuckled. "Not much, and that's the truth! But I want to tell you a few things you don't know and that might be helpful to you!"

"That you and your brothers are smugglers?" Ardith said.

"No," McLeod said. "That is no news. Everyone knows that. But you don't know that the bid for the property here came through an Edinburgh lawyer from the McLeods. We are the ones who want to buy Wyndmoor. We have the funds and it can be in the name of one of the family who aren't having trouble with the law."

"You want to go on using it as a smuggling base," William said.

"It is ideally suited to our purpose," the tall man in the cape and mask said. "And when the hue and cry about the smuggling dies down, my brothers and I can safely return."

"You sound very sure of that!" Ardith said.

"I know this country better than you do, ma'am," McLeod said. "There is much sympathy among the people for us. And now, two other matters before we take our leave. I can tell you that we have never plotted against your lives. That is not our way!"

"Thanks," William said with sarcasm. "It would be easier to believe if there were no guns at our backs."

"A safety move," McLeod said. "I'd also like to tell you what many in the village have known but few will admit, because to do so would incriminate them—the leader of that gang who burned Fanny Bray was Henry Gordon!"

"Henry Gordon," she gasped, since she had never suspected the artist.

"Yes, Henry," McLeod said. "Drunken and reckless. He led the murder gang and then, like the coward he was, he ran off. That was what sent him to study art in Italy! But he left a daughter behind! Illegitimate, she was, but a daughter nevertheless. She lives here in this house, you know her as Meg!"

"My wife's personal maid," William said.

"That's right," McLeod chuckled with satisfaction. "That is as much as I care to tell you. And I would be thankful if I were you. You can repay your debt to us by selling the property to those lawyers in Edinburgh!"

As he finished saying this he moved swiftly out of sight and was lost to them. They stood there prisoners still, the cold metal of the gun muzzles in their backs.

A low, grating voice told them, "Count to twenty before you move. Anything less and you'll get a bullet through you!"

The pressure of the guns vanished and they could hear retreating footsteps. William soberly counted to twenty and even then waited a little. After that he dropped his hands and turned to Ardith who at the same time dropped her stance of surrender.

Her doctor husband stared at her. "What did you make of that?"

"They always insisted McLeod was not a murderer," she said.

William grasped her urgently by the arm. "Let us get out of here!"

"We won't be bothered again," she replied as he literally pushed her inside.

He closed the door and bolted it again and returned the pistol to his belt. They stood together in the softly-lighted hall. He said, "Do you think he told us the truth?"

"Yes," she said.

"Then we made a bad mistake in Henry Gordon!"

"I have had times when I've wondered about him! And it was he who led those crazed villagers against Fanny!"

"McLeod says so. And Meg is his illegitimate daughter. Do you think she knows it?"

Ardith gave him a significant look and in a low voice, said, "I'm beginning to think so. And something else has just occurred to me. She has been so particular about setting out my medicine every night. And my hallucinations and sleepwalking started here. After I began taking that nightly medicine.

"How do we know she hasn't placed something in the medicine on selected nights? Some drug which makes me walk in my sleep and have distorted dreams?"

"Where would she get such a drug?"

"From her father, who seems to be our enemy for some reason I can't explain. And he, in turn, could obtain it from a very real enemy, Dr. Carr. No one would know the shrub berries and poisons here better than he!"

"You may have something there," her husband admitted. "But what can we do about it?"

"More than you think," she said. "No one knows we've been told these facts."

"That's right."

"I have an idea I'll see the ghost of Fanny again tonight," she said.

"Because it is on these nights when you've presumably been given some drug that the phantom appears."

"Exactly," she said. "So we must prepare ourselves for the advent of the ghost."

"How?"

"I will tell you," she said. And she did.

The house had settled down for the night. The crisis over, all the servants had gone to bed. However, as a precaution, William had suggested to Mrs. MacDonald that the lamps in the various sections of the old mansion continue to be left burning.

He and Ardith returned to their rooms. But not to their beds. They placed pillows in both her bed and his, and drew the clothes up over them so that the pillows resembled sleeping figures. Then, on her suggestion, they took up a vigil in a closet beyond the bed in her room and near the connecting door which led to his bedroom. They allowed the door to be open a crack so they could see what was happening.

For a long while nothing happened and they were both very weary. Then, shortly after two, the door of Ardith's bedroom slowly was opened. She watched with bated breath and William held on to her arm firmly. As the door opened a figure appeared. A figure in a cloak with an attached hood. The cloak was drawn to in the front and entirely hid the body of the phantom. Only the face showed inside the hood! The glowing face of Fanny!

The single lamp left burning in the bedroom let Ardith and William make out details of the phantom. She saw a gleaming knife in the ghost's right hand and had all she could do to stifle a cry! The ghostly Fanny moved near her bed and, seemingly satisfied that she was asleep, then crossed to the door to the adjoining bedroom and stealthily opened it.

From the closet she and William could see the cloaked phantom with the glowing face hesitate in the doorway and raise the knife a little in preparation for an attack on what the ghostly Fanny must surely believe was William. It struck Ardith the plan must be to murder her husband, carve the usual Devil's hoof on his cheek and have her blamed for it! In her confused, drugged state, the plotters would think it easy to make her seem the criminal!

William moved slightly and she saw he had reached for the pistol. Now he opened the door of the closet gradually and, as the phantom made its way to the bed and his supposedly sleeping figure under the coverings, William followed on its trail. The phantom halted by the bed and poised the knife to plunge it down!

At the same moment William fired at the phantom's back! The flash and smell of gun powder filled the air! Then the phantom dropped the knife and turned around. With a frantic gesture, the phantom clawed off his mask and pulled back the hood to reveal the stunned face of Henry Gordon!

William said sternly, "All right, Gordon. We're on to your game!"

The wounded man swayed a little. And then he let out an oath and, in a surprise motion, bent down and swooped up the lamp from the bedside table. He threw it at the long window drapes and it exploded there and the drapes burst into flame. At the same time, the wounded man ran out of the room and made for the stairs. William raced after him while she vainly tried to pull down the flaming drapes without success!

She saw the fire could not be put out, and so ran out after her husband and the fleeing Henry Gordon. Again on the stairs there was a fire started where the mad Gordon had thrown down another lamp. And when she reached the doorway of the living room, it was the same. Gordon had smashed both the lamps there, causing fires in each instance. Flames ran up the side of the wall and along the carpet in another place. The French windows to the garden were open, and she assumed William and the wounded man had gone out there. She followed!

She found them a short distance away on the lawn. Henry Gordon had finally collapsed and William was bending over him. He looked up at her as she came breathlessly to him and said, "He's dead! He ought to have died instantly! I don't know how he managed to get this far and do what he did!"

Ardith turned from the dead man on the grass to look at the house. Inside the drawing rooms the flames had grown to huge proportions. In a shocked tone, she said, "He's finished Wyndmoor!"

William was on his feet and at her side. His grim face was highlighted by the rising flames from the house. He said, "I don't know! It depends on upstairs and the water supply!"

The stablemen and other servants were gradually coming out and their shouts indicated they were organizing to battle the flames.

William left her to help with suggestions for battling the flames. She stood there with the dead body of Henry Gordon stretched out behind her. Now all the drawing room area of the great house resembled a bonfire. She could hear the cries of the servants as they tried to stifle the flames with pails of water and other futile means. And she saw clearly that Wyndmoor was doomed!

Flames began to shoot through the roof on the other side of the mansion, no doubt from the fire which had started in William's bedroom. Now the servants merely stood back in awe and watched the house gradually being devoured by the leaping flames!

The stablemen were removing the horses and cattle in

case the stables were next engulfed. Sparks from the house were falling near them and in some cases lighting on the roof! A dog was barking and acrid smoke began to fill the air!

Out of the flames and smoke there emerged two figures. She saw it was William and he was bringing Meg over. She waited for them, caught between sympathy and anger at the maid who had most certainly betrayed her.

Meg's face was white except for some smudges of soot. She wore only her nightgown with a cape over it and her straw-colored hair tumbled to her shoulders. She gave Ardith a frightened look and then went on to kneel by her dead father and begin a broken sobbing.

Ardith said, "She knows?"

"Yes, I talked with her. She's been terrified since she guessed her father killed Margaret Gordon and Mad Charlie. Henry was bent on making himself the heir to the family title and money."

It was the morning of the following day. Wyndmoor was now only a mass of ruins, still smoking, and a memory. Happily the stables had been saved and so had the other outbuildings. The men who slept in the stables remained to look after the stock and the property, but the other servants had been paid and sent away.

All save Meg, who was occupying a room at the inn where William and Ardith had taken her. Now the frightened girl, along with them, was seated in a large room at the inn and Lawyer Macree was severely questioning her.

Lawyer Macree asked Meg, "When did you first learn that Henry Gordon was your father?"

"When I came back here from Edinburgh," the girl said in a small voice.

"And was it then that he proposed you seek work at

Wyndmoor?" the lawyer asked her.

Meg said, "Yes."

"Did he tell you that he wanted you to help him in a plot against Dr. Davis and his wife?" Lawyer Macree wanted to know.

"Yes," the girl said.

The lawyer was stern. "Why did you agree?"

"Because of the story he told me," Meg said.

"What story?" Lawyer Macree wanted to know.

Meg gave William and Ardith an uneasy glance. "They will be angry with me!"

William spoke up, "We are puzzled and angry now, Meg. If you will explain to us perhaps we'll feel better towards you."

The girl swallowed hard and then with difficulty said, "He told me Dr. Davis was a poor doctor and ought to be frightened away. He said he had a plan to do it. One of the ways was to put things in Mrs. Davis's medicine at night and Dr. Carr would supply a mixture of herbs which would make her ill. So on nights when he told me, I put the drops of the herb compound in her medicine glass."

Lawyer Macree said sternly, "You know that was a dangerous, criminal act."

"I didn't like doing it," Meg said unhappily. "But my father told me that a young woman he loved took arsenic while they were living together in London. He said the doctor attending to the young woman was Dr. Davis. And he claimed that it was neglect by Dr. Davis that caused her death. She could have been saved!"

The old lawyer turned to William. "Do you know anything about this?"

William's handsome face showed a frown. "There was a girl! I remember! She was brought into the hospital in a bad state. I did all I could for her, but she died. And for a while after I received mad, threatening letters calling me an incompetent butcher and a lot of other things. I brought them to the attention of the hospital chief and he advised me to pay no attention to them. His theory was that the letters would cease. And they did. After a few months I received no more."

"Could the writer of those letters have been Henry Gordon?" the lawyer wanted to know.

"It's possible," William said. "They were never signed."

"Then you were in no way responsible for the unhappy young woman's death," Lawyer Macree said.

"I did all in my power to save her. She was bound to die from the moment she entered the hospital."

"You hear that?" Lawyer Macree asked the girl.

Meg nodded. "I'm sorry. But my father really believed it. I'm sure he did. He said he wanted to settle accounts with the doctor by driving his wife mad just as Fanny Bray became mad!"

"That was another grave mistake," Lawyer Macree sighed. He told the girl, "Go back to your room while I talk with the doctor and his wife. We will decide about turning you over to the law."

Meg stood up, and hesitated, then she blurted out, "I never did anything wrong like that in all my life before!" And sobbing, she ran out.

Ardith sighed after she'd gone and said, "I don't know about you, William. I can't feel angry towards that poor girl. She was led astray by her evil father. She was bound to have a sort of hero-worship for him. Up until he came into her life she had no one."

"So it was easy for him to bend her to his will," Lawyer Macree agreed.

"I have an idea," William said. "With her father's death she has become the most direct heir to Sir Douglas Gordon and Lady Mona. They have lost a daughter; Meg is attractive and has good health. If her uncle could be persuaded to adopt her they could mold her into a proper lady and suitable heiress."

The lawyer shook his head. "I can't see Sir Douglas agreeing to that."

Ardith spoke up, "Let me talk to Lady Mona about it."

"Excellent idea," her husband said.

Lawyer Macree raised his eyebrows. "Then you plan to make no charges against the girl or old Dr. Carr?"

"No," William said. "Let us keep what we know to ourselves. Henry Gordon can take the full blame, and he has already been punished by death. He was twice guilty, first for leading the gang against Fanny and then through what he tried to do here."

"I have already talked to the constabulary," the lawyer said. "There will be an inquest, but it will be a mere formality. They agree you shot and killed him in self-defense."

"One other thing," William said. "You can tell those lawyers in Edinburgh we gladly will sell the house. I know who the principals are, and I fear we owe a debt to them."

The older lawyer showed surprise. "You are sure you want to do this?"

"Yes," he said. "We will leave Harwick now. I plan to follow my mother's advice and establish a practice in Edinburgh where my grandfather was a successful doctor. The air is as good there as anywhere in Scotland, so I think my wife will be well situated there."

So it was settled. Ardith's last duty in Harwick was seeing Lady Mona. And she was pleased that the titled woman at once embraced the plan of adopting Meg. Oddly enough, when it came time for the two of them to present the suggestion to Sir Douglas, the bad-tempered man showed remarkable tolerance.

"She has Gordon blood," he said. "Why not?"

Ardith told the titled man and his wife, "Meg knows now her father was a reckless scoundrel and admits it. But she obeyed him because he lied to her and she loved him."

"Say no more," Sir Douglas Gordon said. "We will give the girl a good home. I only regret that you and your husband are leaving. We do need a good doctor."

She smiled ruefully. "I think Dr. Carr will try harder now that he knows he could lose his practice. And no doubt in time another young doctor will come along."

So Meg was well on the way to a new life in the Castle Gordon. On the last day as they were loading their luggage on the stage which would take them to the railway line, Lawyer Macree came waving a sheet of paper above his head. He rushed up to them and, mopping his brow, told them, "I was afraid you'd get away before I brought you this news. My answering cable from John Bray." And he passed it to William and Ardith to read.

The cable was terse but pointed: "Discovered Mary's madness soon after arrival in Canada. She was placed in hospital and died there two months ago. John Bray".

Ardith said, "So Fanny's name is completely cleared. I wanted that before I left. And I'm happy James Burnett was not involved. I understand he went to Edinburgh."

"Yes," the lawyer said, taking the cable. "May I say again how much you resemble the late Fanny Bray!"

She nodded. "More than that, I have come to feel very close to her."

So the last one they talked with before boarding the stage was Lawyer Macree. But, when they took their places inside, they found themselves seated across from a fellow passenger. This passenger was Jeannie Truffin, the young woman who had been living with Henry Gordon.

She said, "I hope you won't mind riding with me."

"Why should we?" Ardith asked her.

"Henry was a bad one," Jeannie said, sadness clouding her pretty face. "But I loved him. He could make a girl fall in love with him easy. Plenty of them did. Including that one in London he thought you let die, doctor. The funny thing was she took the poison over him being unfaithful in the first place. I think it hit him hard, and he had to blame you to live with himself."

"Maybe that was it," William said. "I tried to save her."

"I guessed that," Jeannie said. "But Henry wanted it his way. And he had the girl and the doctor helping him. Well, it's over. Harwick is no place for me now. It's back to the bars of Edinburgh for Jeannie!"

"Harwick is not a place for any of us," Ardith said as the stage got under way. It rolled down the dusty main street and headed for the green Highlands. Next day they'd board the train for Edinburgh and she'd see Ian! It would be a new start. And a better one!

William took her hand in his. "It will soon all be behind us."

"I know," she said, glancing out at the evergreens and the blue mountains in the distance. It had been a strange, frightening experience, but she did not entirely regret it. She had been a means of clearing the name of the lovely, long-dead Fanny. And she would always believe that just for a brief time or two she had become Fanny. That across the years their two spirits had merged. And even now an inner voice told her that at last the spirit of Fanny was at rest and satisfied.

Watch for the next book in this series: "The Stewarts of Stormhaven." It is called "This Evil Village!" The time is 1913, and the story takes place in an abandoned entertainment park just outside Edinburgh. In this enchanted village, a forerunner of today's Disneyland, Sophie Davis finds herself the new owner and threatened by macabre figures straight out of the fairy tale castles in the park!